BY THE AUTHOR OF
FANNY HILL

The woman of pleasure was not a figment of John Cleland's imagination. She lived and moved among the colorful figures of 18th-century England. And she had her male counterpart: the coxcomb . . . *man* of pleasure.

John Cleland knew this life intimately. In *Memoirs of a Coxcomb*, as in *Fanny Hill*, he wrote of it with complete frankness and honesty.

Suppressed until now, it is a major work of exotica.

Franklin S. Klaf, M.D., is a New York psychiatrist who studied at New York University, Columbia University, and Bethlehem Royal Hospital in London (the world's first mental institution). He has written many articles for leading professional journals and popular magazines. His latest book, *Strindberg: the Origin of Psychology in Modern Drama,* is regarded as a major contribution to the literature of the theatre.

COMPLETE AND UNABRIDGED

MEMOIRS
OF A
COXCOMB

BY JOHN CLELAND
Author of
FANNY HILL

The Companion Volume to
MEMOIRS OF A WOMAN OF PLEASURE

in an Unexpurgated Edition
with an analysis of the life
and works of John Cleland
by Franklin S. Klaf, M.D.

LANCER BOOKS • NEW YORK

MEMOIRS OF A COXCOMB

Printed in the U.S.A.
Published by
LANCER BOOKS, INC. • 26 WEST 47TH STREET • NEW YORK 36, N.Y.

MEMOIRS
OF A
COXCOMB

with an introduction

by Franklin S. Klaf, M.D.

ABOUT THIS BOOK AND JOHN CLELAND: AUTHOR OF "FANNY HILL" AND "MEMOIRS OF A COXCOMB"

AT THE AGE of forty, John Cleland was a failure. He had spent the first half of his life in a variety of dissipations, from the harems of Smyrna to the fleshpots of the Orient. He had squandered his father's inheritance, fought with superiors, and finally languished in a debtors' prison.

Now he was free, without a profession or other means of subsistence. Only a few intangible assets made him feel optimistic in the midst of his dilemma. He had received a sound education at Westminster College, and liberal training in how to be a rake from his father, Colonel Cleland. He was literate, in fact an accomplished linguist.

Enter Ralph Griffith, a bookseller of St. Paul's Churchyard, a man in similar circumstances. The two opportunists became partners in a publishing venture. Cleland was to distill his experiences and write a book called "Memoirs of a Woman of Pleasure," a novel which was to become the most sensational piece of erotica in English literature. In 1747 Fanny Hill was launched into circulation and immortality.

Both men achieved their financial objectives. Griffith became a millionaire, and John Cleland was temporarily saved from insolvency. Then came the repercussions. Griffith was put in the pillory, and Cleland was summoned before the Privy Council to explain his activities.

Eighteenth century English aristocrats were austere on the surface and licentious underneath. The members of the Privy Council had known old Colonel Cleland, and some of them had probably shared some of his youthful indiscretions. Here was their friend's son, who had dared to describe in public what many people were doing in private. How could he be silenced?

The answer seemed simple. He needed money. No British

officer's son should be left without funds. So the Privy Council gave him a pension of £100 a year, exacting his promise not to write a sequel to "Fanny Hill."

For a while the scheme worked. Cleland retired to the country, amusing himself by writing political pamphlets, poetry, and plays. Anonymous friends sent him treatises on the origin of the Celtic language, and he became absorbed in philology. None of Cleland's neighbors realized that this peaceful, scholarly man was England's foremost living pornographer.

The Privy Council, diligent though they were in their duty to the crown, possessed little knowledge about the psychology of writers. No man who has ever written a best seller can resist the temptation to try his luck again. John Cleland's mind teemed with ideas for his next book. It would be a successor to "Fanny Hill." Griffith, unchastened by the pillory, set up another printing press and anxiously awaited the first pages of the new manuscript.

Cleland called the sequel "Memoirs of a Coxcomb." He used the same basic plot, substituting a rake for a whore. Although the book is a work of fiction, it is based on personal experience and social custom. Rakes were not rare in mid-eighteenth century England. Taking their credo from the letters of Lord Chesterfield, they went through basic training on the Grand Tour of the continent before settling in London to pursue English girls. Hogarth's idelible portrait of "The Rake's Progress," with its sad ending in Bedlam, failed to stop a growing moral laxity.

Fanny Hill's male counterpart follows a career of debauchery familiar to English society. The description of his character represents a masterful blending of fine writing, subtle humor, and psychological acumen. Cleland's talents had matured by the time "Memoirs of a Coxcomb" was written. The years of silent contemplation of his tempestuous past had quickened his perception. Freed from financial pressure, he wrote leisurely, polishing each episode, achieving a series of special effects. Whereas "Fanny Hill" was a potboiler written to pick up some quick money, "Memoirs of a Coxcomb" is the work of a skilled craftsman.

Unfortunately, Cleland's reputation had been tarnished beyond redemption. "Fanny Hill" kept appearing in foreign and domestic editions, with and without illustrations, while his second erotic novel was ignored. His notoriety was assured, but critics failed to see any literary merit in his writing, consigning his books to the underworld of private editions. Cleland retained the £100 pension and retired to Petty, France, where he enjoyed his bottle of wine and memories of past pleasures until his death at 82 years of age.

Needless to say, Victorian critics did not strain themselves resurrecting his work. The name "Fanny Hill" passed into legend as the heroine of a book everyone had talked about but few had ever seen. Even Freud failed to find a copy of the German edition, which was never in plentiful supply. Early twentieth century scholars also ignored Cleland, and many failed to include his name in the index of anthologies.

Now, at last, John Cleland's writing is being published in an erotically charged atmosphere. Once again, as in his own lifetime, he may be dealt an injustice. Cleland was no eighteenth century Kinsey embarking on a one-man sex survey. He was a man who profited from sensual experience, a man who knew all about women from their physical charms to their subterranean nature. Like Balzac, he became a bedroom philosopher, tolerant of human ineptitude and fascinated by man's frailty.

Cleland's writing can transform our age of analysis into an era of emancipation. Sexual instincts existed long before Freud pointed his finger at them. Women were driven by the same cravings and men were possessed by the same polygamous inclinations before they were able to tell their troubles to a friendly, but expensive psychoanalyst.

No man can ever hope to fully understand the psychology of women without reading the works of John Cleland. Cleland was an erotic scholar who practiced before he wrote, not some aged commentator suffering from disuse or atrophy of the vital functions.

Cleland is a guide to the sexually perplexed, a gift to the inhibited. His books are alive with fresh insights and vivid portrayals. Although he wrote two hundred years ago, what he had to say is timeless.

Literary history often produces strange turns of fortune. The stodgy, pockmarked Samuel Johnson, who read five hours a day and married an elderly, sexless widow, became an eighteenth century hero. Boswell, who faithfully recorded his own eventful career as a rake in an obscure journal, has now eclipsed his master's fame. Both Boswell and Cleland were social commentators, venting their dislike of prudery, gossip and pretense. But Boswell kept his private papers buried in a trunk, and Cleland made the fatal mistake of publishing his memoirs.

What motivates a man to write and publish erotica? Some hints are available to explain Cleland's behavior. We know that his father was a rake, and that he spent his own youth in pursuit of women. Is the "Coxcomb" of this book a combination of father and son? No one will ever be certain, but this is probably the case. Why did Cleland publish? This question has already been answered—he needed money. Boswell, with a profession and a wealthy father, could afford to write for his own amusement.

Cleland's history is unfortunate in another respect. His was the tragedy of an excess of gifts. He failed to achieve recognition as a writer because he was too effective as a pornographer. After the fame of "Fanny Hill" no one took him seriously. The Privy Council paid him a pension not to write, and he was quietly put out of circulation like an English *enfant terrible* who had disturbed the status quo.

Now he has emerged from seclusion to be read by a generation that is gradually freeing itself from shame and guilt. He has a foot in both camps, as a scholar dedicted to the old traditions, and as an advocate of the new enlightenment. His skill will be praised, his style imitated, and his daring admired.

For years libraries kept these books under lock and key, out of reach to all but erudite professors. The shackles have finally been removed, and one of the finest eighteenth century writers has the opportunity to take his rightful place in English literature.

Let him speak for himself.

—*Franklin Klaf, M.D.*

MEMOIRS

OF A

COXCOMB.

PART I.

S O DELICATE is the pleasure, so superior to defending is the dignity of confessing one's follies, that the wonder is to see so few capable of it. Yet, what does such a confession cost, but the sacrifice of a paltry, miserable, false self-love, which is for ever misleading and betraying us? And of all its illusions there is not perhaps a more dangerous or a more silly one, than that which hinders us from discerning that there is scarce a less merit in acknowledging candidly one's faults, than in not having been guilty of them. For my own part, I speak experimentally. I never felt so pleasing, so sensible a consolation for the misfortune of having been a coxcomb, and an eminent one, too, as this proof of the sincerity of my conversion, in the courage of coming to a fair and open confession of the follies I drove into, in the course of that character. And though nothing is truer than that the desire of pleasing the ladies first engaged me to take it up, and seek with uncommon pain to shine in it, it is but justice to subjoin that, if I owed to that amiable and unaccountable sex my having been a coxcomb, I owe to a select one of it, too, the being one no longer. But let the following history of my errors and return to reason, which I now go into without further preamble, substitute facts to reflections. These ever follow with a better grace than they lead.

My father and mother died long before I knew all that I lost, in losing them. I was their only child, and under that title heir to two of the best estates in two of our richest counties in England, besides a sum that did not want many thousand pounds of making what is called, in the language of Change-Alley, a plumb: and which was secured to me much more effectually, as it happened, than a good education. For to say that I had not a bad one was barely all that I dare venture, and keep any measures with truth. Being left as I was, under the care and tuition of an old, rich aunt, who was a widow, and past the possibility of having any children herself; her declared and real intention to leave me all her fortune, which was very considerable, though most certainly I could not want it, engaged my guardians to acquiesce in my education being trusted without the least interposition or control, on their part, to her management and direction. There was the less reason, too, for this choice, for that a woman who had from her infancy constantly lived in the country, and of course had been but little acquainted with the world, could not be the fittest person in it, to superintend the bringing up of a young gentleman of my pretensions to make a figure in it, both from my birth and my fortune. But such is the power of interest. My aunt insisted, and the expectation of that distant, superfluous addition to my fortune formed in the eyes of my guardians a sufficient excuse for giving way to my aunt's fondness.

I lived with her then till the age of eighteen at her own seat in Warwickshire, where she had spared to the best of her knowledge no pains or expense to have me taught all the accomplishments, indispensably necessary to one of my rank and condition. But she would have most certainly disappointed her own good intentions by her extreme fondness and over-tenderness of me, if my tutor Mr. Selden, whose name I shall ever mention with the greatest gratitude, had not found out my weak side, and with that the secret of engaging me to make what progress he pleased, by properly piquing my pride. All correction or severity were forbidden him: and I do not know whether, after all, he did not succeed as well, by the emulation and value for myself, he inspired me with, as he would have done by those harsh and, indeed, disingenuous methods, too often used to youth, and which breed in it such a fund of aversion to learning, that they do not afterwards easily get rid of its impressions.

This flattering of my pride had, however, one bad effect, in that it laid too much the foundation of that insolence and presumption, which I carried into life with me, and made me, by thinking more highly of myself than I deserved, lose a great deal even of that little merit, I might otherwise, and perhaps not unjustly, have pretended to.

However, very unluckily, just as the heat and impetuosity

of my age, barely turned of seventeen, most required the guidance and direction of a governor, mine was taken from me by the circumstance of a very advantageous preferment, which required his attendance on the spot, and which my aunt had procured him, in recompense for the care he had taken of my education, and which she, more partially than wisely, considered as wanting nothing of being complete.

Mr. Selden then left me, and, I confess, I saw him set out with a regret, soon dissipated by the pleasure of thinking that I should have a greater swing of liberty, for though not much, he was still some check on me, and that it would the sooner bring on my going to London, which I languished for, and had indeed no hopes of; till on his departure, my aunt, whom nothing could have dragged out of her country-retirement but a resolution not to part with me, declared she would go there in the winter season, purely upon my account: and now the spring was little more than set in.

As soon then as my tutor was fairly gone, my first fling out was into the pleasures of the chase. My aunt who had, through him, been mistress enough of my conduct, to keep that passion within some bounds, for fear of the dangers which attend it, was no longer able to control me, in that, or indeed anything else. I knew her weakness, and turned a little tyrant upon it. A few weeks, however, of an unbounded pursuit of hunting put an end to the violence of my passion for it. My blood, now boiling in my veins, began to make me feel the ferment of desire for objects far more interesting than horses and dogs. And a robust, healthy constitution, manifest in the glow of a fresh complexion, and vigorous well-proportioned limbs, gave me those warnings of my ripening manhood, and its favourite destination, by which nature prevents all instruction, and suggests the use of those things that most engage our attention, without putting us to the blush of asking silly questions. I had not indeed waited till then for the dawn of certain desires, and wishes: but besides their being only imperfect ones and crudities of over tender youth, my hours and opportunities had been all so confined either to my studies, exercises, boyish amusements, or my aunt's fondness for my being as little out of her sight as possible, that I had not the least room to encourage such ideas, or give them hope enough to live upon. Accordingly, they generally died away of themselves, like a faint breeze that had just blown enough to ruffle the surface of my imagination for a few instants, and flattened into a calm again. But now, those transient desires, inspired by this rising passion, began to take a more settled hold of my imagination, and to grow into such tender pantings, such an eagerness of wishes, as quite overcame and engrossed me entirely. Woman it was, that I may say, I instinctively knew, was wanting to my happiness. But I had as yet no determined object in that sex, but yearned and looked out for one everywhere. This was not, however, a point very easy, especially for me, in the house and way I lived in; where strictness of decency, and above all my aunt's constant assiduities, planted such a guard upon me, that few virgins could have found it a harder matter, to get rid of their burthen, than I had to do of mine, which was indeed become an intolerable one.

Yet this passion had a contrary effect on me to all others. For, in place of that impatience of check or control, that wilfulness, with which I rather commanded, than obtained, a compliance with them, I was really mastered by this. A kind of native modesty made me shy and reserved of letting any one know the cause of my inward disorder. From fierce and insolent, I was now, I may say, transnatured to somewhat a more civilized savage. Gentleness and softness are almost ever the character of that passion in its infancy, perhaps from its feeling that it must depend on the will of another for its gratification. I was now then in prey to that tender melancholy which is generally a state of meditation on the means of accomplishing our desires, and which makes us find a solitude everywhere, and an empty void in every thing, that has not a relation to the cure of this disorder, for which, however, there is no great fear, in these times, of dying for want of physicians. Yet, strong as this youthful passion ever is, it was fated for some time at least to give way to a stronger and a nobler one, even love itself.

About a mile from our seat, on the skirts of a wood, stood a lonely house, thatched, and scarce too large for a cottage, but more defended from any danger of thieves, by its appearances of poverty, than by a few palisades, which formed a kind of fore-yard to it, for the conveniency of a small stock of poultry.

Here I had often called, as it lay in the track of my diversion of shooting. The tenant of it, an old woman, who farmed it of my aunt, had by her care and officiousness to offer me any refreshment her house afforded, when I used to stop there, dry or fatigued with my sporting, so much won upon me, that I easily prevailed upon my aunt to let her have her house and spot of gardening rent-free.

She had nobody to live with her but a young lad, a grand-child of hers about eleven years old, whose sprightly answers, and affectionate readiness to go with, shew me the game, and carry my gun, took with me so much, that I begged him of his grandmother, with an intention to do better for him than what there was any appearance of from her.

The poor old woman let me have him away with no other reluctance than what her natural fondness, and being left entirely alone gave her. As for his part, he was in rapture at the proposal, and a fine livery which I ordered him, joined to the appointment of him to wait entirely upon me, soon drove all mother-sickness out of his head.

Taking him then out, as usual, to carry my gun, I often called at the old woman's: and but a few days after this being regularly fixed in my service, being more than ordinarily fatigued, I stopped there, purely to drink some cyder, of which I had ordered a provision for that purpose from our house. But my surprize will not be easily imagined, when slipping familiarly into a little room, always appropriated to my reception, and which was indeed the room of state, though before no better set out than with an old crazy table, a few sorry prints, a funeral escutcheon and the widowed frame of a departed glass, I found it now very neatly furnished, and two women, whom I had never yet seen, with a tea-equipage before them. A tea-equipage too! no, never had there before been such a circumstance of luxury heard of, much less seen, under that thatch.

As I entered the room, somewhat abruptly too, the old woman who was waiting on them, not having had notice enough of my coming, to stop me, the two strangers got up, and making me a curtesy, seemed a little confused and disconcerted by my intrusion, though they had even been prepared for it, by the old woman's telling them that the young baronet often called at her house.

I was, however, out of all figure to inspire much respect. A sportman's frock, and the rest of my dress in that style: my face reasonably covered with dust, mixed with the perspiration of pores opened by heat and fatigue, all together composed me an air of rusticity, which the beginning of the most quick-sighted of all passions, made me on the instant sensible of. The first character of love is a diffidence of pleasing.

My eye hardly glanced over the elder of the two strangers, who was, however, a very agreeable figure. She might be about forty, dressed plainly but with an air of decency and deportment, far above the rank of life such a lodging supposed her.

But then the youngest! With what a command of beauty did she not attract my eyes, and engross my attention? Fifteen was her utmost; but to the charms of fifteen, nature had joined her whole sum of treasures. The shape of a nymph, an air of the Graces, features such as Venus, but Venus in her state of innocence, when new-born of the sea: a complexion in which the tints of red and white, delicately blended, formed that more than roseate colour, which is at once the painter's admiration and despair. Then there was such an over-all of sweetness and gentle simplicity, diffused through her every look and gesture, as might disarm the most determined votary to vice, and turn him protector of her virtue. I say nothing of her dress; her personal charms hardly gave me leave to observe it; and indeed what blaze of jewels could have tempted away my gaze from that of her eyes?

At my age then, and with my desires, when every woman began to appear a goddess to me, in virtue of the power I attributed to that sex, of bestowing on me the mighty, unknown happiness I languished by conjecture, no wonder that a form, to which exaggeration could not lend a perfection that she had not, should make so strong an impression, where I was already so predisposed to receive it.

I stood then, like a true country-corydon, a few minutes, motionless with surprize, in a stupid gaze of admiration. At length, I articulated, in awkward breaks, and with bows that certainly did no great honour to my dancing-master, my apology for the rudeness of breaking in upon them, offering immediately to quit the room, and trembling for fear they should take me at my word.

The eldest, whose name I afterwards learned, Mrs. Bernard, observed to me, with great politeness that I seemed very much fatigued, and that she should take it for an honour if I would accept of a dish of tea. The youngest still stood with looks modestly declined, and unconcerned, as if not warranted to join in the invitation.

I sat down then: and the conversation presently from gen-

erals grew to particulars, in favour of the curiosity I could
not escape expressing, at the oddity of seeing persons of their
fashion and figure in such a mean habitation.

Mrs. Bernard, who doubtless chose I should learn whatever
she wished me to think concerning them rather from herself
than from the old woman, acquainted me, that having been
charged with the education of that young lady who was with
her from an infant, certain family disagreements (which she
very falsely took for granted were insignificant to me), had
reduced them to seek the shelter of the greatest privacy, till
the storm should be overblown. That she was not unacquainted with the danger of a retreat so far removed from
the defence of neighbourhood, but that the reasons of it were
above even that consideration. She added, too, but with a
very sensible shyness, that she hoped the accident of my seeing them there, would neither interfere with the continuation
of their obscurity, nor the plan of retirement, which she
begged at once my discretion and protection in.

Whilst she was giving me this account, I sat mute, and absorbed in feelings utterly new to me. What wretch is there
so unhappy, so disinherited by nature, as not not to have been
sometime of his life in love! Those indeed alone, who have
paid the tribute of humanity to this passion, can conceive to
what a point I was struck by all I now heard. I was, however,
only affected relatively to this new object of another set of
sensations, than those merely instinctive ones, which nature
furnishes in the rough, and which love alone can give a pol-
ish and lustre to.

The answers I made to Mrs. Bernard, however unfit to give
any great idea of my breeding or understanding, were perhaps the more pathetic for the vivacity and confusion which
reigned in them, and which are so sensibly the eloquence of
the heart. What I felt then rather disordered than weakened
my expressions. My tongue, too, directed my discourse to
Mrs. Bernard; but my eyes addressed it to Miss, who did not
so much as look up at me, whatever pains I took to catch her
if but glancing towards me.

I stayed then as long as was consistent with the advance
of the evening, and the measures of respect, which the little
I knew of the world, and the fear of displeasing, suggested
to me the propriety of. But in all that time, Lydia, or Miss
Liddy, which was the name of the youngest, had scarce
opened her mouth, and that only in monosyllables; but with

such a grace of modesty such a sweetness of sound, as made every string of my heart vibrate again with the most delicious impression. I could not easily decide within myself which I wished for most ardently, to be all eye, to see her beauty, or all ear, to hear the music of her voice.

Forced then to take my leave, I did myself that violence, but not before I had obtained the permission Mrs. Bernard could not very politely refuse me, and which I protested I should not abuse, to visit them during their stay in that part. But as I had observed that there was not a soul in the house except the poor, old woman, I could, without any affectation or obtrusion, order the boy, her grandchild, to stay behind, to be at hand for any service they might want; in which, too, I had a second view, of knowing from him all that should pass in my absence: an employ he was admirably fitted for by nature, who had bestowed upon him one of those simple, harmless, unmeaning faces which are invaluable, when joined to wit enough to make the most of the little guard one is on against them.

I was scarce got half way down the little sort of lane, which led to the cottage, before the wishful regret of what I left behind me, made me stop and look back. Then, then I perceived all the magic of love. I saw now everything with other eyes. That little rustic mansion had assumed a palace-air. Turrets, colonnades, *jet-d'eaux*, gates, gardens, temples: no magnificence, no delicacy of architecture was wanting to my imagination, in virtue of its fairy-power of transforming real objects into whatever most flatters or exalts that passion. I should now have looked on every earthly paradise with indifference or contempt, that was not dignified and embellished with the presence of this new sovereign of all the world to me.

Nor was the transformation I experienced within myself one jot less miraculous. All the desires I had hitherto felt the pungency of, were perfectly constitutional: the suggestions of nature beginning to feel itself. But the desire I was now given up to, had something so distinct, so chaste, and so correct, that its impressions carried too much of virtue in it, for my reason to refuse it possession of me. All my native fierceness was now utterly melted away into diffidence and gentleness. A voluptuous langour stole its softness into me. And for the first time in my life I found I had a heart, and that heart susceptible of a tenderness, which endeared and ennobled me to myself, and made me place my whole happiness in the hopes of inspiring a return of it to the sweet authoress of this revolution.

I naturally hate reflexions. They are generally placed as fescues to a reader, to point out to him, what it would be more respectful to suppose would not escape him. Besides, they often disagreeably interrupt him, in his impatience of coming to the conclusion, which facts alone lead to. Yet, I cannot here refrain from observing, that, not without reason, are the romance and novel writers in general despised by persons of sense and taste, for their unnatural and unaffecting descriptions of the love-passion. In vain do they endeavour to warm the head, with what never came from the heart. Those who have really been in love, who have themselves experienced the emotions and symptoms of that passion, indignantly remark that, so far from exaggerating its power and effects, those triflers do not even do it justice. A forced cookery of imaginary beauties, a series of mighty marvellous facts, which, spreading an air of fiction through the whole, all in course weaken that interest and regard never paid but to truth, or the appearances of truth; and are only fit to give a false and adulterated taste of passion, in which a simple sentiment is superior to all their forced productions of artificial flowers. Their works in short give one the idea of a frigid, withered eunuch, representing an Alexander making love to Statira.

Let me not lengthen this digression by asking pardon for it. It may be more agreeable to promise as few more of them as possible. I resume then the thread of my narrative.

Returned to my aunt's: it was easy for me to give what colour I pleased to the having left the boy at his grandmother's; but it was not so easy, for one of my age and inexperience, to conceal the change of my temper and manners, which betrayed itself in every look and gesture. My aunt was surprised at the gentleness and softness which now breathed in all I said or did. Unacquainted with what had happened, she could not account for a novelty that so much delighted her. At supper, too, I forced a gaiety, very inconsistent with the state of my heart, which was not without those fears and alarms inseparable from the beginnings of so violent a passion; but I made the pains of it, as much as I could, give way, at least in appearance, to the pleasure of my recent adventure.

The day had hardly broken before I was up, and disposing everything for the renewal of my visits. And as I well knew it would be impossible for me to pay them so often as I fully proposed to myself, without the motives being presently known and published, I resolved, so far at least wisely, to disappoint the discovery, by determinately braving it. I ordered then, without any air of mystery or reserve, my servants to carry to the old woman's everything I could think of, such as tea, chocolate, coffee, fruits, and whatever might not probably be come at in such a country-habitation, in that delicacy and perfection, as we abounded in at this seat of my aunt's. The worst of which conduct was, and here is the place to set it down, that my aunt was soon informed that I had a little mistress there, that I kept to divert myself with. And though the falsity of it shocked the delicacy of my sentiments, I preferred it, however, as a less dangerous disturbance, than if my aunt had been alarmed so as to view my resort there in a more serious light. She once, however, ventured to touch upon it to me, in a taste of remonstrance, but I gave it such a reception, and she was so thoroughly subdued by the superiority I had managed myself with her, that she was not tempted to renew in haste the attack. Perhaps, too, she comforted herself with thinking it was the less of two evils, that I should carry the war abroad, rather than make it at home amongst her maids; one of whom, by the bye, in spite of all the caution used to prevent it, I was on the point of consummating an impure treaty with, when chance threw this new passion in my way, which erased every thought of any but the object of it out of my head and heart.

At ten in the morning then, the hour I guessed might be my charmer's breakfast time, I set out in my chariot, dressed in the richest suit I was master of, with my hair trimmed and curled in all the perfection it was capable of; in all which my intense wish to please had even a greater share than my vanity. Thus equipped for conquest, I landed at the bottom of the lane, and walked up to the house, where I was immediately admitted to the ladies, who were just set down to their tea.

The eldest had not in the least changed her clothes; but Lydia was, if possible, yet more modestly and undesignedly dressed than the day before. A white frock and a glimpse of a cap, lost in the hair that curled everywhere over it, and eclipsed it, whilst a plain cambric handkerchief covered a bosom easily imagined to be of the whiteness of snow, from what it did not hide of her neck, and which in the gentlest rise and fall seemed to repeat to me the palpitations of my heart. Such was her morning dishabille, in which simplicity and neatness clearly triumphed over all the powers of dress and parade.

After the first compliments were over, Mrs. Bernard thanked me for my regard, the excess of which she obligingly complained of, remarking to me at the same time that they were of themselves abundantly supplied with all necessaries towards making their retreat agreeable, and concluded with a civil but firm request, that I should not put her to the necessity of sending back what was superfluous to them, and which they had, for fear of offending me, accepted for the first time and given to the landlady in my name.

This stiffness in persons I supposed under some misfortune surprised me a little: but not, however, so much, as their perfect and unaffected indifference to the change of my figure, in point of dress. I had then doubtless in me those seeds of coxcombry, which afterwards ran up to such a height as for a while over-shadowed the other good qualities I might be indebted to nature for. The suit I had on was entirely new, and had but the sunday before given the stares to a whole congregation; but I could not, unpiqued, remark that they glanced over the glitter of it, with that inattention which persons of true taste, and true distinction, have especially for dress, when they perceive it made a point of.

These mortifications, however, contributed doubtless to throw more modesty and humility into my answers. I made proper apologies for the liberty I had taken, and which I had grounded on the situation of their retreat. I added, too, that I was so perfectly convinced of the respect owing them, as well as so interested to serve them, that I conjured them by the regard they had even for their own safety, if not for their conveniency, to accept of an accommodation at Lady Bellinger's, my aunt's, where I was sure they would be treated with all the highest honour and regard; and at the same time without the least impertinence of curiosity to penetrate any secret they should be pleased to reserve.

"Though," answered Mrs. Bernard, "nothing can prove " more demonstrably the purity of your intentions and the " nature of your sentiments in our favour than such an invita- " tion, you will forgive us if we cannot accept it. We depend

"on persons to whom, for many reasons too immaterial to
"trouble you with, such a step would be highly unaccept-
"able. The greatest privacy is at present all our object. We
"could not expect it so entirely in a house crowded with
"servants and visitants; besides that the *incognito* we are
"forced to keep, gives us an air of adventurers, that not all
"our consciousness to the contrary could reconcile us to the
"enduring. All then, Sir, that we have now to fear, and wish
"you to avoid, is the giving, by your resort here any uneasi-
"ness to your family, or room for scandal to fasten its malice
"upon."

During this harangue, I had kept my eyes entirely fixed
upon Lydia, who kept hers fixed upon Mrs. Bernard, but
with such a calm of countenance, that I could not perceive
whether she approved, or not, these her conclusions. Finding, however, that my steadiness of gaze began to embarrass
and give her pain, I forced away my eyes, and had only power
to say all that I thought necessary to soften Mrs. Bernard into
a toleration, or rather renewal, of my leave to visit them,
which, as she soon saw it was a point I would not easily give
up, she seemed to acquiesce in, under such restrictions and
precautions, as were decent for her to prescribe, and which
indeed I meant too well, not even cheerfully to accept of the
compromise.

As soon as these preliminaries were adjusted, so greatly to
my heart's ease, I presently grew more cheerful, more frank,
and especially more particular to Lydia, who received everything I addressed to her, with the most shy timidity, or the
most complete unconcern. Nor did she ever recover herself
into any show of gaiety, but as I desisted from particularities
to herself. I was not long at making this remark, nor at being
heartily chagrined at it. I pouted a little, I discovered my uneasiness at the reception she gave these preludes of my passion, but equally in vain. She behaved towards me as if she
rather wished me to continue the coolness of a pique, as a disposition less irksome to her than my fondness. But whatever changes of countenance she shifted to, coyness, unconcern or mirth, she pleased in all too much for me to obtain
even an interval of freedom. I loved, and I did not despair.

I gave, however, this second visit the less length, for the
impatience I had to enquire of Goody Gibson, the old
woman, by what means these ladies had fished out and

planted their habitation in so uninviting and out-of-the-way
a corner.

After then taking my leave, I easily managed an interview
with the landlady, who gave me the following account. That
a little, oldish man had been directed, as he pretended at
least, to her house and had bargained at the first word for all
the apartments she had to spare; and that the very next day
he had sent in a waggon load of furniture, and would have
sent more, if her house could have held it. And that a few
hours after Mrs. Bernard and the young gentlewoman, accompanied by this little, old man, came and took possession
of their new lodging, since which she had not seen him, but
believed he would come soon to them, as he promised that
he would. That they seemed in the meantime to regard no
cost; for they had sent Tom, her grandson, last night to Warwick market for partridges and the costliest fish: and that
Mrs. Bernard had put her in the way, as well as helped, to
dress them. That she paid vast respect to Miss, who now and
then wept bitterly.

This was the sum of the information I drew out of the
good, old woman; which, by the way, very little enlightened
me as to their real character and condition in life. I easily conceived, however, that this little, old man, she spoke of, had
the key of the whole mystery. And accordingly I gave Tom
strict charge, to be alert and watch all he could, that I might
take my measures on his report.

I was in the meantime so prejudiced in favour of these
incognitas, that whatever unstately aspect or derogation there
appeared in their present circumstances, I could readily have
taken at least the youngest, for one of your princesses, such
as romances paint them, when forced to wander in distress,
only she had clean linen, and no jewels, at least that she
thought proper to make a show of.

One provision, however, for their safety I could not refuse
my own ardent concern for it the satisfaction of procuring.
Our park wall had a gate, which had been long condemned
as useless, and which opened within a few yards of this
house. Here, in a lodge, that had been, of course, long unin-
habited, contiguous to the gates which I new ordered to be
set open, I planted a guard of two of the park-keepers or ten-
ants, who kept constant watch at nights, to prevent even the
fear of any insult in that remote place. The fellows, too,

did their duty the more cheerfully, as I was obliged to give
them double pay, both on my own account and on that of the
ladies, who had offered to satisfy them, and from whom I
charged them not to receive anything, in a tone that convinced them I was not to be trifled with. By this step in favour of their security, I found I had made my court very effectually to Mrs. Bernard, who thanked me cordially; Miss
only in a short perfunctory way made me a cool compliment, upon the occasion. But even that overpaid me. Surely,
what one does for the person one really loves, is ever a more
delicious pleasure than doing it for oneself.

I had not, in the meantime, been so pressing for leave to
wait on them at their hours of convenience, not to make use
of it. My assiduities were alert and incessant. I had found
that they neither wanted, nor would accept presents of any
sort. But as flowers, fruits, birds, and the like, are never included under that denomination, and carry with them that
character of simplicity, so peculiar to the country, I exhausted every invention, to gratify Lydia with these marks of
my passion. She received them, but received them with that
air of dignity and reserve, which shewed I owed her acceptance more to her politeness, than to any attention she had to
the motives of the presenter.

One day that I had received from London a very curious
and neatly bound edition of Telemachus in French, a book
I knew she was very fond of, and was actually, under the instruction of Mrs. Bernard, translating little extracts of it, for
her improvement both in that and her own language, I was in
hopes, from the nature of the present, that I should not risk
a refusal of it. Accordingly, I carried it myself, and offered it
her in the presence of Mrs. Bernard; but she declined receiving it, under the civil pretence of her having one already. I
was, I looked, mortified. Upon which, Mrs. Bernard very
good-naturedly observed to her, that though receiving presents from men was an encouragement she never should recommend to her; yet there were certain bagatelles, which by
the courtesy of custom were always excepted, especially in
certain circumstances. And that there was really a greater
dignity and indeed a justice owing to one's assured superiority, in accepting things of so little importance, than treating them as matters of consequence by rejecting them.

Miss, on this remonstrance, with a smile of ineffable sweetness, as if by way of reparation, almost snatched the book,

which I held extended in my hand, and making me a low
courtesy, said, "Sir, I thank you not only for the favour itself,
"but for the lesson it has procured me, which, I am satisfied,
"is perfectly just."

I was, however, so transported with carrying my point,
that I could have hugged Mrs. Bernard for the vexation she
had spared me, and for the pleasure she had procured me.
And, indeed, whatever cruel chagrin her fidelity to her
charge afterwards occasioned me, I must do her the justice
to own, that never woman more deserved to be entrusted
with the care and education of a pupil. Without one weakness
of her sex, she had all the essential virtues, all the good qualities of a man of honour. Her real personal history was as
follows.

Young, she had been married to the son of her lady's steward. Brought up entirely as her lady's companion, she had
shared in common with her all the advantages of the most polite education, and seen the best company on a footing of apparent equality. Her husband, by whom she had several children, none of whom lived, died, and left her with a middling
provision for life, which did not hinder her from re-attach-
ing herself to her lady, to whose family she now devoted all
her care and tenderness, and became deservedly her humble
confidant and friend. The little, old man, whom I have before
mentioned, was no other than her husband's father, to whom,
too, she endeavoured, as far as was in her power, to make up,
in duty and affection, all he had lost, in losing his son. And
it was in virtue of these relations, and of her tried discretion
and trustworthiness, that she became the guardian, or rather
preserver of Lydia, in the most critical conjuncture, when
all the happiness of her life was at stake; all the particulars
of which, it was not till long after, that I came at the nature
and truth of. So much, however, was precisely here necessary to premise, concerning her character and connexions
with Lydia. Let me add, too, that next to that great master
love itself, I owed to the conversation I had with her more
true, more essential knowledge of the world I was preparing to launch into, than to all the lessons or instructions I had
received either from my tutor or Lady Bellinger. Nothing,
I found by experience, forms a raw young man so effectually,
as the conserving with an agreeable, well-bred woman.
Though to say the truth, I could not with impunity have, at
my age, and with my warmth of constitution, seen so famil-

iarly one of Mrs. Bernard's sex, with her qualifications, and even remaining personal merit, had not Lydia's victorious superiority drove all thoughts of that sort out of my head.

Mrs. Bernard had, in the meantime, perfectly penetrated the nature of my sentiments towards her amiable charge. But sure of herself, sure of Lydia, she seemed, at least, entirely unalarmed. Content to watch my every motion and attempt to engage her to a private conversation, but naturally, and without the appearance of watching it. The impossibility then of coming to such an explanation with Lydia as I languished for, whilst they stayed at that house, where my visits were under too severe restriction of time and place, suggested me the renewal of my invitation to them, to remove to my aunt's, upon a motive I thought Mrs. Bernard would, with difficulty, parry.

I broke to her then, not without trembling and with the utmost delicacy, the reports which my assiduities had occasioned, and which in country places are unavoidable, reports unsavoury to that footing of respect and innocence, on which they had permitted me to see them, and which I could now part with my life sooner than renounce the pleasure of. But I had to do with one prepared and determined. She observed to me that I neither surprised, nor discomposed her with an intimation of a suspicion attending my assiduities, which she had bespoke, from the nature of their situation, and which they deserved too little, not to despise. That she owned it a duty in general to guard against the appearances of wrong, but that their particular case absolved her insensibility in otherwise so delicate a point; and ended with desiring me not to press them any more to a removal they were averse to, unless I would drive them to the inconvenience of seeking once more a covert, that should protect them from such persecution.

I shuddered so much at this last menace, that I took special care from thenceforward not even to drop a hint that might dispose them to put it into execution. Nor could I help redoubling my admiration at the well-supported air of dignity and state, which breathed in all their conduct and expressions, and increased my ardent curiosity to find out their real character and rank in life. This last I had soon reason to imagine myself in a fair way of satisfying. Tom came one day, just as I had dined, to acquaint me that the little, old man

was certainly to be with the ladies that evening having sent a
message to that purpose from Warwick.

I easily knew that it would be in vain, and indeed im-
proper for me to give them the interruption of my visit at
that juncture, and consequently stayed away that evening, at the hazard of their conjecturing, as they doubtless
did, the true reason of this novelty.

Thus far was right, but I took a measure, on the other
hand, full as foolish, as the event did not fail to prove it.

I ordered my horses, and immediately set out for Warwick, which was at a small distance from our seat. There I
presently found out by the description the very inn, where
this old man had put up, and where his horse still stood, for
he was himself gone, as I expected, to the habitation of the
ladies.

In a room then, which I had taken up, and where I was
very well known, I waited patiently enough for his return.
As soon as he came in, I ordered the landlord to acquaint
him that a gentleman would be glad of his company for a few
minutes.

On this he complied without any hesitation, and came in,
with an air of modest freedom that shewed he knew the
world, and would alone have disposed me to treat him with
respect, even had not his connexion with the idol of my heart
inspired me with that regard for him, which extends to no
person so powerfully, as those whose service our passions
stand in need of.

He was very lean, low statured, and had something of an
acuteness and sagacity in his countenance, that his real character was far from giving the lie in, to the rules of physi-
ognomy.

The preface, leading to the favour I had to ask of him, was
in substance, that it was from no motive of impertinent curiosity, much less from any design himself would not approve
of, that an acquaintance which chance had given birth to, had
created in me the warmest, the tenderest interest in the wel-
fare of two persons, who, I was not ignorant of, were dear
to him, and in some sort under his protection, and, telling
him withal my name (which he knew as well as myself),
assured him that no confidence he could favour me with in
respect to them, should ever be abused by me; that the greatest good might indeed result both to the ladies and myself

from my being let into their secret, but that in all events, there could no harm come of it, since I gave him my honour, I would religiously conceal it from all the world, and even my knowledge of it from themselves, if he required it. That I would also inviolably adhere to the strictest rules of honour, with regard to them, and in short, not take one step, in consequence of his discovery, without his previous avowal and approbation.

He heard me out, with the greatest patience and attention: when, master as he was of his face, I saw it overspread with such an air of ingenuity and candour, as gave me the greatest hopes, and might have duped one of more experience and knowledge of the world than myself.

"Lord, Sir!" says he, "are you the gentleman to whom my " daughter, and the young lady have such great obligations? " Well! I protest, I am highly pleased with this opportunity " to return you my thanks. Poor souls! indeed they stand " greatly in need of your goodness. But, as to what you " desire to know, I cannot say but Mrs. Bernard had it strictly " in charge not to discover the occasion of their retreat to " anyone; but you seem such a worthy gentleman, that I think " there need be no reserve to you, whatever there may be to " others. So, Sir!—but hold! Now I think of it, I would not " have them know neither that I have acquainted you with " the mystery: for, it may make them less on their guard to " find their secret in a third hand. Upon that condition " then——"

Here I renewed the most solemn protestations that I would never directly, nor indirectly, drop a hint, or give them the least overture of my discovery: that I approved even his caution, and would do honour to his confidence, by my conduct on it.

"Well then," says he, "you have doubtless heard of Mr. " Webber, the great banker in Wellington-street?" "I cannot " say that I have," said I: "Good lack! Good lack! that is " much" replies the old gentleman. "Why he was one of " such extensive dealings, that I thought everybody knew " Mr. Webber in Wellington-street. But indeed, poor gentle- " man, his case is very bad at present. He has lately had such " a run upon him, that though he is a bottomed man, and " when his affairs are made up, is able to pay twenty shill- " ings in the pound, he has been obliged to step aside for a " little time, till he can turn himself, and see clearer into his

"affairs. In the meantime, as it was inconvenient for him
"to have his daughter with him,—and he is a vast proud man,
"that to be sure he is,—he has sent Miss Lydia out of the
"way, under the tuition of Mrs. Bernard, who has lived a
"long while in the family, with a strict injunction to live as
"private and out of the world as possible. It may be, too, he
"may have other reasons, but I do not know them. I am but
"his agent in the case, and should be ruined for ever with
"him, if he comes to the knowledge of my having revealed
"so much without his consent. Oh! he is very scrupulous, a
"very scrupulous man."

All this he circumstantiated so gravely, so naturally, too,
though in a low language occasionally affected, that I swal-
lowed every syllable of it, for truth. For my part, who was
more romantically in love than all the Celadons that ever
owed their existence to fiction, I was so deeply affected at
this Mr. Webber's misfortunes, on the account of his amiable
daughter, that the tears were ready to start into my eyes.
After an instant's pause then, granted to the vehemence of
my emotions and my reflexions on the occasion, I broke silence, and told him that his confidence had penetrated me
with the deepest concern: that I did not, however, confine
myself to a barren protestation of it: that though I was under
age, and could not dispose of my own fortune, I was so much
the master with my aunt, that I could assure him, and myself, of raising immediately a sum from ten to twenty thousand pounds, or even more, if that would extricate or make
Mr. Webber easy. And to leave him no doubt of the nature
and innocence of my designs, I promised him that, whatever
violence I did myself, I would not even see Miss again, but at
her father's house under his express sanction and consent.
That, for the rest, his acceptance of this aid would be the
greatest favour he could possibly do me.

I saw my gentleman's face at this, in spite of all his command over it, covered with so much surprise and confusion,
that I was very near not being the dupe of his story. He was
so moved, so staggered, as he afterwards told me, by the
frankness and generosity of my offer, and the candour I
backed it with, that it was not without some pain and compunction that he continued a deception, which he could only
answer to the innocence of his motives, and to diffidence of
the discretion of my age.

Continuing then on the foot of the false confidence he

had begun, he told me that he believed there would be no occasion for his employer's being driven to any extraordinary resource for assistance: that he would however acquaint him with what I had so generously tendered, intimating withal that he was withdrawn out of England: that it would of course take up some time to receive his answer, and that he advised, nay begged of me, by no means to make any further enquiries: that time would shew the reasons of this caution. And concluded with assuring me, in all events, that I should not lose the merit of what I had so obligingly offered to do for persons who had really not deserved their distress. And in this he was sincere, and kept his word with me.

On these terms, we parted. I returned that evening to our seat. And now, in the first opportunities of being in private with myself, I found the solution of all my doubts and difficulties, with regard to my passion for Lydia. I had never before expressly told myself, or indeed knew my intentions towards her. Nothing was truer than that I had never once harboured a thought about her inconsistent with the most rigid honour and the purest virtue. But I had, also, never once dreamt of my passion driving me the lengths of a serious engagement with her, especially in the uncertainty I laboured under of her condition. My birth and fortune gave me a title indeed to pretend to the daughter of the first duke in Britain. But then, a banker's daughter was neither according to the maxims of the world, or my own notion of things, an alliance anyways dishonourable. As to his misfortunes, whether temporary or not, I never once hesitated about treating them, but as a reason the more for confirming myself in my resolution, to sacrifice every consideration to my love. I was not of age, my family might exclaim: these and every other objection I held cheap in comparison with the possession of a heart, it became the highest plan of happiness I could form to triumph over. Besides that, wilful as I was, fiercely impatient of control, especially in so tender a point, I was very capable of plunging into that sort of mad ingratitude, with which often fools, at their own expense, so cruelly repay the tender concern of their best friends.

After thanking myself then for a firmness, on which I conceived all the future joys of my life to depend, and clear, that since I was fated to play ALL FOR LOVE OR THE WORLD WELL LOST, I could never meet with an object so fit to justify me, I resigned myself up to the blandishments of sleep, which became the more welcome to me, from the agitations of the day.

Waking pretty early, my little spy, Tom, was at the bed-side with his yesterday's gazette. He brought me then the no-news of the little old man's having been there in the after-noon; but added, that pretty late in the evening, there had come from Warwick, a small band-box directly to Mrs. Bernard, the contents of which he knew nothing of.

Now, had I had at that time, but the thousandth part of brains that I had of love, I might easily have conjectured that this band-box was no other than a cover to a letter of advice, concerning the attack I had made, the preceding evening, on their agent's secrecy. But prepossessed as I was, that he had made me a sacrifice, which he was as much concerned at least as me, to keep from their knowledge, I thought no deeper of it, than its being some commission he had complied with, of procuring some ribbons, head-dress, or the like.

At my usual hour then in the morning, I repaired to my darling haunt, where I had the pleasure of being received by the ladies with even an air of welcome. I had not, it seems, been ill served by the step I had taken, and which I little suspected their having been acquainted with. Nay, such was the delicacy of my sentiments, that I looked on myself, as half a criminal towards them for having dared to penetrate into their condition, without their leave, and of which, I promised myself, not to give them the least glimpse of suspicion, nor did I, unless in what escaped me, by a redoublement of respect, and attentions.

I could not, however, help observing that Lydia's behaviour to me marked some alteration, but whether in my favour or not, I had too much fear, and too little experience to determine. My intrepidity, more founded on the consciousness of the innocence of my intentions, than on my natural vanity, had deserted me, at the sight of her. I trembled, because I truly loved. Lydia, it is true, had never from the first once departed from that shyness and reserve, with which she had begun to treat me. But now a certain confusion, an air of tender timidity mixed with her reception of me, that I had too little knowledge of the sex to account for. No! never before had I seen her so amiable, and so sweetly austere. She blushed as I spoke to her, and hardly brought herself to answer me. Ignorant as I was, and ingenious to torment myself, I began to fancy she had taken some strange aversion to me, and saw me with uneasiness. Coxcombry is certainly not the vice of a lover. That passion never produces, and generally cures, where it finds it. My propensity to it was then in its infancy. I was as yet only a coxcomb in bud. And at that time all my pride stood in such thorough subjection to the imperious power of love, that I was far from presuming myself dangerous enough for Lydia to take alarm at, or feel a flutter in my favour at the approaches of an enemy generally more feared than heartily hated.

Her confusion, however, bred mine; and it was awkwardly enough I brought in the mention of my having been obliged to repair to Warwick the day before, on a business of the utmost importance. For I durst not give my reason for staying away the air of an apology. Lydia blushed, said nothing, and smothered a smile. But even that did not open my eyes on her being acquainted with my errand.

Mrs. Bernard, who had seen the enemy, and knew his marches, observed our painful situation, and came in to our rescue. With an address familiar to her, she soon brought the conversation into a flow of more ease and freedom. Lydia by gentle degrees resumed that cheerfulness which never left her, but when any thing particular from me to her, whether in looks or words, turned her grave and reserved. I often, indeed, endeavoured to bring the discourse to land upon love, a subject from its nature inexhaustible and eternally new, and which I was far from master of; since it was actually the master of me. But still I was sensible I should not talk impertinently upon it, since whatever I would say, would come immediately from my heart, the only true source of eloquence and persuasion. But all my eagerness, for art I had none, to engage or lead them into a topic introductory to an overture of my sentiments, produced me only the pain to observe that the subject was highly disagreeable to both Mrs. Bernard and Lydia. Mrs. Bernard, indeed, eluded it, in the style of an ambassador, when he is sounded upon untreatable matters. Lydia, like one who was entirely a stranger to it, and desired to continue so.

These rigours which my whole tenour of thinking towards them, told me I so little deserved, had half awakened my pride. I endeavoured at least to act indifference, but I put on my airs of contumacy so awkwardly, that I perhaps never betrayed more love, than when I aimed at appearing to have the least. One look of Lydia disarmed and deprived me of even a wish to rebel; nay redoubled my submission. I thought myself but too criminal for having dared to form one.

Youth is an age, love a passion, not overburthened with judgment. Had I been capable of any, I might easily have considered that Lydia's modesty, honour and the fears natural to her tender age, to say nothing of the persecution she was under, (for I did not then know the nature of it), very rationally accounted for all the coyness I had to complain of.

As for Mrs. Bernard, who was too well experienced and too penetrating not to remark my passion, and to do justice to the respect, it was evident that the purity of it inspired me: she was not without her anxieties and fears, that the consequences might prematurely take too serious a turn, for her check or control. If there was then nothing in my rank or condition, nothing in the nature of my sentiments that could reasonably alarm her; the nicety of her trust, the peculiarity of the conjuncture and the tenderness of both our ages sufficed, however, to determine her to keep off all explanations that might carry us too great lengths, before a proper foundation should be laid by a discovery, which discovery could not well take place, 'till the motives which forced them to resort to this romantic refuge should cease.

Possibly, she carried her caution too far, from her not conceiving me so independent as I really was; and she never gave my approaches on that point encouragement enough for me to set her right, by a proper representation of this circumstance.

After then staying as long as I durst that morning, I returned home, more in love, and more in despair than ever.

Several days passed in this manner, without my being in the least more advanced than the first instant. Mrs. Bernard's polite but firm vigilance and Lydia's frozen reserve supported, no doubt, by all the remonstrances of this her Mentor in petticoats, were an overmatch for all my attempts to soften them, and indeed for all my patience.

I had besides no confidants that I could well seek advice from. My companions were chiefly of my own age, as young, as unexperienced, and as thoughtless as myself. Besides that, a passion, so violent as mine, never goes without a spice of jealousy. I looked on Lydia as a hidden treasure which I could have wished, for security's sake, to have been kept buried from all eyes, but my own. I conceived, by myself, what impressions such a form must make on every beholder, and imagined no age proof against them. Love alone inspired me these ideas of caution. I had not been taught them: and they were far from unjust, or even unwise.

My aunt, Lady Bellinger, whose tenderness for me was pushed even to a weakness, and who deserved from me other returns, than those made her by my native character, by a pride rendered yet more intractable from her indulgence, at an age when I could not do the justice I have since done to it. I had then yielded to the torrent; but I soon saw the pain and uneasiness I had occasioned her by my conduct, the seeming indecency of which scandalized and afflicted her. But what she did not say to me had more effect on my stubbornness of temper than all she could have said.

Urged then by the double motive of doing justice to the ladies, whose fame and honour were as dear to me as my own, and of giving a satisfaction which I judged indispensably due to her, from the moment she did not require it, I seized the first convenient opportunity, of acquainting her with the perfect innocence of those assiduities, which had borne so base and undeserved a construction: in short I let her sincerely into all that I thought myself at liberty to reveal, or blameless for suppressing, under the uncertainty I myself was in, of the issue of my wishes and pretentions.

Truth is irresistible. The vivacity of its colouring has quite a different effect from the daub of falsity or invention. My good aunt, who loved me too fondly for me not to have easily deceived her, was surely less capable of rejecting the force of reality; besides that, transported as she was to find me at once innocent of the grossnesses imputed to me, she was possibly more so, to find me recovered into respect and duty enough to give her an account of my conduct. I saw the moment then, that she would have ordered her coach, and by way of reparation, have drove directly to the house where the ladies were, and have invited them to all the accommodations and protection of her own. But this good-natured impetuosity I was obliged to restrain, from my knowledge of their sentiments on that point, though I wished for nothing so ardently, for many obvious reasons; especially, too, as such a step would have effectually stifled the scandal which so great an affectation of privacy, and my resort, had given birth to, and which, however, soon died away of itself under their cool contempt of it.

One circumstance, however, on my explanation with my

aunt, somewhat surprized and alarmed me. As the ice was now broke, for her to say what she pleased to me, she told me that even the family of the young lady was no secret in the neighbourhood: that her father was a merchant, whose affairs were in some disorder, and that his name was Webber. That she, Lady Bellinger, had been the more hurt by the supposed irregularity of my conduct, in that it was insinuated that I had taken the advantage of their family distress, and employed it in aid of my seduction.

I blushed with rage and indignation at such a hint, and was but the more won and softened by my aunt's silence to me, on so tender a point, as I knew the pangs it must have cost her heart to suppress hitherto her sentiments upon my procedure.

That haughtiness of spirit, which is not owing to meanness, as haughtiness generally is, is not always the worst part of a character. No art could have suggested to Lady Bellinger, so efficacious a method of reducing me to her point, as the measures she kept with my pride, by not shocking it with remonstrances, which it would certainly, at all events, have rejected. But now instead of growing insolent or obstinate, on the indulgence she shewed my errors, real or supposed, that indulgence quite disarmed and overcame me. I loved, I adored Lydia, and would have renounced my life sooner than my passion for her, yet I resolved nothing so firmly as not to take one decisive step without my aunt's previous participation or consent. This last I knew neither humour, pride, nor interest, would overbalance her inclination to satisfy me in, on her being herself satisfied that it was necessary to my happiness. But my advances were not yet in forwardness enough, for me to enter upon a confidence of that sort with her.

To return then to Lydia. I was not without my perplexity to find her story divulged. Nor did my innocence quite tranquillize me upon it. I sometimes imagined that chance alone had occasioned the discovery. It served, too, to confirm to me, the old agent's information. The truth, however, was that he had with the greatest air of mystery recommended this sob-secret to two or three persons in Warwick, whom he judged the properest to give it a quick circulation. And as to me, he had shewn me so little mercy, that independent of the other particulars, he had even overstretched his fiction to the name of the street, which was no more existing than the imaginary Mr. Webber himself. He thought, it seems, nothing too much to quiet my curiosity, and to put me off the right scent, as he judged me the most likely to exert myself in tracking out the truth. And to clench my deception, there were not wanting some of those male-gossips, who pretend to know every thing, and whom, to be sure, Mr. Webber could not escape. Who knew him better than they? They had often smoaked how things would go with him: often had they been afraid of his over-living his abilities: then his wife was such an extravagant woman! It was no wonder matters were as they were. Now, when the truth came out, in sequence of time, that no such person ever had existed, they were, to be sure, confused and ashamed? Not at all: they were only mistaken: it was Mr. such an one they took him for, and for whom they found some name, as much of invention as the other.

In the meantime I still continued my visits to the thatched-house, or rather the enchanted palace, where still I found Mrs. Bernard inaccessibly entrenched, behind the utmost civility, against all my attempts to come to the point. Great expressions of acknowledgment and gratitude, but not a syllable tending to encourage any overtures whatever concerning her charge, from whom she was inseparable even for an instant. I had tried, in vain, several innocent stratagems, to come at a private audience from Lydia; but all my art and invention were in default against her superior skill and management. Argus was indeed lulled asleep with all his hundred eyes. But Argus was a man, and a simple couple in a woman well on the watch, is worth a thousand of them. Whence are eunuchs so vigilant, but from their resemblance, in some sort, to women?

As to Lydia, there was no circumstance of regard or attention, to prove my passion for her, omitted by me. I exhausted then the whole chapter of such presents, as were consistent with her delicacy to receive, without forgetting any thing that might be agreeable to Mrs. Bernard, whom I saw the necessity of keeping measure with. The choice of all the gardens round me in fruit or flowers; every rarity that the country afforded, as well as the town, the newest patterns, the newest music, every thing in short that could contribute to their pleasure or amusement in that wearisome solitude, I made it the delight of my life to procure them. Books, pamphlets, newspapers were especially Mrs. Bernard's share in my provision.

So much importunity, to give these marks of my passion the harshest name, could not fail of making some impression on Lydia's gratitude, if they did not even touch her heart. I began then at length to flatter myself that I perceived less and less rigour and reserve, every day, in her countenance and behaviour to me. She seemed now more familiarized to all the passion I threw into my looks, or into what I said to her. I thought I read in her eyes expressions of softness and languor, which did not threaten me with a declaration of hatred, if I could but have got an opportunity to make her one of love, out of Mrs. Bernard's hearing. But that was impossible, so that I was forced to content myself with these constructions, too favourable indeed to my wishes, not to give my hopes leave to live on them.

All my assiduities, too, only served to rivet my chains. The more I studied Lydia, the more I was forced to admire her. Possessed of all the power of perfect beauty, without the insolence of its consciousness, or the impertinences it serves so often for a privilege to, she gave all she said or did the sweetest of graces, that of pure nature, unadulterated with affectation, that bane of barely not the whole sex, which so many of ours are either the dupes of, or coxcombs enough to catch the contagion of from them. Her native modesty suffered her to say but little, and that only on subjects proper for her age. But that little, how elegant without pretensions, how correct without stiffness! One could have indeed wished she had spoke more; yet there was no reason to complain that she had not said enough.

One day, that I found her embroidering a rose on a white satin, and that I took it for my text to place some silly, common-place compliment, on its being an humble type of that freshness, and superiorly beautiful colour of her complexion, she observed to me, (blushing the original she was copying from, out of countenance) that this flower much better represented the fate of maidens' hearts in that the instant it unlocks its bosom, it betrays its approaching ruin.

This was giving me a fair opening to have gone essentially into the merits of my cause; but Mrs. Bernard's perpetual presence interposed, and barred me the reply. Sensible of the advantage given me by this comparison, which I was pre-

paring to improve, under the favour of due distinctions, she
started an abrupt transition, which I thought I saw Lydia, by
her colouring, construe into an admonition, which she respected more than she was pleased with. In short, at every
turn or avenue, paved for me by chance or my own unwear-
ied industry, to come at a declaration of my sentiments, I
found Mrs. Bernard unremoveably in my way.

I was now almost at the end of my patience, when I was to
undergo yet an infinitely severer trial of it. I was then fully
determined, by the uneasiness of my situation, to come to an
explanation at all adventures with Mrs. Bernard herself, and
waited only such a space of time as I assigned within myself,
for some answer to the proposals I had made, and supposed
to have been conveyed by their agent, to Mr. Webber, which
time was now on the point of expiration.

Already did I hug myself on the joy I anticipated, with
transports, on being delivered from the torture of restraint,
and pouring out my whole heart to Lydia, under sanction of
its purity. I was not indeed vain enough to hold myself sure
of hers, but I had not withal reason to despair of its declaring
in my favour.

My rank and fortune I had most assuredly counted for
nothing, in respect to my pretensions to Lydia herself, though
I did not doubt of their weight and influence on Mrs. Bernard. I was at that time indeed, and ever, too proud to appeal
from my personal merit to that of my possessions. This
worthless and ignoble meanness I constantly left, with the
contempt it deserves, to our lords of the new creation, or
the greasy money-grubs of the city.

Having then fixed within myself a short day for the fair
and open disclosure of my views and designs to Mrs. Bernard,
I waited for it with the anxieties of one who is to throw the
dice for his life on a drum-head.

One evening then, that I had been preinformed of their
having received a packet from Warwick, I visited them in
course, as usual. In Mrs. Bernard's looks I could indeed
perceive little or no alteration, except a certain air of increased kindness, and forced obligingness, in which her design to throw dust in my eyes had perhaps less share, than
the consciousness of the cruel stab she was meditating to all
my hopes, and the sort of reparation she intended me, for
the part her duty constrained her to act in it.

But as to Lydia, less mistress of her emotions, less capable of art and dissimulation, the change of her countenance was considerable and manifest. Her face was paler than usual, her accents faltering, and her reception of me rather tenderer and more engaging than ever I had found it. Industrious to deceive myself, I immediately imagined that they had received some disagreeable accounts of Mr. Webber's affairs. I was not even scarce sorry for it, from the hopes of such a circumstances adding to the merit of my disinterestedness, in the proposals I was on the point of breaking to them, and even flattered myself, I should now, instantly, receive a privilege for, in the advices I expected from their agent.

With all the warmth then of the most passionate concern, I ventured to ask Lydia if she was well, or had received any news to discompose her; but she had her instructions, and pleaded an indisposition, which she had not, and which Mrs. Bernard seconded the excuse of, in order to shorten my visit. I did not then make it so long as usual, but I had full time to observe that Lydia was exceedingly disquieted. I caught her eyes often fixed on me; they brimmed with tears, which she endeavoured to keep in, and she immediately, but with reluctance, averted or declined them to the ground, on their encounter with mine. I thought them uncommonly softened towards me. At that instant I hoped it was love: but, soon after retracted that opinion for another, less flattering. I attributed then afterwards these appearances to the reproaches she might think she owed herself for the cruel returns she was preparing to make me, for the most delicate, though the most violent passion, I had betrayed for her, by symptoms that could not escape her; amongst which even my silence was not the least, and added to the merit of my sentiments towards her, that of a timid respect, which however ridiculous to the women of the world, could not but find favour in the eye of her unaffected innocence and modesty. Perhaps too, the thoughts of a removal from a place, where she was habituated, as it were, and which I had endeavoured to render as pleasing to her as possible, might give her part of the uneasiness she expressed: but however, I had not so much as conceived the shadow of a suspicion of their intentions at that time.

I took my leave of them with an ominous heaviness of heart. The next morning I was waked very early by my *valet de chambre*, who acquainted me that the boy Tom was at the door, and pressed hard for admittance. I instantly ordered him to my bedside, not without a secret presentiment, which made me shudder. He came, and with tears in his eyes delivered me a letter, trembling, and scarce able to bring out "they are gone, they are gone!" "Who is gone, you "block-head?" said I, in a tone of madness which shewed at least my apprehensions. "The ladies, Sir," answered the boy, with an increased fright, at the rage I expressed. "How? "when? with whom?" I demanded in one breath, holding the letter still in my hand, without the courage or heart to open it. The boy, in substance, gave the following account.

That I had not been gone a minute before they retired to their apartment, in which they locked themselves up, without coming out, 'till one in the morning; when the little old gentleman knocked at the door violently, and alarmed the grandmother and him. They were afraid of thieves. But looking out of the window, they saw that the two watchmen from the park-lodge were talking with the gentleman: and the ladies themselves came and told them it was their friend, and came for no harm. They opened the door, and the ladies met the old gentleman, and Mrs. Bernard told him they were ready; and so they were, with their bundles of clothes and linen, and a small casket. These the old gentleman gave the watchmen to carry, and the ladies gave them five guineas for their trouble. They walked down the lane, at the bottom of which was a coach and six, with only one person in it, and that a lady, who on Miss's stepping into the coach, threw her arms about her neck and kept her embraced for above a minute. They told them they believed they should come again next day, but if they did not, that what they left was a free gift to the landlady. They gave the boy, too, a purse with some guineas in it, and bid him be a good boy. Miss wept both before and after she got into the coach, and delivered him with her own hands the letter, which she bid him be sure to give to nobody but myself. The lad ran after the coach 'till he tired himself, to see which road it took, 'till he lost sight of it, and was bewildered so that he could not easily find his way back again. And by all that he could make out they did not take the road to London or Warwick, but rather towards the sea-side.

All the time he was giving me this account, I remained motionless, petrified with surprize, vexation and anger. Surprized at the suddenness of my misfortune, vexed at the loss of the whole treasure of my heart, and angry at the unkind-ness of their usage. In the injustice of my passion I was near giving orders for turning the parkkeepers away, for not stopping them, as if I had had given it in part of their charge to them; when, on the contrary the poor fellows thought they were serving me, in serving them, and obeying their or-ders.

Recovering then, a little, my spirits. I sent every body out of the room, that I might read this fatal scroll with less dis-turbance. I broke open the seal, still trembling with compli-cated emotions. The letter was Mrs. Bernard's, and these were the contents.

To Sir William Delamor.

Sir,

"*In our present procedure towards you, there is only the ap-*
"*pearance of ingratitude. We leave this place with the justest*
"*sense of your politeness and civilities. Irresistible conjunc-*
"*tures force us away, in this manner: you will, perhaps, one*
"*day acknowledge, and do justice to the violence of them.*
"*In the meantime, if any entreaties of ours can have weight*
"*with you, we conjure you to suspend any enquiries about*
"*us. You have been with our privity, but so innocently, mis-*
"*led about our name and condition, through the extreme pre-*
"*caution of our agent, that you will, if not thank, at least not*
"*condemn either him, or us, for it. I once again beg you will*
"*not think more about us, till time and circumstances shall*
"*give us leave to explain the whole mystery to you. Above*
"*all, it is of importance to Miss Lydia's safety that you do*
"*not undeceive the country, of the notion they have of our*
"*rank, such as is already diffused of it. In the hopes of this*
"*your compliance, we shall always remember you with grati-*
"*tude and esteem. I quit the pen to miss, who insists on it,*
"*and am,*

     Sir,
       Your most obliged, and
         obedient, humble servant,

       Catherine Bernard.

The following was added at the bottom of this letter, in Lydia's hand, in form of postscript.

"*I confirm what Mrs. Bernard has said to you, and I add*
"*from myself, that I should be sorry you did not think I*
"*leave this retreat with regret.*

LYDIA.

As shocked, as thunder-struck, as I was at this unexpected
revolution, which awakened me out of my dream of the
completest happiness I could form an idea of; the sight of
Lydia's hand, and the glimpse of tenderness I thought I perceived in her postscript, gave me a sensible consolation, a consolation even necessary to keep me from sinking under the
blow. I read it over and over, I bathed it with my tears rather
of rage than of love. Yet I devoured it with my kisses. Her
name broke from me in exclamations of grief and rants of
despair. I expostulated with her, as if she was present, on the
cruelty of her treatment. What had I done? How had I deserved to be deserted in this manner? Then what reproaches
did I not make to myself for having postponed the proposals
I had intended? Might not they have changed their plan and
softened the rigour of their procedure towards me?

I sent for the boy in again. I asked him a thousand questions, and made him as often repeat every particular of their
departure: how they looked: what they had said: but nothing he had to tell me, could give me the light or satisfaction
I wanted.

Harassed, at length, even to faintness, with all the vexation and grief of disappointed love, I got up, and my first and
early care was to repair to the cottage, though I was sure of
meeting there with nothing but subjects that would refresh
my pain and regret.

Arrived there, so far from the paradise my raptured ideas
had once erected it into, it now wore to me the aspect of a
cold, dreary, disconsolate desert. I seemed like a poor travel-
ler, who, cheated by his imagination, has at a distance
formed to himself the appearance of superb palaces, towers
and delightful gardens, but, on advancing near, discovers the
illusion of the perspective, and finds with horror nothing but
shapeless rocks, stunted yews, and an uninhabitable wild.
Such was the discount that habitation was now at in my present sense of things.

The poor, old landlady came to me, and very innocently
sharpened my affliction by her praises of her lodgers. They

had been, as she said, a blessing to her house, and she hoped in the lord they were not gone for good. Her grief in short was so sincere, that she seemed to have forgot their leaving her in goods and money about fifty times the amount of their agreement.

All this liberality plainly, however, denoted their being persons of fortune and condition, as indeed the whole uniform tenor of their carriage and air had left me no doubt of. But still, I exhausted every conjecture that could lead me to a discovery of who they really were. Yet I naturally enough imagined, that if any young lady of quality had been missing, or on any account had left her family it must have made noise enough to have reached our notice, and we had not heard an accident of that sort even whispered.

Concluding then, that there must be some very extraordinary occasion for such exquisite privacy, and powerfully restrained by the intimation of Lydia's safety being annexed to my silence and discretion, I determined to obey implicitly their orders of desistence from any enquiry, or mention of their half-confidence to me. I hoped, too, that such a submission would the sooner produce me the *éclaircissement* they had left me the hopes of; hopes, which alone hindered me from setting out that instant, and acting the part of a true knight-errant, in pursuit of a wandering princess. And indeed, there was something so singular, and out of the ordinary road of things, in my meeting, falling in love with, and losing of Lydia, that did not make the less impression on me, for carrying a spice of the romantic through the whole adventure. I found, it seems, something flattering in the idea, that such a peculiarity was reserved for me.

Returned to my aunt's, I told her, according to my plan of secrecy, no more than that the ladies were gone, which indeed she might have read plain enough in the change of my air and countenance. Seeing then how seriously I was effected, she openly said every thing she could think of to lessen my affliction, and hugged herself, no doubt, at what an escape I had had.

My sense of Lydia's absence was not, however, soon, nor indeed ever, thoroughly got over. For some time, I remained melancholy, stupified, and feeling severely the want of something essential to the enjoyment of my life. It had been, during her stay, deliciously indeed filled, and taken up with the pleasures of seeing and attending on her. But her desertion of me had made such a sensible gap, so irreparable a void, that I had no longer a relish for my existence. All the women I saw, and who had once inspired my desires, were now nothing to me. I looked just enough at them, to satisfy myself they were not Lydia, and I sought no more. Hunting, country sports, conversation, studies, all grew insipid to me; every thing put me in mind of Lydia, but nothing could supply her place with me.

By degrees, however, the violence of my grief subsided and softened into a certain languor and melancholy, which was not even without its pleasure. Lydia, present to my memory, always engrossed my heart: but time, that great comforter in ordinary, introduced intervals of insensibility, which other objects, other passions seized the advantage of. I still did not love Lydia less, but now I did not think of her so often, or with that continuity as at first. The number of things that made impression on me, augmented in proportion as that of my grief grew fainter and fainter. I was of a constitution, too, which began to interfere powerfully with that system of constancy and Platonics, which a world rather spoilt than refined has agreed to banish into the corner of those old musty romances, that went out of fashion with ruffs and high-crowned hats, and which is most certainly exploded out of the present practice: perhaps with less profit to true pleasure than is generally imagined.

I pined now for the term fixed for our going to London; still in the hopes of hearing from, or tracing Lydia out. But in the meantime I felt more than ever the insipidity and wearisomeness of a country life, in which, generally, one day is the dull duplicate of another. What, in short, I now found most wanting to me, was amusement: whilst the promptership of nature, and the solicitations of a curiosity which began to resume its rights, left me no room to doubt about the sort of it. I had, besides, soon an opportunity to ascertain, and indeed realize, all my wants and desires.

Mrs. Rivers, a relation of our family, distant enough to annihilate any scruple about our nearer approaches, and widow of a gentleman of a very good estate in M——, whose constitution she had broke by overdrawing upon it, was the instrument, it seems, allotted me, to make my first experiments upon. She had accepted of an invitation to our house, for a few weeks of the summer season, where she accordingly came down, preceded by such a character of virtue, and devotion to the memory of the poor dear deceased as, joined to the narrow notions I had imbibed by a country education, assorted me no more prospect of an affair of gallantry, than if I had been told my grandmother was coming.

Well! down she came, powdering in a coach and six, and arrived about noon in our house, where I was then with my aunt: who, after the usual ceremonies of reception, presented me to her, and desired I would do the honours of the house, as became me. Most certainly I then imagined as little as my poor aunt herself, how completely I was destinated to do them, and to teach her the true English of *chère entière*, in return for the lessons I was to receive from her.

I was just then returned from hunting, in the dress for that diversion, and had not amiss the air of a young, sturdy fox-hunter, breathing all the florid freshness of the country, and all the vigour of that character. This appearance of mine, she was too knowing to be displeased with, for she received my hearty salute and compliments, with a certain warmth and encouragement, which her first glance over my person had not, it seems, indisposed her to, and which as great a novice as I then was, I could perfectly distinguish from the reception my caresses were used to meet with from women, in the days of my incapacity for any thing but innocence towards them. This, however, did not give me the least glimpse of hope. I construed it no other than a mark of superior civility, or good nature, being too much prepossessed with bug-bears and invincible obstacles in the character of this lady, to think of any designs upon her: me I say, to whom, once more, every dairy-maid, in virtue of her sex, was now as good as a duchess, and the woman the easiest to be come at, the woman for me, at that time.

Mrs. Rivers had, however, in her person, wherewith to justify the liking of any, even more delicate than the nature of my wants suffered me to be. She was about twenty-three, and had not been married above eight months to a husband who had done her more justice than himself; and to whom she had probably been more sparing of lectures of moderation, than of her readiness to oblige him at his own expense. He had been at Bath for the recovery of his shattered health, but in vain, through the ignorance or neglect of his physicians, who had omitted the most material prescription, that of leaving his wife behind him. It was even whispered, with how much justice I do not pretend to decide, amongst the dealers in secret anecdotes, that a fit of the jaundice he took at a young officer's assiduities, which she had not enough discouraged, had given him the finishing blow. Be that as it may, he died quietly, out of the way, and Mrs. Rivers, whether out of gratitude for so much kindness, or from a persuasion that her grief and her weeds became her, had very ostentatiously prolonged the usual term of both.

As to her person, she preserved yet all the graces, all the bloom of the first spring of youth. Her complexion was of that delicate, smooth, glossy brown, which one is not only satisfied with seeing. Her eyes, amidst all their langour, betrayed certain sparkles of fire, of no bad omen to those whom it should concern. Then she joined to all the dispositions I could have wished, and was then far from presuming, all the experience necessary to bring things to their true and natural conclusion, without spinning them out impertinent lengths.

After a short retreat, she came down, dressed, and recovered from the fatigue of her journey. Dinner was served in, at which her eyes pleased me more than her tongue, for she talked away unmercifully of the good man Hector, but her looks, (and what looks!) were pretty constantly levelled at me: I did not then know that woman rarely or ever speak of the dead, but with an eye to the living.

I was not, however, long imposed upon. The expression she threw into her eyes, her attention to consider me, a number of little distinctions, easily seized by an inclination so warm as mine now was towards the whole sex, gave me hints, and those hints created hopes, readily embraced by my desires, and cherished by my native vanity and presumption.

Compelled, however, by decency, as well as policy, to conceal my new-born pretensions from the observation of the company, it was not, however, without difficulty that I at once constrained myself, and yet kept up the dialogue of our eyes, just enough to prove to her that her advances were not entirely thrown away upon me. And here I still style them advances, less out of coxcombry than justice, for I had certainly then not the courage to have made any, both on account of my inexperience and my high prepossession of her prudery.

After dinner, I very zealously took charge and exercised the functions of my aunt's master of ceremonies, with respect to our new guest. It is easy then to imagine how affectionately I acquitted myself of it, considering the sentiments she had inspired me with, and which her conduct towards me in private, gave me no room to think her over displeased with, whilst her carriage to me in public set me lessons of discretion and reserve, which I concluded were necessary, and conformed accordingly. It was but natural that I should suppose she had most experience. She must have seen service, and I was modest enough to take her for my leader in my first engagement.

All vanity apart, I was at that time certainly not without pretensions to please. I had, at least, the merit of a fair, ruddy complexion, shapely stature, promising strength of limbs, and all the native attendants of a healthy, untainted youth. I was at that nice point, in short, when imminent manhood brings on essential maturity for action, without abating any thing of the smooth of youth, or of those tender, bloomy graces, which endear that age to those women especially who have rather delicate than craving appetites.

Mrs. Rivers, who was far from insensible, had been, at least as she afterwards told me, determined in my favour at first sight: but she had still great measures to keep, and appearances to respect: and she was reasonably afraid of the indiscretion of my age. But where are the objections that love, or a passion like love, cannot triumph over?

The few days after her first arrival, which had been taken up with the insipid ceremonial of neighbours' visits, had the more harassed my patience, from my having conceived the liveliest hopes of success, from her behaviour to me, in those intervals of private audience I could snatch from the hurry and importunity of company. It was then that her countenance, which had worn the air of the greatest austerity and reserve, visibly relaxed and softened towards me sufficiently to encourage my attacks. Her looks of parade and her looks of nature were at least as different as her dress and undress; but their shift was quicker.

My aunt, who had been alarmed at my particularities to her, which I was not yet master of art enough, to conceal entirely, thought herself obliged to represent to me the impropriety of my entertaining any thoughts of a serious engagement with my cousin, as she called her; and though her reasons turned chiefly upon her fortune being unequal to mine—reasons I should have spurned, had I been really in love—they had the more weight with me, as all the desires I had, violent as they were, still had nothing of that passion in

them. And when love is out of the question, the head, unin-
fluenced by the heart, is generally pretty cool and numerical.
I easily then tranquillized my aunt, on the strength, which
truth impressed on my assurances, of my having no such
thought or intention: but she was not of a character for me
to venture any thing more than a half-confidence to, upon
this occasion. As she herself certainly never had the least turn
to gallantry, an idea of that sort probably did not present
itself to her, and it was not my place to start it.

At ease then from that quarter, I was determined to push
my fortune with the widow, who, on her side, very happily
did not do me the honour to throw any thing further into her
designs upon me, than taking me into the service of her pleasure. This was a sympathy of sentiments with mine, extremely
fit to abridge matters, and bring us post to that grand conclusion, which neither of us were of a humour to languish
long for.

My progress then was so rapid, that after a few preliminary objections, in which decency and an air of resistance, for
the honour of having resisted, had a greater share than sincerity, I obtained an assignation, but an assignation in form.
And where? In her very bedchamber: where I was not to
suppose, she would admit me merely for the sake of display-
ing her virtue: a bedchamber is rarely the theatre of it.

To form then any idea of the raptures I swam in, at having
brought her to this point, one must conceive all the enchant-
ment, all the power of novelty, in the first gratification of the
senses in their highest and perhaps their noblest pleasure. Even
my vanity added to the raptures I prefigured to myself, in
satisfying a curiosity so natural at my age. Having too little
delicacy then in my sentiments towards this new object, the
reflexion that I owed my conquest as much at least to her
desires, as to any merit of mine, never once occurred to me;
and such was at that time the intoxication of my senses, that
I was near mistaking, for a true passion, that coarser homage
I was about paying to the whole sex, in the person of Mrs.
Rivers.

Luckily, too, for my purpose, I had none of those difficulties to encounter with, in coming at an interview, which some
authors in the serenity of their closets, or by a good fire-
side, embarrass their heroes or heroines with, at a great expense of invention, and to the no small discomfort of those
readers who love the last page of a romance better than the

first. There were no eternal duenas, no under-ground sweats, no scalade of walls, no ambush of bloody rivals, of the glitter of sabres in a critical instant, to perplex or romancify my schemes of delight.

Our plan then was laid with the utmost simplicity and ease. The window of a closet to Mrs. River's bedchamber corresponded with a gallery, separated only from that which a door from my apartment opened into, by a ballustrade, easily overleaped; after which I had nothing to do, but to lift up the sash and step in, under favour of the secret of midnight, which is the hour at least as much consecrated to assignations as apparitions.

Panting then with the anticipation of all the bliss in view, and dressed like a bridegroom for this expedition, I repaired to my appointed place at the appointed time. I found the window faithfully disposed for my opening, and every thing prepared both for my reception and the privacy of it.

I was soon then on the right side of it, when, after fastening the shutter, I went a tiptoe to Mrs. Rivers's bedchamber, with unequal paces, between the trepidation of fear and the urgency of desire. Here I found her, still up, leaning in an indolent attitude on a table, with a book in her hand, which she threw down, at seeing me.

She was in that sweet dishabille so much more engaging than the most declared dress, the studied negligence of which costs art so much, in its imitation of nature. A blush of surprise and confusion flushed into her face, whilst her eyes now sought, now declined the encounter of mine, and movingly expressed that tender diffidence with which women seem to beg good quarter, when on the point of surrendering at discretion.

I threw myself at her feet, and kissing one of her hands, which she abandoned to my pressure, I had not words to express the force of what I felt.—So much the better. Women do us admirable justice, on a silence owing to a disorder that moves them at least as much as it flatters them. It is not eloquence that on such occasions makes its court most successfully to them.

It was very happy for me then, that the ceremonial of an assignation at that hour and place, must naturally be an enemy to the flourishing of harangues and protestations. I was so confounded, and unequal to this rapturous scene of a virgin pleasure, that I should have said a thousand impertinences. And I was now more impatient to prove, than profess the force of my desires. Yet finely disposed as I was, my youth and inexperience threw into my words and actions such an awkward bashfulness, such a timid disorder, as soon made Mrs. Rivers sensible of my being at the first act of my novitiate. But this was only a recommendation the more to her.

My observation was indeed too much lost in the tumult of my imagination, and the riotous crowd of my ideas, for me to give an account of her looks and deportment towards me, in these critical instants. I do not doubt but my embarrassment, (though pleasingly, in regard to the cause of it) still, however, somewhat embarrassed her too. Nature is, nevertheless, of itself a wonderful instructress. One has but to abandon oneself to its impulses, and there is no fear of making any very wide mistakes.

It is generally said of women, that the pleasure procured them by their first engagements is the most lively, and the most delicious: that it makes, too, the most lasting impression. Thence their fidelity and grateful kindness to the first author of its acquisition to them. Not so with men, and the young especially. Their first introduction is commonly effectuated in such a hurry, and disorder of the senses, that it robs them of the attention necessary to dwell upon the joys of their present fruition. Overwhelmed and bewildered they enjoy indeed, but it is in a confusion of sensations which resembles the delirious dozings induced by opium, in which the soul is out of itself, and awakens when the agency is over, as from a dream, which the memory scarce preserves the traces of. A just maturity is the only true age of consistence, and delight. Impetuous youth worries its pleasures too voraciously, and impotent age mumbles them, even to palling.

This night, however, fully initiated me. And surely no woman was ever more qualified by nature, and a reasonable experience, than Mrs. Rivers, to form a young novice, even with less apt dispositions than myself to this great branch of natural philosophy. No one ever better understood the art of dalliances, or of keeping longer the desires up to their edge.

Herself then agreeably flattered with the notions I doubtless gave her reasons for, of being the first collectress of my tribute of manhood, she spared me no marks of her satisfaction. All the most engaging caresses, all the sweet successions of toying, and of more solid essentials, brought on the break of day upon the spur, before we were aware of having worn out the night. It was now a necessity for us to separate. Full then of gratitude, full of a passion, which resembled love enough to be mistaken for it, I took the most tender leave, and returned to my own bed, on which I threw myself, and was soon composed to a rest not unnecessary to me; and I resigned myself up to it with the delicious calm of a conqueror sleeping over his laurels.

Pretty late in the morning, I waked, and my imagination, now less inflamed, I reviewed coolly enough the operations of the night, and was not yet so ungrateful to the pleasures I had reaped, as to think of them with regret. Yet methought, they had lost much of their vivacity: the recurrence of Lydia to my memory, of Lydia still perfectly adored, and only sacrificed for the moment to the power and pressure of present objects, dashed my exultation, and vitiated my triumph: but I became too soon reconciled to myself, by a distinction the more dangerous, in that it was a real one. I was now clearly sensible that love entered for nothing into my sentiments towards Mrs. Rivers, and that my heart still reserved a sanctuary sacred to Lydia alone, on the altar of which burned the purest incense. Under favour then of this stale, but commodious sophistry, I grew more quiet, and more hardened to the reproaches I could not help, at intervals, making myself, whenever the flame of love, ill-smothered under a heap of rubbish, flashed in my face.

Our passions are but loose casuists, and what is worse, our reason is often too bribed over to their side; in which case we fall like a client sold by his attorney, or a prince murdered by his guards. Thus it was pleasant enough that the more virtuous, the more respectful light I placed my passion in to Lydia, the less I conceived myself guilty towards her, from my not confounding it with those sentiments of a coarser nature, which composed the foundation of my commerce with Mrs. Rivers, whom I considered merely as a woman; but Lydia, purely as a superior being, with whose worship it would have been a profanation to mix ideas of flesh and blood. And it was on this plan of latitude and distinction that, now the fence was broke, my heart soon became a thoroughfare for the whole sex.

As nothing is more exactly true than that satisfied desires are easier kept secret, than the endeavours to bring them to that issue generally suffer them to be; my discretion, now well seconded by Mrs. Rivers's perfect talent of dissimulation, had no hard task of laying even suspicion asleep. But then her fondness, with which she in private made herself amends for her constraint in company, produced an effect unfavourable to the wishes she pretended, and perhaps was sincere in. Mrs. Rivers was, it is true, as amiable, as handsome, as any reasonable person could desire: but, what with that excessive fondness of hers, joined to the facility of access to her, even in night-gown and slippers, what with my own turn to inconstancy, I soon abated of my first ardours: and grew every day to wait for the return of the night with less impatience. Her charms, in short, had not power enough to keep off that languor of satiety, which generally steals upon uninterrupted enjoyments, especially when the heart has nothing to say to them.

Women, on these occasions, have a quickness of sense and resentment, that is neither to be lulled, nor imposed upon: and, to say the truth, there are certain test-acts, in the number and mark of which there is no trifling with their penetration. At the first alarm of this change, and before I was well satisfied in it myself, Mrs. Rivers, with an impolicy too natural to violent passions, first cleared up the situation of my sentiments to myself, and afterwards lessened to me my compunction at it, by the repetition of complaints more just than wise to give vent to. It is only for love to subsist after enjoyment: but here my desires had died of their natural distemper, a surfeit: and the querulous tone of expostulation is certainly not the secret to recall, or revive them. I pushed even my injustice so far as to find new matter of disgust, in all the passionate endeavours, which her taste, if not her love for me, engaged her to employ towards bringing me back again, to the point we had set out from. Her tenderness grew at length so burthensome to me, that I now resorted to my appointments with reluctance, sure as I was of hearing nothing but a love-sick jargon upon constancy eternal, and eternal constancy. Most women are in this point like impertinent singers, whom the trouble is not so much to persuade them to sing, as when they have once begun, to get them to have done with it.

Yet it was not with impunity, neither, I was thus to play fast and loose with this engagement. A conquest of the importance I had affixed to that of so fine a woman as Mrs. Rivers indisputably was, had inspired me with a vanity, which was not lessened by all the apprehensions and regret she shewed for losing me. They made me, to say the truth, more vain, but not one jot more disposed to dissipate them. Her revenge then, without her designing it, was sufficiently taken care of, by her laying the foundations for my commencing the coxcomb, the character I afterwards so splendidly consummated. Could I have at that season made that reflexion, when it would have been of service to my correction, or cure, I perhaps had not thought her punished enough for the follies I was indebted to her for, by all the pain my infidelity, or rather coolness could put her to. But I became yet more unjust, even from a sense of my injustice, which having been riveted by her remonstrances, appeared so criminal, and cruel even in my own eyes, that I was half angry with Mrs. Rivers for being the cause, however passive and innocent, of my making so bad a figure to myself: for I was not yet quite so fine a gentleman, as, in affairs of gallantry, to make a jest of ingratitude, or of not using a woman well, who has put it in one's power to use her ill.

Happily, however, for my quiet, the term was at length at hand for Mrs. Rivers to return home upon indispensable obligations. She had protracted it as long as possible, but now her going was a point decided. The sense of this would have alone revived my tenderness; but I was besides influenced by the desire of repairing the wrongs my indifference had done her, of soothing at least her resentment, and of expressing so much gratitude for her favours, as might make her forgive my being nothing more than grateful. With these dispositions, it was no great matter of violence to me, to restore to my commerce with her the warmth which I had been some time wanting in to it, and which, if I did not feel myself in the same degree as before, I gave proofs enough of, to reingratiate me, especially where pride and self-love were sure to welcome the deception.

In the instants of our separation, persisting still in the same plan, I took special care, not to let her perceive, how little expense it was to put me to, in regrets. Whether or no she was the dupe of it, I will not venture to say. I had reason to believe not; for soon after we heard that she had not been a fortnight in town, before she made the fortune of a young fellow, whose personal merit was his greatest recommendation. I was then embarked in another pursuit, so that I received the news with a most meritorious tranquillity, and had almost a mind to insult her with a letter of congratulation, which she escaped more through my indolence than my good-nature. This, however, did not raise the women in my opinion, nor sink me in my own. But I became the more hardened in my designs to deal with them henceforward, as if nature had only made them for my pleasure. In which general degradation I was, however, still far from including my still-worshipped Lydia. My sentiments for her, though they defended me so ill against the irruptions of my constitutional warmth, still subsisted, as they had nothing in common with those I felt for the rest of her sex. And I place here this illusive abstraction rather as a mark, than a vindication, of my errors: but I was, it seems, predestined not to arrive at wisdom but through a course of follies.

My descent, too, from that elevation of sentiments, only known to true love, was a truantry the more culpable, in that I had fully tasted the difference. How could I then renounce, or exchange its incomparably greater charms, for the worthless ones of male coquetry; or prefer the dissipations, the heartless joys of even conquests of this sort, to constancy in a passion, of which even the pains carry with them their peculiar pleasure, and are never without dignity and self-esteem. But he has little knowledge of the human heart, little acquaintance with its prodigious inconsistence, who does not at least admit, if he cannot account for these transitions from one extreme to the other.

Mrs. Rivers then was hardly out of my sight, before I began to think of filling up the vacancy she had left, with another amusement of the same sort; for I now had no relish for any other, and thought it neither no great compliment to the sex to prefer the chase of that game, to any other, however out of all taste this may sound to a staunch fox-hunter.

My next pursuit was rather a frolic begun and ended in a few days, than a serious affair. Chance threw it in my way, just in the nick of my loss of Mrs. Rivers, and very opportunely to fill up the tedious interval left 'till we should set out for London. And here I am heartily sorry that the laws of history, which are the laws of truth, do not permit me to ennoble the subject of my adventure, for the sake of those whose delicacy will be wounded, and their curiosity struck dead, when they shall know she was no more than one of the prettiest nymphs, or minor-goddesses of the household, in the whole country. I cannot find in my heart to call her by

her true title of chambermaid, I have been so sick and sur-
feited with the old story of masters falling in love with
mamma's maid, and heroically making a match between pure
love and naked virtue.

For me, however, to whom at least in those days of simplicity, and before what is so impudently and falsely called
high-life had debauched my better natural sense, I readily
preferred the title of right-handsome, to that of right-hon-
ourable, and any girl with beauty was to me a rank above
that of a royal highness without it. I was not then fool
enough, however, since a coxcomb, to let my pride set the
dice on my pleasure; nor am I clear to this day, that
the herald's office can issue out charms as it does bearings, or
that a sallow, sickly countess's visage can so naturally provoke desire, as satisfy a paltry vanity. So much for those who
may snuff at the dignity of my conquest. I promise them,
however, that if they pity my taste, I shall hardly envy them
theirs.

This girl, whose name was Diana, had been but a few days
come to her place; and had already turned all the heads of
our menservants, insomuch that there was some difficulty in
keeping any of them sober, they were so taken up with cele-
brating her charms, in horns of october to her dear, dear
health. In short, she was the general toast, from the butler
down to the stable-helper.

One of my footmen, Will, whom I had been twenty times
on the point of turning away for his slovenliness, by the sudden transformation of it into all the finical spruceness and
nicety his condition was capable of, gave me occasion to enquire into the motive of it, and finding it was owing entirely
to his being smitten with this fair disturber of our domestic
peace, I became curious to examine her more particularly:
for I had just cast my eyes on her, seen she was handsome,
and thought no more of her.

She was about nineteen, and lately came from a place
in a country boarding school, where, by her waiting on the
misses, she had just picked up crumbs of education enough
to bridle upon, and give her an air of superiority to the common run of servants in the country. Half a dozen French
words, which she had learned like a parrot; two or three
tunes, as *Blow Winter's wind*, and *Come Rosalind, Oh! come
and see*, which she sang passably, and played lamentably on a
cracked spinnet, that was a piece of garret lumber, some tags

of tragedy, out of the *Earl of Essex*, and the whining characters in *Cato*, and her deep reading at stolen snatches, in the
Virtuous Orphan, and *Fortunate Country-maid*, and the like;
all these composed her, amongst the subalterns of our family,
such a transcendent merit, as provoked their indignation,
that such an accomplished creature should be in *sarvice*. And
indeed her own little head was so giddied with this wonderful elevation, she was so spoilt with the affectation and value
they inspired her with for herself, that had she not really
been one of the prettiest figures that can be imagined, she
would have been insufferable. Her dress, too, was always neat
and clean, unless when, on extraordinary occasions, she mis-
took her interest so much, as to take a little tawdry finery
for an addition, and which only served to prove that no dress
could entirely destroy the impression of her person. Then
her hands had happily escaped the havoc which hard work
generally makes with them. Probably she had never been put
to any.

The minx's behaviour, however, amongst her fellow-
servants, whom she kept at a distance, with a scorn awkward
enough, and fitter to create ridicule than respect, had so effectually awed them, that there was no talk in the house, but
of the fools she made, and the proposals she would not stoop
to. This reputation, then, of reserve piqued my curiosity, and
I was soon determined, by an attention to her person, and the
liking I took to it, to divert away a little time with her.

Upon this resolution I began to take a little more notice
of her, and to drop occasionally some marks of my distinction and of my good intentions towards her, which completely finished her self-conceit. The simple girl, it seems,
imagined that the same airs of prodigious virtue might be
played with the same success on me, as she passed them on
those of her own rank. I had opened my attack by some little
presents, which she returned me with great dignity and spirit.
She wondered, that she did, what I meant by it.——She hoped
nothing in her conduct had given me any encouragement for
bad designs.—She knew she was indeed too mean for me to
think of her for a wife, and she was sure she was too good to
be a mistress to the highest lord in the land. If she was poor,
she was virtuous.—With all this cant stuff that has so often
ruefully taken in many a country booby of more fortune than
intellects. As for me, who was out of all danger of being led
greater lengths than were proper by a passion that I had not,

I could with great coolness project my plan of operations: and master of myself, I was the more likely to become hers upon my own terms. I had, it is true, thrown my handkerchief to her, a little in the sultan-style, and her refusal to pick it up, at my nod, had hurt my pride, but I was determined that hers should give me my revenge. Convinced then that all her dread virtue lay in her vanity, I happily hit on the expedient of making that subservient to my designs on her pretty person.

In this view then, I for a while redoubled my importunity, and seemed to keep less measures with myself than before, as if hurried away by the force of my passion. All which only served to feed her insolence, and proportionally increase a resistance, which I could never think of the impudence of her aim in, without applauding and confirming myself in my designs to punish it, to my heart's content.

My good aunt, who very gravely took umbrage at the show I made of my designs upon her, was on the point of sending her out of the house, but I interposed my authority with her so effectually, that she submitted to let her stay, with a reluctance I could scarce forgive her, so much I thought myself dishonoured by the motive of her apprehensions for me.

My declared intentions had now driven all competition out of the field, and I saw nobody in the house who durst dispute my Dulcinea with me. And I did not give myself amiss the comedy to see all the airs she swelled into, at the ardour I expressed with all the humiliation of a true lover, which I the better supported in the double view of pleasure and revenge. The more flame and impatience I threw into my solicitetions, the more miss stiffened and stood upon her virtue, 'till, infinitely more deceived by her wishes than by any reason I had given her, her vanity had screwed her hopes up to the ridiculous pitch of forming serious designs upon me. No wonder then that a virtue no better guarded than by a vice, should not be a match for an attack on so corrupt a sentinel. And to say the truth, the ruin of women is often begun at home, and their fierce exclamations against the men, for want of justice to them, often proceed from their not having done it first to themselves, and that in more than one sense.

Diana, in the course of those parleys, which she indulged me in by way of drawing me in with the most theatrical protestations of a most inviolable virtue, had perhaps, under the notion of having inspired me with a great deal of love, taken a little herself: and that little might not ill second the effect of the mine I had laid the train to blow up her pride with.

And here I cannot with any degree of candour, omit remarking, that in that eternal warfare which nature seems to have established between the two sexes, and which, in one shape or another, subsists in every period of life, the men are not guilty of a little injustice, in imputing as a crime to the women that very dissimulation which they force them to in their own defence. If they love, and are sincere enough to confess it, we hold them cheap for their easiness: if they, in favour even of our pleasure (ever made more poignant by resistance) gratify that weakness in us, then we abuse them for their dissimulation: we who, in general, scarcely ever triumph over them but by employing it, with this excuse indeed, that sincerity is never more successful than when more praised than practised on either side.

Bent then, on playing all the game upon Diana, and satisfied I had at length brought her to the point I wanted her at, by proper progressions and that every thing was finely predisposed, I made the grand move, which soon decided the fate of the match, in my favour.

In one of those meetings which I had, not without affectation of great earnestness, humoured her belief of my attributing to chance, when I owed to her own art the giving me the opportunity of it; and when she was wound up, to expect the disclosure of some solemn, important resolution, in the style of my not being able to live without her, I gave her to understand, in the terms of the most cool and deliberate respect, that I was at length a convert to her virtue,——that I entered perfectly into the reasons of her reserve to me ——that such exalted, pure innocence should never be the object of my loose desires,——and that I would always be the friend and admirer of a modesty I had no longer any designs upon, and of course should not pester her with any more of them. Poor Diana, with all her chastity at her tail, and totally unprepared for this most reverential declaration of desistence, appeared now more disconcerted than pleased. She was not, in short, equal to her surprize at it. Probably she had not read, or at least remembered any circumstance like it, in the novels by which she had formed her scheme of cruelty. I would not, however, give her time to falter out a most false approbation of my new sentiments; but left her to chew the cud upon them, with an air of the most triumphant indifference. And in this I was not entirely a comedian, or perhaps I had not given so good an account of my undertaking.

I waited then a few days to see the effect of my stratagem, with a patience very fit to ensure the success of it, and soon found that neglecting is not always the worst way of courting. Diana, thus deserted by me, and unprovided with admirers of comparative weight enough, to think of playing the stale game of alarming my jealousy with, had no consolation, no resource, left for it, but her conscious virtue, which began to be inwardly the less dear to her, in proportion of its being the less in danger from without. The enemy was now within, and her pride treacherously taking side with it, made pretty quick work with that violent chastity of hers. Nor was it hard for me to perceive the gradual change, my still civil, but cool behaviour had brought on: the more she had acted her rigour, the more fiercely she had displayed it in the eyes of the whole house, now a witness of my most decent desertion, the more she was fretted to have laid out so much in high heroics to a neat loss. A woman piqued is a woman subdued, if a man discerns but his advantage, and properly improves it. And I now stood upon master-ground enough for both.

That I may not then expand this achievement of subaltern gallantry to an unconscionable length, I shall pass over all the little arts and doublings she employed to decoy me back, and which only confirmed me in the policy of keeping aloof till they entangled her in such advances, as put it past her power to make an honourable retreat. I nicked the exact instant then, when a gentle extension of my hand served to pull her in out of her depth, and drowned in the joys of re-engaging me, at any rate, all the cries of that maiden modesty she had made such a fine fuss about.

This pride of hers, however, had had such a fall from the height she had stuck herself up at, that it could not miss breaking its neck so effectually, as never to get up again, at least to give me any trouble with it. My triumph was complete, and the pleasures which attended it, so great as to keep down for some time at least, my rising remorse at the guilt and disorder of it.

Diana, had indeed dropped to me in a manner that, without increasing my esteem for her, had disarmed my resentment for a resistance which my pride had taken offence at. I began now to think her too severely punished. My senses had been too exquisitely gratified, for my heart not to take charge of their gratitude, since it could not be touched with love. I thought then I could not do enough for a young creature, who, having done so much for me, had put it into my power to do nothing but what I pleased for her.

Even libertinism has its laws of honour at least. And to reason only upon human respects, the seduction of maidens in a point so capital to them as their chastity, is a breach of order and decency always criminal, and always better avoided than excused by the force of temptation: but it becomes the lowest of mean villainy, when the unhappy object is sacrificed to satiety, and neglected and thrown to the ground, like a squeezed orange. Cruel return, to expose a young creature to all the consequences of the world's contempt, which with great injustice falls less on the author of the injury than on the more innocent and the weaker party, which has been the victim of it.

I was then coxcomb enough in all conscience, but not villain enough not to think of repairing, as far as superior considerations would allow me, the mischief I had done.

Time pressed. Our preparations were already in forwardness to set out for London, and I knew I could not ask of my aunt a favour she would sooner grant me, than not to take Diana along with her. The truth was, the girl's fondness and indiscretion had, without my having any share in the blame, revealed the nature of our intimacy to the whole family: so that I risked nothing in making a confidence to Lady Bellinger, of what she knew already, had groaned over, and was the readier to forgive, from her joy that it was no worse, at least in the world's sense of things. This was a confidence, too, which before would have been little less than an insult, and which, in the turn I took care to give it, appeared in the eyes of her partial tenderness, a sort of reparation for my want of respect to her, in this irregularity, committed, as it were, under her nose.

I did not then consult her in vain. Charmed as she was that I had consulted her at all, she indulgently entered into my designs and motives; and, accordingly, took a pretext for discharging Diana, so very remote from the real cause, and accompanied with so much kindness and liberality, that she could neither see the drift of her dismission, nor object to it.

Probably too, she had flattered herself with an invitation apart from me to go up to London. But this I eluded, by desiring her to go to her friends first, where I would signify my intentions to her, and most assuredly take care of her fortune: of which last I was very sincere both in the assurances and execution. But a day or two, then, before we went for London, she repaired to her friends, tranquillized, if not satisfied, about our separation, which I easily afterwards managed, so as to cure her of any hopes of shortening; at the same time that I provided effectually and, I may venture to say, generously, for her future support, in a way that could leave her no room to reproach me for her ruin, so far as that word implies wordly want or distress. My aunt, too, had enabled me to make her a very handsome present at parting.

Thus I saw myself disencumbered, at the expense of no more than a mere trifle to such a fortune as mine, of some little remorse, and of a few moral lessons from my aunt, which I was too much obliged by her goodness not to receive with a docility and respect which made her almost not sorry that I had deserved them. Her affection for me was in truth her weakness: but mine for her was a virtue, since it was a just gratitude I must have been a monster, not to have repaid that parental fondness of hers with, which it was not at least for me to find fault with the excess of.

And now the long-wished-for day arrived for our set-out for London, where I had never before been, but for such short spaces of time, and at such an age, as could afford me no insight into what is called the town, and which I was now determined to launch into, and get into the heart of life.

I took leave then of our mansion without one single regret, and from my whole heart left the country to the cattle it may be good for, and to those serene individuals, who withdraw from society to indulge themselves in its innocent joys. I took no poetical adieu of all the verdant woods, flow'ry lawns, mossy fountains, purling streams, gliding in sweet meanders through the enamel'd plains they are loth to leave; grottos glooming with a tender shade, natural cascades, and the whole train of rural beauties, which make such a figure in *soft* pastorals and lyric description, and are so often sighed for through affectation, or by those who have not experienced them, as I had, whom they had tired a thousand times. Nor could they make me but consider the country as one of the last places in which I should choose to wait the coming of old age upon me, or to which I should ever sacrifice, unless the air of it was medicinally prescribed me, that venerable season when the tumult of the passions is over, and experience has the most qualified one for society, the choice of which, never to be come at in a country retreat, is so much the charm and essence of life, at a time it stands most in need of the refined and gentle dissipations of intellectual pleasures.

END of the FIRST PART.

MEMOIRS

OF A

COXCOMB.

PART II.

ABOUT the middle of autumn I made my joyful entry into the great metropolis of our British dominions, the season when that company flocks to town out of inclination, which had mobbed out of it, in compliance with the fashion of going periodically to tire oneself heartily in the country, or to watch one another upon party-motives.

My first care on my arrival was consecrated to the memory of Lydia: my perquisitions after whom ended only in new matter of vexation at my not being able to trace out, either who, or where, she was, and of admiration at the singularity of the adventure. The sentiments of melancholy which this disappointment gave fresh force to, suggested to me the idea of alleviating it by all the dissipations of a town-life, and in pursuance thereof, I plunged over head and ears into all the amusements and pleasures which presented themselves in crowds to one of my age, rank and fortune. Lydia then still reigned at the bottom of my heart, but the surface of my imagination, played upon by numberless objects of splendor and gaity, passively took the shallow, volatile impressions; whilst my youthful warmth gave those follies they hurried me into, for the moment, the air, and almost the force, of a passion.

At my first arrival in London, there had been a sort of consultation held between my four guardians, whether I should directly set out on the grand tour.

The Earl of T——, one of them, was clearly for my losing no time, towards gaining that accomplishment, which is held as taking the first degree of a modern, fine gentleman. His reason, and his only reason, was that the Duke of —— and my lord such as one had sent their sons, when they were about my age, on the same errand, for a finishing. But not a word did he allege of the benefit they had received by it. Mr. Plumby, another of my guardians, sided with his lordship, adding with great gravity and importance, that nothing could be more profitable to a young man than travelling, which he was qualified to assert from his own experience. This, indeed, was true in some sense, for though his travels had been confined to the coast of Barbary, he had there laid, when clerk to a merchant at Tripoly, the foundation of his immense fortune.

On the other hand Sir Thomas Kingward, perhaps as much from a spirit of contradiction, that soul of dissent, as from any thing else, or because he had not first proposed it, declared resolutely against my going, observing, at least with more shew of reason, that travelling to any valuable purpose required a proper degree of observation on governments, manners, men and things. That my age was certainly not the age of judgment mature enough to attend to, or penetrate into, points of that importance: and that the superficial acquisition he saw brought home by the pretty, travelled gentlemen of the age, did not give him very favourable impressions of this fashion, since it served to procure to most of them no better than the ingraftment of exotic follies and impertinencies on their native stock, with which they made an unnatural and ridiculous mixture. Sir Paul Plyant, my other guardian, acceded to this opinion, not from his thinking it the best, but as it happened to be the last delivered. Upon this equal division, the point was then referred to the umpirage of Lady Bellinger, who did not hesitate a moment in giving her casting vote for my stay. I dare swear she would not for the world have trusted me out of her sight, in those bloody-minded papist countries, of which she had, like a true, good protestant, more direful apprehensions, than a very exact conception.

As for my own inclinations, they were so equally balanced, that I was very much obliged to any one who should save me the trouble of a decision, so that I cheerfully acquiesced in my aunt's determination: glad to give her a mark, which cost me so little, and pleased her so much, of my readiness to comply with her desires.

Fixed then for some time at least in London, I took a firm resolution to lose as little of life as possible. Happily, however, amongst all my follies, I was constitutionally free from an itch of gaming, a dislike to which I never saw reason to regret. As I was soon known to have a liberal command of cash, though I was not of age, through my aunt's lavish fondness and the indulgence of my guardians, the whole gang of sharpers had their eye upon me, from my lord Whiskem, down to beau Hedge, whose first rise was a guinea, given him by mistake for a halfpenny, his reward for shewing a link to a gentleman coming out of the playhouse. He immediately ventured this at my lord M—d—n's gambling-shop with a spirit, which fortune was so charmed with as not to leave him, till she had niched him in a chariot, and thus more properly introduced him to the notice, than raised him to a very suitable companion to our modern nobility.

I was soon then considered as a pigeon very fit and easy to be plumed, on its first flight from the dove-cote. All their bubble-traps were presently baited and set for me. But if these gentry are not more dangerous than they appeared to me, I should think the general outcry against them did them too much honour, and that the persons who fell a prey to them, "well deserved their woe." For though I certainly then knew little, or rather nothing of the world, the chariot and bay horses, and the embroidered suit, and all the technical show, so necessary to carry on their trade, never once imposed on me: the rascal glared so transpicuously through all their false finery. Even their smooth complacency, their eternal grin of assent, and indeed all their mock-courtliness, which tempts one rather to spit in their faces, than to be taken in by them, wore no more the air of genuine gentility, than a mask does of a face, and could as difficultly be mistaken. It was in short so impossible for wretches, actuated by principles so infamous and abasing, to counterfeit that frank, open, noble air, which distinguishes the true gentleman, that their dupes must be dupes indeed!

Guarded then as I was by an invincible contempt for all gaming, as a most wretched, tasteless destruction of time, my natural penetration had the fairer play. I felt, I may say, instinctively the hollowness of their insiduous approaches, and my pride was so enraged at their remarking the country put enough wrote in my face to attempt me, that I kept very little measures with my rebuffs, as I should have been very sorry that they had not perceived I saw into them. But if they could defraud me of nothing else, they did of the pleasure I had so just a title to, and had bespoke of mortifying them. I had, however, misreckoned. Those, who are capable of their meannesses, are not extremely tender, or susceptible of confusion. The regret of their prey escaping them is all they can feel, and even for this baulk they did not want their consolation, in the reflection that one sheep's escape from bleeding did not absolutely thin the market.

I might expatiate more in so fair a field for it, but that it might look too much like playing the old saving game of pride, the miserable finesse of which consists in thinking to compound for those follies one has a warm or weak side towards, by declaiming against those one has naturally no delight in. I have not, however, mentioned my aversion to play here as a merit, but as a happiness.

The whole bent of my inclination then lying towards the pursuit of women, of which I had made an experience that gave them sovereignly the preference of every other allurement, I was now only undetermined as to my choice. Sure of liking all, as of loving none, since Lydia had exhausted and still engrossed my sentiments of that passion, I sought no farther than the satisfaction of those desires inseparable from one of my age and unruliness of constitution.

I had been now but a few days in town, and had gone through the whole tedious round of visits of business and ceremony, when I was at length left at liberty to indulge my own notions of life, from which I had not been restrained without some impatience, even for so short and necessary an interval.

But of all the follies and fopperies of high-life nothing had more suprized, or sickened me, than that which goes under the name of visiting; and indeed can there be any thing on earth more ridiculous than for women, who heartily despise one another, very probably with equal justice on all sides, to play over so often the dull, stupid farce of rapping at doors, where one wishes, and pray for nothing so heartily as not to be *let in*.

Poor Lady Featherweight! Could I ever remember her distress without laughing, if it was not doing her too much honour even to unsettle a muscle about her? This most consummate trifler had, one afternoon with great importance, scrawled out six and thirty names of her acquaintance, whom she owed visits to, not one of whom but without giving her the least trouble, would have gladly sent her a receipt in full for the debt. Thus equipped with her beadroll, my lady sets

out one afternoon in her chair; and had already dispatched
five and thirty, not one of whom, but had, to her great joy,
refused her the door. The six and thirtieth, and the last to be
sure, was the plain, untitled Mrs. Worthy, who with a fortune
not more than middling, enjoyed life with ease and dignity.
Content with acquisitions, which made her a companion for
the elegantest, noblest and learnedest of our sex, she took
care not to corrupt the merit of her superiority with affectation or female pedantry. She had, withal, friends amongst her
own sex, whom she really loved, because she esteemed them.
Even the triflers of it she tolerated with unaffected tenderness, and always made good-natured allowances for the mere
defects of nature or education. Thus she never insulted the
present, or wounded the absent. It was at this door then Lady
Featherweight stopped. She had so slight an acquaintance
with her, that Mrs. Worthy hardly knew her name, whilst her
own was probably put down on that illustrious list, only as
an expletive of the three dozen, or for the air-sake of having
it to say she visited one who saw familiarly none but the best
company. Mrs. Worthy happened not to be out, and no particular orders being lodged at her door, it was answered to
Lady Featherweight's footman, that Mrs. Worthy was at
home. As soon as she heard it, she flounces out of her chair,
with a muttered ejaculation: "I think she is always at home,"
and was shewn up-stairs, where, after she had heartily tired
poor Mrs. Worthy with a wretched hash of subjects, such as
ribbons, marriages, laces, fops, scandals, balls and routs, she
ran out of her house, whipped into her chair, and came in a
hurry to my aunt's, whom she dishonoured by an exception,
that was to saddle her with her nonsense for the rest of the
evening, and lamented to her in the most pathetic terms the
misfortune of meeting with one person at home, when she
had, with so much fashionable politeness, laid her account
for a general exclusion. My good aunt, with very little acquaintance with the world, and just plain sense enough to
discern the extreme folly of this street-errantry, contented
herself with observing to her, that if they were friends or
acquaintances worth cultivating, worth in short the trouble
of a visit, she should think it a misfortune to miss seeing
them. "Oh, my dear!" says Lady Featherweight, "you can-
"not be in earnest!" And then she named us, in a breath, such
a cluster of duchesses and countesses, who had visited for
years, and never seen one another, as when, I came to know

them afterwards, confirmed me heartily in my contempt of a childishness scarce pardonable in pretty misses, that have not outgrown the christening of their dolls. But to see the tawdry, frippery, overdressed figure of this fine lady, without one grace of beauty, youth or wit, to intercede for her; to hear her complain of her misfortunes, and to think at the same time of the distress she must have put the person to, who was so much out of luck as to be plagued with her visit, was so rich a jest, that I burst out a laughing in her face, which she made me redouble, by very cordially joining in it, in the idea of her succeeding in her pretty airs, without dreaming that the joke was of her personal subscription.

Folly does not amuse, or even employ one's notice long. The one I have just mentioned soon grew even beneath my contempt, and it is only by way of regret for the disappointment and loss of time, it has too often occasioned me in my dealings with that sex, that I have deigned to mention it at all.

To return then from this insignificant digression. As soon as I was at leisure to turn myself, I found that, towards carrying my plan of pleasures effectually into execution, I should need a companion and confidant of more experience and knowledge of the town than myself. Such an one the difficulty lay not in the finding, but in the choosing. I had several pretty near my age, and animated, like myself, with the prevailing spirit of our season of life, the love of pleasure, who offered me their service. Chance, however, more than any judgment, determined me in favour of Lord Merville, a young nobleman, just of age, whose father was still living, and with whom he lived in the strictest friendship, ever attentive to repay his paternal tenderness with all that filial respect and confidence withal, so infinitely more honourable to both, than that servile subordination, with which some fathers so sagaciously purchase the hatred and distrust of their children. A conformity of inclination soon drew us into a free communication of sentiments and pleasures.

Merville had, at an age when most young men are held to begin the world, essentially exhausted all its variety. No body knew it better, or was better acquainted with all its pleasure and all its ridicules: but blessed with that sort of good-nature which never goes without good sense, his taste for the first soon inspired him with a necessary toleration of the last. His complaisance, always without design, was indeed a kind of constitutional indolence, which would not suffer him to give himself the trouble of maintaining his dissent from the humours or inclinations of his acquaintances, of which he had, as the natural consequence of such a character, a great number, and few friends, though none more deserved them. Yet yielding, as he almost always did, to the opinion of others, it was never without a graceful dignity that he yielded. Did he, which was indeed rare, give you his advice, it was ever with such a soothing sweetness, such a regard to your self-love, as freed it from the disrelish, which generally attends that office, even in the best of friends. But if too just to oppose a tendency to weaknesses he was himself not exempt from, his notions of friendship were, however, too high not to bestow on those he honoured with it, the assistance and benefit of his experience. One was sure of his company, nay his guidance, certain lengths, but not a step beyond safe or honourable ones. Whereever he found any invincible indocility in any of his friends or companions, in points essential to the preservation of character, health, or fortune, he constantly, without coming to a disagreeable rupture, gently dropped them. His friendship, in short, was that of a Mentor rather too much mitigated; but that was more the fault of human nature, than his. He was more for regulating pleasures than rigorously restraining them: his morals were relaxed, but his heart excellent, sure sign that they were not always to continue so. I began then by being his companion and associate to his pleasures, and, in process of time, had the honour of becoming his friend.

With too much discernment not to penetrate the ply of coxcombry I was taking, and to know at the same time the inutility of combating it directly, he leaned with me, in order to bring me back again, and, in the mean time, gave me all the instructions and insight I wanted towards my avoiding any gross mistake in my first launch into life, when the first steps are so decisive.

It was under his directions then, that to soften the inconvenience of my living, as I was obliged to do, at my aunt's, and to secure me from the necessity of recurring to the mean expedient of appointments at bagnios or bordels, that I hired in a genteel, though remote street, a neat small pleasure-house, which was committed to the care of a trusty domestic, well versed in schemes of this sort, and recommended me by Lord Merville, who vouchsafed to direct the furnishing it, in the greatest simplicity, but with all the greatest elegance of taste: without one single article granted to show, or denied to the most voluptuous luxury. In this retreat, so commodiously fitted for the reception of my company, every want of nature was refinedly provided for: and it was here we occasionally resorted, to unbend in select parties, and to find again that lively pleasure which always languished, died away, or deserted us, amidst the magnificence of fretwork ceilings, history'd tapestries and apartments too spacious for pleasure not to lose itself in. Delicacy of manners presided at our entertainments, and gave poignancy to those enjoyments, from which it is never excluded but to their detriment. Even our most sensual gratifications were those of rational votaries to pleasure, and had nothing of the grossness of tavern-bacchanals, or brothel-orgies. Comparatively, too, with which I may venture to lay down for a maxim, that true taste not only adds to the pleasures of life, but moderates the expenses of them.

My little pleasure-house was not, however, entirely finished and settled, before I was engaged in an adventure of gallantry, with which I opened my first campaign in town. One evening that Lord Merville and I were at the play together, the boxdoor opened behind us, and let in a lady, who rather dragged after her, than she was led by, a pale meagre, spectre-like, young man of quality, whom she very cavalierly shook off, as soon as she saw Lord Merville, and with the greatest familiarity came down and seated herself next to him, in a place that happened to be empty. "Where do you "keep?—One never sees you.—Were you at the last opera?— "Have you got your snuff-box?—*A propos*, when were you "at Lady Drumly's?—Did you win or lose?", all this was pronounced in a breath, with a volubility of tongue, and a disengagement of air, which plainly pointed her being used to the best company. Merville, who guessed by my looks my curiosity to know who this original could be, and knowing that barely naming her was enough to satisfy it, said with a bow between grave and careless; "Indeed, Miss Wilmore, I "am charmed to see you; you look extremely well." This was an answer full to the purpose of all her questions, which she had herself very probably forgot. Presently, after seeing Merville speak to me, she lolled upon him, and asked him loud enough for the galleries to have heard her, who I was. He spoke softly to her, and told her my name and family. This was enough; I had now her eyes, in full stare, upon me, without the least concern or confusion at my catching them. And presently, with an air of unconstraint and superiority to all that might be said or thought of her, on that occasion, she got between Lord Merville and me, that I might not, I suppose, lose my share of the happiness of sitting next to her.

What Miss Wilmore had been in her early bloom was hard to say. I have been told she was then delicate, and even handsome: but she was now five and twenty, and was not at all the first, and had some remains of the last. She was an only child. Her father dying when in his fond opinion she was of age and sense sufficient to take care of her estate, he left her one large enough to give her pretensions to the first matches in the kingdom and that entirely at her own disposal. Hurried away by the impetuosity of her passions, and naturally an enemy to ceremony, she had not waited for that of marriage, to acquaint herself with the most essential mysteries of it. Having then satisfied her curiosity on that point, and supported her resolutions by a great and independent fortune, she was determined that it should not play her the trick common enough of purchasing her a tyrant. As she heartily despised her own sex, she soon kicked off its trammels, and declared openly for unbounded liberty, in defiance of the tyranny of custom, and the usurpation of the men, whom the interests of her pleasure only engaged her to admit as their mistress and her own, but to whom she disdained to stoop as a wife. Fixed in these sentiments, she braved the public, which by the way she heartily despised, with an intrepidity and spirit that might have done her honour in a better cause. That many women are rakes at their heart may be, and is, I believe, true. That all are so, in a sex evidently formed for domestic happiness, seems more a poetical licence, than a truth warrantable from nature or experience. But that not one could ever gracefully support that character, when openly professed, I believe will hardly be disputed. Miss Wilmore at least proved no exception to this general observation. The first use she made of the loss of her reputation, was to turn it to the account of her taste for gallantry, which she now gave full scope to, without excluding, however, every other pleasure, that her inclination led her into, and which she could easily gratify with her command of fortune, and her sense to live up to it, without hurting it.

Throwing then off entirely the restraints of her sex, she made parties of pleasure with young fellows to all public places, and held them play at cards, at table, or over a bottle, with all the freedom of a man: but for these liberties, she only chose such companions as she could either entirely command their complaisance, or were too well-bred to encroach upon the familiarity she allowed them, beyond her own bounds: for she kept up some decency even in the midst of her disorders. It was then natural for those of her own sex, whose conduct and education had taken a different turn, to condemn and fulminate a sentence of civil excommunication against her. And this she neither complained of, nor regarded. But what diverted her, and confirmed her the most in her scorn of the opinion of women in general, was to find that some of the most worthless of them, the most ulcerated with every vice, hypocrisy not excluded from under the black cover of the last, declaimed the most fiercely against her, who had at least to plead for herself that she had one vice, and that one the very worst, less than they. Some indeed, equally guilty, but less barefaced, declined her acquaintance, out of policy, as the timid herd drives the blown deer from amongst them.

Her person had, however, suffered by her boundless indulgence to all her passions. It had robbed her entirely of that grace of modesty and delicacy, which distinguished and embellishes female softness. A masculine air had taken the place of it, and appeared as unnatural, though not so disgustfully shocking, as effeminacy in a man. Her bloom was already worn off, and her features enlarged and grown towards coarse. Yet still there was great fire and spirit left in her eyes, and an unaccountable something about her, which engaged and took with one, the more one knew or conserved with her, especially in her cooler intervals, when her passions gave her natural sense fair play.

Lord Merville knew her, and it was his own fault that he had not known her better: but he had undertaken her with such a security of succeeding, founded on her character, as had alarmed her pride, which would not suffer her to be taken thus, as it were, by insult, and put her on the defensive, who probably would otherwise not have scrupled being the aggressor. As he immediately withdrew, and had really had no very deep design upon her, a few days absence had made her either forget or forgive his attempts, and on seeing him

at the play she treated him, as if no such misunderstanding
had ever existed. However, whether I was as a new face welcome to her, or had not at least any prepossession against me,
to get over, as Merville had, all the distinctions and favours
were for me. We presently engaged in a conversation, carried
on in breaks and pauses, such as Merville's occasionally inter-
posing, or our looking round the house, naturally bred. For
attending to the play was fashionably out of the question.
For my part I was coxcomb enough to meet, and encourage,
all the advances she made me, without the least reserve,
though I was sensible I was subscribing a scene to the whole
house. Merville frowned, bit his lips, lifted up his eyes in
vain. I looked on Miss Wilmore as a kind of heroine, whose
character and temper piqued my curiosity, and whose person had not yet lost all its pretensions to please, or at least
amuse. As for her poor conductor, who had the air of a figure of straw stinted in the stuffing, he was, it seems, one of
those insignificant danglers by trade, whom she could take
and leave without consequence, and who was not absolutely
without some merit, since he did himself justice enough to
pretend to none, and humbly contented himself with handing the ladies to public places, and held it for the greatest
honour, if they would let him fancy a suit of ribbons for
them, or play with their monkeys, and to say the truth he
looked as if favours of another sort would have cursedly embarrassed him. Miss Wilmore had picked him up, she did not
well know how herself, at an auction, and he had continued
ever since occasionally her most humble and most innocent
servant. He saw himself then deserted by her as a thing too
much in course, to give us any interruption with his very
modest pretensions. As soon as the play was over, Miss Wilmore scarce waited for the tender of my hand, which she
seized, I will not say grasped, and I led her with an air of triumph to her chariot, that diverted more than Merville, who,
however he laughed at seeing me spirited away in that manner, was not without some concern, surely on my account,
for the consequences.

I had told Merville loud enough for her to hear me, that
I would instantly return, and take him up with me, so that
she had but the time between the play-house door and her
chariot, to settle the point of an invitation to me, to come
and spend the evening with at her own house the next day,
which I accepted as readily as she could desire, in the full de-

termination to push the jest as far as it would go. As for this precipitation on Miss Wilmore's side, it was so much in character with her, that the wonder would have been, if she had omitted it.

This great preliminary being thus adjusted, I went back to Merville, who complimented me with much sneer and some malice, on the dignity of my conquest, which he observed, could not but give high impressions of my nicety and distinction. But I was not easily to be bantered, especially out of a folly that I had unaccountably enough set my head upon. As for my heart, I had no reproaches to make to it, for any breach of my peace on this occasion.

At the hour appointed, I repaired to Miss Wilmore's, and found myself not mistaken, in bespeaking a clear stage and all favour.

I was immediately introduced to her, and found her sitting in her drawing-room, in a dress of design. But though she inspired me neither love nor respect, I could not help observing that she still very well deserved my desires. I approached her then with that air of triumphant certainty, which, presuming victory, not seldom commands it. I had myself, too, neglected no advantage that dress could give me. After the usual compliments then, I took post in the chair set for me, and spread myself out, in full display of my figure, and all its decorations. Miss Wilmore, who, however, was really above being pleased with the coxcomb-part of me, was too solid in her views not to forgive that, in favour of the taste she had taken for my person.

The tea equipage was set in order for my reception, which is generally a necessary part of the ceremonial in an afternoon visit to women. It serves like wine amongst men after supper, to open and engage conversation. It was over our tea-cups then, that we came to leading explanations, when, notwithstanding all that I had heard, all that I believed of her easiness, great enough even to spare one the trouble of advances, which she used liberally to take upon herself, I found such a fear of hurting herself in my opinion by the idea of cheapness she knew was annexed to her character, as threw an air of modesty and reserve upon her reception of my gallantries; an air that bore the double merit to me, of distinguishing me enough to depart from her usual freedom, and of letting me see her sincere motives in it without pretending to place her shyness to the account of a virtue that she had not, and which she was above affecting.

At first indeed, on finding a certain elusion of my attacks, where I had bespoke even a forwardness to meet them, I was half piqued, and half disgusted. The copying it with me, which I should naturally have expected in another woman, appeared as trifling ill-usage, if not impertinence, in one I had been made with reason to look on as a most determinate Anti-Platonic. I was even inwardly afraid of the ridicule I should incur, in having a blank *tête à tête* with her. I pouted a little, I even drew back, and threw out hints of taking my leave of her for that time, in the hopes of my having another opportunity with her, when she should be in a better humour. Miss Wilmore, who took this, as I really meant it, for a kind of menace, and divided between her fears of disobliging me too far, and of giving me too much reason to contemn her facility, sustained, for a while, this struggle between her decency and inclination, when the last in right of habit and accustomed sway prevailed, and determined her in favour of my ardour. The declaration of her eyes, preceded that of her tongue, which was delivered with all the disorder incident to those critical occasions.

"Well," says she, "Sir William, I feel I deserve your man-"ner of treating me too much to complain of it. I disdain to "hide from you that the desires you express, are my own "wish. I should be sorry you had not them. The step I have "taken proves it. All my regret and confusion is that they "cannot be accompanied with your esteem, however, I may "have hitherto acted, to the discredit of this sentiment, which "I have too sovereign a contempt for the falsities of form, to "feign, if I did not feel, and feel it for the first time. May "you hereafter do me the justice to reflect, that if I have sur-"rendered to others on my own terms, I yield myself abso-"lutely to you, on yours; that even my easiness has its merit "to you, since you alone could change the motives of it, from "those of the senses to the more noble ones of the heart, "which now lay me low at your mercy, you alone".———She was going on, in this strain: but though it flattered my vanity extremely, I was too impatient, too complaisant indeed to the confusion I saw she was in, to prolong it, by giving her capitulations a calm audience. I interrupted her then, I closed up her mouth with a kiss of energy enough to take her breath from her. I had insensibly shifted my post from my chair to the couch she sat on, and soon found her too much subdued, too much in earnest in her passion, to trifle long with my attempts to prove mine. Sincere in her desires, sincere in her expressions of them, she at length met mine with a meltingness that restored her even to her beauty, and to her sex. All her masculine airs were now softened into tenderness. The rakish, the bold, the indelicate Miss Wilmore disappeared, and in her place I held in my arms a true female with all the timidity and modesty of a new-made bride. I could scarce conceive her change, nor my own. I had, I may say, achieved a victory without a resistance; I had enjoyed without esteem; yet, such was the force of my gratitude, such the visible alteration that new-born love had operated on her, and which stamped on her caresses an impression not to be mistaken for that of mere sensuality, that gave a point to my happiness, the keener in that I had not expected it, and that my vanity was agreeably feasted with the preference I imagined I had obtained over my predecessors. I stayed then 'till two in the morning with her, in which time we supped together, waited on only by a faithful confidante; and in the returns of our privacy, I employed myself full efficaciously in quelling or rather drowning her tender doubts and fears of my inconstancy, but withal in a way that would give her reason to redouble her regrets, whenever they should come to be verified.

Respects of decency obliging me to take my leave of her for that night, I did it with such apparent, and what I should never have imagined, with such real reluctance, as was, to say the truth, but a just return, for all she expressed at our separation.

I got then into a chair that had been kept in waiting for me, and in my way home I could not help reflecting on what had passed.

To dispose as I had done of Miss Wilmore's person, a circumstance I had so much in common with many others who had preceded me, was nothing. Perhaps the justest matter, to have made trophy of, would have been, not to have *had* her; but the idea of being the first to inspire her with sentiments of love, to fix her, to show her all over the town as my captive, and tied as it were to my triumphal car, carried with it something so soothing to my vanity, that I could not help giving it a dominion over me. My pleasure, too, had found its account in her, far beyond what I had anticipated, which I take to be often the case of those who, engaged with women of not more than ordinary beauty, and not having had their expectations over-raised, have been less subjected to disappointments, than others have been with those striking beauties, who promise too high a feast, for reality to make good. There are women again, who are wise enough, either for their own interest, or that of their pleasure, to do themselves justice on the indifferent state of their reputation, or the mediocrity of their personal merit, by employing so much art and attraction, in supplement of these wants, as often to make and maintain the conquests they snatch out of the hands of ungraceful, indolent virtue, or insipid beauty.

The next morning I dressed and went to breakfast at Miss Wilmore's, whom I found at her toilette, and Merville with her, which I could not observe without a sentiment that had something of jealousy in it. She received me, at first, with a certain air of embarrassment and confusion, which delighted and informed Merville of the pass things were at between us, as clearly as if she had made him the confidence in express terms. But Miss Wilmore soon recovered herself, and as she had taken her resolution concerning me, and imagined she should please me by a sacrifice made to my vanity in the avowal of her sentiments for me, she declared me from that instant her sole favourite, and even desired Merville not only to take notice of it, but not to thwart or oppose her in it. Merville assured her he was so pleased with her frankness, that, since he was not to hope for himself, he would not be above accepting her confidence, though, he added, maliciously enough, that it was an honour he expected, considering her known discretion, to share with the whole town. And in this conjecture he did her no injustice, for a long habit of indifference to what should be thought or said of her conduct, was not to be suddenly changed, especially when the strength of her passion added its usual impatience of dissimulation to her natural disdain of it.

The alteration withal in Miss Wilmore's deportment, her now softened tone, her less boisterous vivacity, compared to what Merville had known of her in her former gallantries, neither escaped his observation, nor surprize. Himself could hardly believe she was the same individual woman, who had so openly renounced all modesty as a weakness of her sex, and seemed now as thoroughly reconciled to it, as could be

consistent with her open confession of the motives of her
conversion. I received then Merville's congratulations on it,
with an air of coxcombry and exultation, which could not
fail of giving him the comedy, and which proved how ill I
deserved the distinction and power now attributed to me. I
little then knew that women as rarely confer their favours
upon merit, as princes or ministers. Then the event soon
shewed how ill Miss Wilmore had judged, in giving me the
honour of reclaiming and fixing her. Merville, however, was
soon so sensible of her mistake, that his concern for me was
now transferred to her, from his thinking her new-adopted
sentiments merited another fate than he bespoke for them,
with a certainty that did his penetration no dishonour.

Miss Wilmore, whose eyes were now opened, in virtue of
a passion she had never before experienced, felt, and deeply
felt, because too late, the hurt she had done herself by the
irregularities of her former conduct. She now found that
that very esteem of the world, which she had been rash
enough to sacrifice irretrievably to her grosser pleasures, was
become indispensably necessary to procure her the duration
of those infinitely more valuable ones, the pleasures of the
heart: which are never to be well, nor long enjoyed, where
that private esteem, which always follows that of the public,
is not of the party.

In vain then did she change, and sincerely change, her way
of thinking and acting. The severest reserve to all but myself,
the dismission of her train of flatterers, gallants, or companions of her pleasures, and the exactest adherence to the decen-
cies of her sex, served indeed to certify and proclaim my triumph, in a manner which my vanity was highly pampered
with, but which could engage no returns from me but gratitude; and what a weak, insufficient sentiment is gratitude,
where love can only satisfy! and love was neither in my
power, nor in my inclination. The world ever more constant
in its condemnation, than in its approbation, now took its
revenge of Miss Wilmore's former neglect, by refusing its
favourable opinion of her reform, and carried even its injustice so far as to attribute it to designs upon me, which love
might indeed have secretly suggested, but of which interest
was, I am still persuaded, perfectly innocent.

But none gave her less quarter than some of our titled ig-
nobles, who to my certain knowledge would have gladly
married her, and passed over every thing, in favour of her

fortune, which was great enough to wash out, in their eyes, stains ten times deeper than what she could ever have contracted. This will not, however, seem incredible in this prodigiously refined age, when, if the hangman's daughter was but *worth* money enough, she would hardly escape being run away with by the *proudest* of our nobility; nor would they who know the world, be at all surprized to see in the news-papers the following paragraph. "On —— last my "lord—— was married to miss *Thrift*, a young lady pos- "sessed of every accomplishment that can render the mar- "riage-state happy, and a fortune of one hundred thousand "pounds." It is even scarce to be queried, whether the condition of consummating the nuptials at the foot of her father's sign-post would be an objection, their delicacy would not overleap.

Miss Wilmore, however, did me and herself justice enough to consider her former conduct, as an eternal bar to an union, which as it could never have entirely healed the wounds of her reputation, so it must have for ever dishonoured mine. Making then a merit to me of this sentiment, she would often assure me that she would be the first to despise and oppose such a weakness, even were I capable of it, and that all she wished or aimed at, was the possession of my heart, which was the less likely for her to succeed in, as it was really not in my own disposal. Nothing, however, less would content her in the turn she had now taken, and as her passion made her extremely tender and quick-sighted, she soon discovered that she had no other hold on my inclinations but gratitude, which was not much, and my love of pleasure, which was yet less, since my desires had been satisfied, and of course satiated. On her sense of this invincible indisposition of mine for her purpose, she soon grew reserved, melancholy, and given up to that tender, pensive grief, which is so engaging, in consideration of its motive. She often obligingly complained to me, that if I had been the first to teach her the pleasure of pure love, I was likewise the first to make her feel its overbalance of pains and anxieties: that I had robbed her of the sweets of liberty, without making her the only amends for her loss, that could make the rest of her life supportable.

It was then that I employed myself to calm her uneasiness, and assure her of a constancy I was far from being capable of. All my ends of amusement and pride had been answered. Repeated enjoyments had unedged my appetite, and the notoriety of my conquest had left my vanity nothing to feed on. I succeeded then as ill as I deserved in my attempts to quiet her just alarms; and, less to my wish than it proved for my ease, she had spirit enough to prevent a desertion she foresaw was inevitable, and by that means saved me the disagreeable sense of its being my act, however I might be the case of it.

I had for some time fallen off both in the number and length of my visits, which in all commerce of this kind, passes for a sickly symptom, that ever threatens an approaching dissolution. Yet her expostulations were gentle, tender, and even friendly: those in short of a woman who wisely avoids giving her gallant the excuse of passion and ill temper for his leaving her. Softened then, by her submissive style of bearing the wrongs I did her, and which was in truth the only method of managing with a temper so hot and impatient as mine then was, I had exhausted the whole chapter of excuses for my visible negligence, and the indifference which grew upon me towards her, even against my will: so true it is that we cannot dispose of our desires as we please.

Miss Wilmore was now no longer that unthinking, giddy flirt, whose wild sallies of whim and gallantry had exposed her to the censure indifferently of the really virtuous, as well as of those who had not the tenth part of her merit, on stating a fair balance of her good and bad qualities. She was now recovered to reason and reflection, from which she soon discovered the necessity of giving me up, and her bearance of my neglect was at an end, on her being well-assured that I had commenced a new engagement. She took then, and what was more, she inflexibly kept, a resolution few women but herself would have been capable of, who had begun life so much at large as she had done.

After ordering with the greatest expedition and secrecy all the necessary dispositions, when every thing was ready, she struck the blow she had so firmly determined; she sent then for Lord Merville to desire to see him at her house, and on his obeying her intimation, she acquainted him with the motive for it in the following terms, as near as he could remember in his relation of them to me.

"The declaration I have now to make to you, my lord, as "you are Sir William's friend, and I flatter myself, even "mine, I own I have not the courage to support to his face, "such is the unfortunate ascendant I have given him over

"me: you will then, I am persuaded, forgive me the liberty
"I take with you, in desiring you would communicate to Sir
"William the sentiment which I prefer trusting to your doing
"justice to, rather than to a letter in heroics, that old and
"trite expedient of deserted and forlorn mistresses. Con-
"scious that I must not hope, what I could not deserve, the
"engrossing your friend's attachment, I am, however, too
"proud to satisfy myself with a divided heart, to have the
"love only on my side: or being no more than the object of
"his transient amusement. Yet my obligations to Sir William
"are far superior to any reasons of complaint against him.
"My passion for him has recovered me out of a career of li-
"centious and folly into the paths of virtue, too late indeed
"for the retrieval of my fame, which the tyranny of custom
"renders impossible to those of our sex unhappy enough to
"lose it, before they know the value of it. You will please
"then to tell him that I leave him with regret, with regret
"I abandon him to the pleasures and dissipations of life, of
"which himself was the instrument in the hand of love to
"show me the emptiness and vanity. It is nothing for him to
"leave me, who does not, nor probably ever did, love me;
"but I who at this instant leave him with unabated tenderness
"leave him, tho' to regret him whilst I live. I neither hope,
"nor wish he should even remember me: and all I earnestly
"beg of him, is not to stir a step either to his disquiet, or my
"own, which last would be greatly the case, if he should seek
"to interrupt my plan of a lasting separation, which I am
"unalterably determined upon, and now resolutely take my
"last adieu."

With this she flung into her closet, without waiting for his
answer, and shut the door after her. Merville made haste to
acquaint me with this new turn, and came to my apartment,
but I was that very morning gone to Richmond on a party
of pleasure, which Miss Wilmore knew of, and had made her
use of that opportunity: so that I could know nothing of
my doom till the next day. As soon as Merville had delivered me this message of dismission, I found my pride at least
piqued, and I was half tempted to consider it as one of those
common finesses used by women to alarm their lovers to
their duty, by their fear of losing them. But on a reflexion
upon the solidity I had observed Miss Wilmore had lately
been taken so sensibly a turn to, I began to apprehend the
reality: I say apprehend, for now the pleasure I should have

found in a peacable riddance, was outweighed by the reproaches I made to myself for deserving this desertion, and the wound it gave my vanity, to think it was she that had thus got the start of me. In the first flutter then of this novelty, I took Merville with me, and drove directly to Miss Wilmore's, where I found the house shut up, with only a porter to answer that his lady had set off at five that morning in a post-chaise of her own, attended with her confidante, but that he could not possibly tell, as he did not know, what road she had taken.

I stared at first, and seemed a little fretted at this cavalier treatment of my fugitive mistress, which I looked on in that light which a prince would on a conquer'd province shaking off his dominion, and in the heat of my passion expressed myself accordingly. But Merville, who knew that I was not only treated as I deserved, but happier than wise, in the painful scenes she had thus generously spared me, soon by half-humouring, half-laughing at my resentment reconciled me to myself, which was what I had more to wish for, than even a reconciliation with my lost mistress. My vanity, too, which was at bottom the greatest cause of my concern, kindly poured its balm into the wounds it had made. I began now to pride myself on having inspired so respectable a passion, and to think it pleasant enough that Miss Wilmore should thus turn the tables upon me, and leave me the poor distressed Theseus on the shore, to lament the flight of my Ariadne.

A few days after, I received a dry and long letter from her, in which she acquainted me with her going to the south of France, where she proposed weaning herself from a passion, the misfortune of which she did not so much impute to me, as to her former misconduct, and giving me a full acquittal of all demands in point of love, she only begged me to maintain a friendship for her, and even not to deny her my esteem, if she should succeed in her firm resolution to deserve it.

This was a treaty, I readily came into, and answered her in terms which, without flattering her with a re-engagement, contained every thing that could satisfy her pride or my gratitude. And as in this I was perfectly sincere, I succeeded to my wish, and had the rare good fortune of keeping the friend, where I lost the mistress.

Miss Wilmore in a short time returned to her country-seat, and from thence to London, where I saw her afterwards on the foot of the most pure friendship. She opened her house to all who had merit to recommend them; and had soon the pleasure to find that, as difficult as the world generally is, in parting with its prejudices, they lose greatly of their force, if they are not often entirely destroyed by the power of time, and that course of conduct steadily pursued, which aims more at deserving than expressing a desire of its good opinion. By respecting then herself, she brought by degrees all those to respect her, whose respect was worth the caring for. As for the formal triflers of her own sex, who held out against the demonstrations of that order and decency which now breathed in all her steps, she considered their estrangement towards her, as so much gained upon the enemy. Disdaining to justify follies she had sincerely renounced, she observed that at least they had procured her a riddance from a number of frivolous acquaintances, which would have been a dead tax upon her time and patience; that she would not indeed recommend the expedient to practice, because over-balanced by superior considerations; but that if the forfeiture of reputation was to be attended with no worse consequences than getting rid of the common run of female visitants, many might be tempted to try the experiment: perhaps, too, with less real inconvenience than some women marry improperly, purely to deliver themselves from the obsession of disagreeable relations.

Here setting down Miss Wilmore, probably with a better grace than I had taken her up, I return to the engagement I had commenced, when, on the umbrage of it, she had so spiritedly dismissed me.

This new acquaintance, too, had been purely the effect of chance. I had left Lord Merville at a gentleman's house a few miles from London, and was returning to town alone in a landau and six, about eleven in the morning; which, over-taking a chariot that was proceeding the same way leisurely before us, ran against it, and carried off one of the wheels clean from the axle-tree, upon which the chariot now tottered in suspense. On seeing this, and hearing the scream of female voices, I sprang out of the coach, and with the help of the servants easily disengaged the two ladies, who were in the disabled conveyance, and who had happily suffered nothing more than the fright.

As it was then impossible for them to get on in their chariot, the roads bad, and the distance from town about two miles; they did not hesitate at accepting my invitation into my conveyance. After I had made them all the apologies and reparation they could wish, for the carelessness of my drivers, which had been the occasion of this accident, I handed them in and seated them, and then gave the coachman orders to drive us to their house.

In the mean time, they were both so muffled up in their capuchins and hats, that there was scarce any pronouncing upon the merit of their persons, till on their being a little recomposed, they took off their hats, and letting down their cowls, shewed me their faces in full view, the one of which marked fifty, at least, and the other about eighteen.

I had already learned the name of the eldest, which was Lady Oldborough, now a widow for the fifth time. Her last husband, Sir Thomas Oldborough, was a young baronet, without a foot of estate, but himself a very handsome person. This lady, whose weakness it seems was to be too much governed by her eyes, had, in the full age of reason, and in her forty-fifth year, married him, made his fortune, and ruined his constitution; which ruin she was not so happy as to have it be directly her work. The truth is, he could not resist the only attraction she was mistress of, which was her fortune, and that a very considerable one, as she was lady-dowager of all the pillage of her four preceding husbands, by none of which she had any child alive. But this fortune became, not without a sort of justice, due to so mean a motive, the insnaring instrument of his destruction. For soon breaking all measures of common decency with a wife he had only wedded in the way to pleasures he could not come at without her money, he launched into every branch of them which that could procure him. And as if to make amends for his former stint, he now abandoned himself to such riotous excesses of all sorts, he drove with such fury, that his constitution failed under him, before it could carry him half way through his fortune. Bagnio-amours, tavern-vigils, the momentary racks of ill fortune at play, in short the whole tasteless, despicable round of the joys of the town, in which so many young fellows of good estates so lamentably consume character, health and fortune, had all contributed to tear him to pieces. Drained then, consumptive, and exhausted, he died, before he was thirty, a very old man, that is to say, as to his favourite ends of living. Thus more properly than she the dupe of this match, which had brought him these fatal acquisitions, he was forced, no doubt to his great vexation, to leave the old woman, as he called her, behind him, whom he had often, with great exultation and certainty, bespoke the joy of burying; and who upon the arrival of the contrary event for known causes, conceiving that her affliction would be treated as a farce, very prudently declined acting it, contenting herself with observing the usual forms, which the world less forgives a failure in, than in the real grief, of which they are, however, no more than the expression, and at the best an apocryphal one.

Lady Oldborough, relieved by this riddance, and grown wiser by experience, determined against putting herself again in the power of marriage-tyranny, or embarking, at least with young fellows, on so crazy a bottom as their gratitude or discretion: yet her taste for them hindered her from absolutely renouncing them. How to come at them, then, upon terms of safety, was the question: and we shall soon see what measures she fell upon for the attainment of her ends.

Her glass had not, it seems, reflected in vain to her her faded sallow complexion, the retreat of her eyes inwards, and the funereal stamp of the crow's foot on their corners. Rare and incredible as it may seem, though a woman, she had not been blind to this decline of her charms: conscious then of what she had suffered by the usual depredations of time, she consulted her greatest interest and acted like a wise minister, who feels himself going out of power, and finding it impossible to hold it in his own person, substitutes a favourite, of whom he can dispose, and thus at least make the best profit of a losing game.

In this view then, she had attached to her, by all the ties she could think of, this companion of hers in the chariot, Miss Agnes, a young woman, without either friends or fortune, but to whom nature had made some amends in the treasures of her person. In truth it was hardly possible to fish out a finer figure for her purpose, or indeed a more tractable disposition. She was, in short, in point of understanding, little better than a beautiful *pantin*, of which Lady Oldborough directed the motions, and played the wires as best suited her views of interest or pleasure: but this game she managed with too much art and secrecy for me to discover, before time and events betrayed it to me.

On my first sight of Agnes, I could not help paying her the admiration which so great a beauty naturally exacted.

Nothing could be more engaging than her face, nothing more correct than her shape, and all together composed a system of attraction, more powerful and more naturally accounted for, than any in all Sir Isaac Newton's works. It was not that I felt that sort of emotion which was reserved for Lydia alone to inspire me, but I felt that quick and sensible desire, which sets all the powers of the mind in action to obtain its satisfaction, and which made me, on that instant, conceive and form designs of pleasure upon her.

Upon this plan, as I did not then know the inside of the cards, it was but ordinary policy for me to imagine that being over particular to the young lady would be a false move, which might prove the loss of my game. I turned therefore all my court towards Lady Oldborough, who, I could not escape observing, eyed me with an attention and a certain expression in her looks, which was not that of dislike. I had then on the side of my intentions that security of pleasing, which rarely fails of investing one with the power of it. I threw, consequently, into my addresses to her, all those easy graces of assurances, which are so irresistible to most women, that they often require no other merit to succeed with them: and I was neither ignorant nor neglectful of my advantages.

By the time I was arrived at Lady Oldborough's house, I had easily made my party so good with her, that I could not get away, till I had passed a promise of coming the next day in the afternoon, a promise which my eyes confirmed to Agnes with a clear declaration of the compliment being paid to her; this she received with such an equivocal and no-meaning countenance, that nothing but the charms of her face could have hindered me from throwing up my pretensions from that instant.

Punctual then, through inclination to my engagements, I went to Lady Oldborough's about the beginning of the evening, where I found her with Agnes, both dressed to receive company, in a drawing-room crowded with visitants, to some of whom I was personally known: and all were prepared to see me there, from the account they had of the accident which had bred our acquaintance.

My own concern had made me tolerably clear-sighted, so that I soon discovered that most of the men were drawn thither by the pleasure of seeing, and by their designs upon, Agnes: a circumstance which at the same time that it answered

Lady Oldborough's purpose, informed me very disagreeably that I should have the competition of rivals to encounter with, besides the opposition I bespoke from Lady Oldborough herself. Nothing, however, could be less rigorous or severe than the order of her house. She had erected it into an academy of gallantry, where none were more welcome than the gay, the young, and the handsome; a disposition very prudentially kept up by the mistress of it, in the view of her coming in occasionally for a share of what was going.

Agnes, however, shone with such superior beauty, that she was incontestably the first figure of the drama, and Lady Oldborough, whose pride was subordinate to her more material pleasure, was so far from jealous of the pre-eminence, that she seemed even not without affectation, to set her up in the first place, and to accept the homage paid her, as a favour done to herself: her motives for which were of so new and extraordinary a nature, such a refinement of art, that they were not readily to be suspected, and her conduct in it had the merit of a delicate self-denial, whilst it aimed entirely at the grossest self-gratification.

Nothing could be more tender, more caressing, more attaching than the reception I met with. All the honours of the assembly were paid to me, in quality of the greatest stranger, and of one, it was already evident, Lady Oldborough made a point of engaging in her society, to which Agnes, who had her cue, contributed all the very little art she knew how to use, in aid of her patroness's intentions.

As my first visit was too purely an audience of ceremony to afford me an opportunity of proceeding upon my business, I made no particular address either to Lady Oldborough, or Agnes. This last, set out for show, like a romish chapel, sat, with all the calm and tranquillity of one of their images, receiving the worship of her idolizers, and a jest or a word from her was as great a miracle. Nothing in short was ever handsomer or stupider. But even this last consideration fortified my desires of enjoying so great a beauty, as I knew it would cost me the less pain or regret, to leave her afterwards. These ideas, thus associated, sufficiently pointed out the nature of my new passion.

It is needless here to insist distinctly on the particulars of a conversation, which turned upon general subjects. Who is there of the least rank or fortune, who has been happy enough to escape the repeated martyrdom of those mixed conventions in which town scandal, characters of players, comparisons of dancers, criticisms upon operas, without the least taste for music, the merciless satires of dunces upon dunces, the control of fashions, the hankwords of the day any how brought in, form the whole frivolous fund of the chit-chat of those, who are far from suspecting themselves of being low company, on the strength of passing vulgarly for the highest?

For my part, I was too glaring a coxcomb not to take with one sex, and alarm the other. The airs of sufficiency and petulance with which I boldly decided upon subjects I had neither dived nor dipped into; the edge I cut up characters with, as they fell under my dissection, the insolent parade with which I displayed my person and dress, all these absurdities, which should have rendered me ridiculous and contemptible, were precisely the recommendations by which I succeeded the most: they were the advantages, in virtue of which I dazzled and captivated the women, and confounded the men, who envied, whilst they could not contest with me, this worthless pre-eminence. I was then without a competitor, the hero of the day.

Lady Oldborough, too, did not a little help, by her visible partiality, to fix my triumph. She caught up all my no-jests, and gave them the weight they wanted by some emphatic comment, or laugh of approbation, whilst she passed by neglectfully, or even condemned, much better things that were said by others, Agnes herself, who scarce took notice of any thing, appeared at least to listen to me, and whatever little meaning shewed itself in her face, it was that of a plain preference of my nonsense to that of the rest of the company.

Thus advantageously introduced and posted, I easily made good my footing, and I soon had the satisfaction of seeing myself reign without a rival. Those who had designs of the same nature as myself upon Agnes, finding themselves totally eclipsed by the happy splendour of my follies, and the favour of Lady Oldborough, mutteringly quitted the field to me, and I experienced no further obstruction from them to the accomplishment of my projects. Some of them, in a fit of despair, were so hard driven as to transfer their homage to Lady Oldborough herself, who was too alert at seizing all advantages, to be over scrupulous about the manner in which they fell to her.

It was then that my assiduities at her house, of which Agnes, as was just, had the honour, were presently divulged, and procured me my dismission from Miss Wilmore, who had never once deigned to come to an explanation with me on the causes of my inconstancy. She saw, it seems, the personages I had to deal with in another light than my passion presented them to me.

Lord Merville, who had occasionally seen Agnes at public places, had, on his side, very undesignedly confirmed me in the prosecution of my designs upon her, by his praises of her beauty in raptures, which in strict justice there was no refusing her. But he was perfectly a stranger to either her, or Lady Oldborough's real character. And I had made no advances towards introducing him, for a very obvious reason. He had too much merit for me not to fear him as a rival, and I had desires too near resembling the passion of love not to carry a little of the hue of jealousy with them: so that I preferred suffering from the want of his advice, to the danger I apprehended from his competition, should I put him into a condition of giving it me, with knowledge of the subject. Merville was not insensible of those fears, which hurt his friendship for me the less, as the motives of them could not be disagreeable to his pride. He was satisfied, too, that in all events this affair would carry me no very serious lengths without my consulting him, and that at the worst I was no marriage-dupe, being, as I had told him, sufficiently defended by the free-engagement of my heart. The attractions of present pleasure might perhaps easily silence the voice of reason, but there was little likelihood of their stifling the cries of love. As for my aunt, whose fondness still continued in the same tenour since my friends found that complaining of my conduct was not the best way of making their court to her, I was perfectly at ease from all remonstrances from that quarter. I even reduced her to the point of respecting the ridiculous sides of character by the air of sufficiency and bravado, with which I rather displayed than exposed them. This is a secret I have often practised with a notable success on more than her, and which I bequeath with all liberality to my brother coxcombs.

In the meantime, my frequent visits and intimacy at Lady Oldborough's were bringing on upon the spur the execution of her designs. She had given me all the fair play, all the liberty I could conscientiously desire, towards carrying on my attacks upon the charming Agnes. I used even to wonder at the intrepidity with which she seemed to deliver her up to me; but she knew her better than I did, though she presumed and trusted rather more upon that knowledge than is, generally speaking, very safe or advisable. But Agnes was only a very distant relation of hers by one of her first husbands, and now entirely cast upon her for her support and dependence: a circumstance which Lady Oldborough had made a merit of not suppressing by way of caution to me, which was not, however, perfectly disinterested on her side.

In the course, then, of the familiarity allowed me, and the opportunities almost industriously thrown in my way, I had taken in deep draughts of what is generally called Love, but had not been able to inspire any. Agnes was, in truth, guarded against me, not only by Lady Oldborough's secret instructions, but by what is much stronger, that constitutional coldness, which takes from chastity the merit of its being a virtue. I had not even with her the chance of finding out the weak side to level my batteries at: for she was absolutely a piece of fine, still life without passions, by which to work or be worked upon. If she repulsed any attempts upon her person, which her easiness invited, and which she always did firmly and coolly, this repulse was as mechanical and as sure, as the effects of clock-work, wound up to strike exactly at certain determined touches or movements. Pride, honour, reason had no share in her resistance, and the instant the causes of it ceased, she resumed, as if nothing extraordinary had happened, the same calm unruffled countenance, the same air of indolent apathy, which was a thousand times more puzzling and provoking, than the most outrageous resentment. In vain then did I employ the whole artillery of gallantry. My presents she would not receive, because she was told it was not right to receive them. And as to all the common-place rhetoric I was master of, it was just so much breath expended in neat waste. I might as soon have persuaded one of the portraits of the Hampton-Court beauties to leap out of its frame into my arms by talking to it, as compass my ends with this fair idiot, who found perhaps more protection in her stupidity, than she would have done in that lively perception, which so ill rewards many of her sex for their trusting to it. Enraged then as I was, not only at the loss of my advances, but at myself for letting my desires get so much the head of me, that I could not command them off this object of adoration and contempt, I endeavoured without avail to play my reason and my pride against my passion, but the more I endeavoured to flounce out of this plunge, the faster I stuck. Her personal charms, recurring strongly to my imagination, re-inflamed me so effectually, that I could not think of parting from the hopes of possessing them. I had even tried the expedient of appeasing my ardours by some by-parties of joy at my little pleasure-house, with some of those easy beauties which London swarms with. But the torrent thus diverted for a moment, returned only with tenfold violence, and served purely to prove that the imagination, once strongly impressed with a particular object, is not so easily to be put off with a change. It is only for satisfied desires to afford one the benefit of inconstancy.

Lady Oldborough, whose observations had waited on me through the whole progress of my passion, and to whose secret artifice I had owed a good part of the obstacles I met with, now saw me sufficiently entangled not to fear my getting off the hook, and began to play off the strength of her stratagem.

Without her giving me any handle for imputations on herself, or to take up notions of her, unfavourable to her designs upon me, I found my opportunities of seeing Agnes alone (for conversing with her was out of the question) greatly abridged, and soon entirely cut off. She was either engaged with some insignificant of her own sex, picked out for the occasion, or she was not well, or detained from me by other excuses, in all which great measures were kept with me. So that had I even perceived they were affected, they appeared natural enough to take from me all pretence of murmur or complaint. This restraint answered a double end of irritating the more my desires, and of forcing me on embracing any expedient which might serve to come at their satisfaction.

Whilst I was thus fretted and disquieted with this new train of difficulties, Lady Oldborough, at the times when I could not see Agnes, took care to throw herself in my way, and to comfort me so obligingly for my disappointment, as closed up my eyes against her having the least share in it. She wondered, for her part, what the girl meant by her foolish coyness, ——that my particularities to her did her more honour then she deserved. ——that she hoped she was not silly enough to think of drawing me in, by her impertinent keeping me off,——that she had a good mind to return her to whence she had taken her,——that though it was true she could dispose absolutely of her (this she often emphatically dwelt upon,) yet she could not say that she could wish to force her inclinations,——she was glad indeed the girl was virtuous,——but there was no general rule without an exception,——that every thing in short had its limits and restrictions,——that if it was ever excusable to swerve from the exactness of duty, it was in favour of such an one as me.

By this strain of condolence and fulsome flattery Lady Oldborough half forced herself into the confidence of my designs, which in truth had never escaped her, and which, had my thoughts of Agnes deserved the name of love, I would never have forgiven Lady Oldborough the grossness of countenancing. But as my desires were without delicacy, so were my views of accomplishing them. She had indeed so artfully insinuated her power to serve me, so indirectly and sparingly opened a glimpse to me of its barely not being impossible for me to win her over to act such a part, that I could not well be shocked with any easiness in her to undertake it; especially as my wishes met her hints more than half way.

I seized then, with the eagerness of a drowning wretch, this extended twig. My eyes all of a sudden opened on the importance of Lady Oldborough to the success of my pretensions. I found without more deliberation, that she must be the key of the wish'd-for-treasure; but still a difficulty occurred, and that not a small one. How was I to engage her in my interest? I knew very well that such offices could not be gratuitous. Her fortune placed her above the temptation of money: though I would not have scrupled the sacrifice of a very considerable sum for the satisfaction of my desires. Our vices are ever more liberal than our virtues, besides there appeared to me so much trouble to be saved by such a method of purchase, as greatly humoured my indolence and love of ease especially in an affair of purely sensual gratification. But Lady Oldborough was really unapproachable in that way: yet convinced that I ought to consider her as a frontier town, necessary for me to make myself master of in my way to the reduction of the capital I had thus laid siege to in vain, I soon found that I must new point my batteries. Determined then not to omit any thing that might level the obstructions to my success with Agnes, I projected the making fob-love to Lady Oldborough, sure that she would surrender on very little summoning, and sure that the other would drop to me in course. I repeat it, this expedient was about as delicate as my desires, and I caressed myself for my wonderful sagacity in having fallen upon it: whereas in truth all the honour of it was due to Lady Oldborough herself, whose art it had been to bring her own designs to seem self-suggested to me, and who waited for me at this very pass, which I had been less brought into by my own driving, than by her insensibly pushing at the wheel.

As soon as I had agreed with myself this noble plan, I resumed, in virtue of the hopes it gave life to, all that air of sprightliness and assurance, so fit to secure my success. Neither this change nor its motives escaped the amorous veteran, whose game, and she did not fail to play it with superior skill, was to give me all the encouragement I could desire to transfer my addresses to her, and to let me see, as through a perspective, what gate I was to knock at before I could have the right one set open to me.

I had likewise another collateral view, in this scheme of trying how far this lovefarce might go towards exciting a jealousy in Agnes, which might be serviceable to me in my design upon her. By jealousy, I mean here, not that which the passion of love is hardly ever less or more unattended with, but that common sentiment of selfishness, which makes one envy others the possession of what one does not care for one-self, and which even children and idiots are not exempt from.

I turned then all my gallantry visibly, and not without due ostentation, towards Lady Oldborough herself, and affected a coldness and indifference for Agnes, which the thorough subordination she was in to this patroness of hers, made her receive at first with a tranquillity, that did not a little mortify me. My courtship had made no impression upon her, and my desertion as little. Still I pushed my point with the other, who met my advances more than half way, and confirmed me in my presumption that, one way or another, I should certainly accomplish my desires, which were more than moderately inflamed by these difficulties, and ultimately enter my port, though I was obliged to steer thus for some time with my face from it.

Lady Oldborough was in the mean time too serious in her designs upon me to trifle with occasions. She knew herself to be at an age, when no time was to be lost, and that I myself was in that dangerous season of life, when I might very possibly slip through her ladyship's fingers. But in the view of omitting nothing that might secure her point, she rather over-shot the necessary, when she went something too abruptly not to be maliciously observed, into all the dress and gaiety of youth, as if it was possible to stifle the truth of her age, by such notoriously false witnesses, as ceruse, carmine, powder, and the rest of the *fourberie* of the toilette. There is not, however, in nature a point, in which the opinion of mankind is more universally clear, nor in which women, especially the old and the homely, are more incorrigible, than in their dress: fine clothes indeed may so far be of use, not as they turn the eye upon the wearer, but as they call it off from a forbidding face, and relieve it more agreeably: but then this avocation never results to the benefit, or answers the intentions of the unfortunate claimant, under these exploded titles. On the contrary, a silent indignation is sure to rise in the men at seeing finery thus murdered and misplaced. How often do we see even the effect of brilliants of the first water spoiled by their unnatural assortment with a system of dim eyes, sepulchral sockets, cadaverous complexions, and flaggy, collapsed muscles, when they can at best be considered but as funeral torches to light round a corpse, exposed in state. On the other hand, those who are ill-treated by nature or time, and who have sense enough to shun, as death, these distinctions, which present their defects more glaring and disgustful, and these pretensions, which render them more ridiculous, are sure to find the finery they thus profitably deny their persons, still more made up to them by the honour, which, from the renunciation of it, redounds to their understandings.

To do Lady Oldborough justice, she was naturally not so weak, as to put her trust in the powers of dress. I had often myself heard her hold in a good hand, at playing off her raillery upon some of her co-evals, for their dressing out of age and character. But passions are unconsequential. Either she was so far hurried away by hers for me, as to go out of her mind, (for love at her age was no better than a temporary madness) or she imagined me more superficially sighted than I really was. Not contented, however, with adorning a winter landscape with all the flowers of the spring, as if it was in nature for December to wear the aspect of May, she now affected the mincing skuttle, the infantine lisp, the giddy simper, the pretty dandle, in short all the airs and the graces of a girl of fifteen. Then she was, with equal silliness, fond of having me constantly at her side in all the public places, and of showing me about as the French did their hostages, for a proof of her still victorious charms. In short, I was so near sharing the ridicules she proceeded accumulating upon herself, that with no great impatience, so far as she was personally concerned, I began to think it high time to shorten my voyage and make my port.

In the mean time, I had the pleasure to find that all subdued as Agnes was to her patroness's will and disposal, her insensibility in a short time began to give way, and herself to betray certain signs of fire and life, which all my direct addresses had not been able to call forth. Her eyes now appeared to me charged with more meaning and expression. Too intent on my designs not to watch these progressions, I soon discovered the growing symptoms of her jealousy in the marks of impatience, pique and disquietude, at the gallantry I directed to Lady Oldborough, and at the tenderness and encouragement with which she received it, all which only determined me the more in the pursuit of my scheme. It was easy to conceive that if I should prematurely alter it, and listen more to my inclinations, than to the policy of ensuring my success, I should run the risk of losing all the pains I had hitherto taken for their satisfaction; since I could then expect no fair play from the provoked and disappointed Lady Oldborough, who might, and doubtless would, exert herself, to cross and counter-work my designs. But, in with her, I was sure of being in with Agnes: such was the situation of my game, and I governed my moves accordingly.

I had no more now to do, than signify my royal will and pleasure to my loving subject, who had, to say the truth, scarce waited for its proceeding from me as my own mere motion. She had not, however, with all her folly, been enough the dupe of her desires, to mistake the point I had in view, in my yielding to the attractions she had thrown out for me. She could not dissemble to herself the implicit compact, not the less understood, for not being directly expressed, of her good offices with Agnes, which was the foundation of our engagement, since it was of her own suggestion, and (I might add without much more insolence than truth) of her own solicitation. Pleasure courts the young, the old court Pleasure, and are often glad to come at it on any terms. It is an age, in short, condemned by the course of the world to have nothing but what it pays for. Those then who have not in strict keeping that rare *winter-fruit*, called *dis-*

cretion, must lay their account with having the forfeit of it exacted from them in some shape or another. They are seldom happy enough to play the fool with a thorough impunity.

It is not, however, improbable that amongst the deceptions of vanity and self-love, Lady Oldborough had somewhat relied on the imaginary remains of her personal charms, or she could never have taken so much pains with plaistering up her ruins. She hoped perhaps that I might still find something in her, which might take off my edge to Agnes, and attach me to herself. We are always ready to apply in one's own favour, examples which flatter our weakness: and there were precedents enough of young fellows, who had been bewitched by superannuated mistresses, to countenance her hopes, or at least wishes, for such an event. But even if this illusion served her for nothing more than stunning her reflections upon the grossness of the implicit contract, which she was now to put the seal to, my purposes were not ill served by it.

Prepared then for my purpose, and mellowed to fall with less than a shake, there was nothing more wanting than to agree the time and the spot for coming to the grand conclusion; and these prerequisites were easily adjusted.

It was not that Lady Oldborough had not some measures to keep with decency. So transient an affair as mine threatened to be, could not make her amends for a loss of character, which might bring on that of her female visitants and all her card match acquaintance, which are so essential at her season of life. She made then a very wide and wise difference between the suspicion she would have been sorry not to have created, and the proof which would rob her of those comfortable resources: and, in truth, since the world is so ready to compound for the saving appearances, it would be rather too impudent, as well as too imprudent, to deny it so reasonable satisfaction.

As soon then as I had, on the foot of the most insolent security, proposed to her by way of a salvo my having the honour of giving her a *petit souper* at my pleasure-house, she wondered at my impudence, and very cordially accepted my invitations, which she most certainly would not have done, had she not counted as little upon my virtue as her own; though she was not ashamed of throwing out some feeble hints of friendship, whilst her countenance betrayed the ea-

gerest wishes for an opportunity to break Plato's neck headlong down the stairs.

Upon this, an evening was appointed for my calling upon
her, with the pretence of escorting her to some Entertainment, whilst it lay upon her to amuse or employ Agnes out
of the way, who used generally to attend her upon most
parties of pleasure, from which a third person need not, from
their nature, be excluded. This was Lady Oldborough's own
affair, and she took care of it accordingly.

For my part, I saw the hour of my assignation approach
with a kind of indolent impatience. It is for desire alone to
beget Pleasure: and every interest but that of immediate
Pleasure itself adulterates and brings with it a disgust very
fit to destroy it. Immediate I say, because a pleasure in prospect rather detracts from the present object, which is only
made use of as a pass to it. How glad then should I have been
to have executed my scheme by proxy! But I had unluckily
no measures of that sort; possibly too they could not have
answered my end. Women, when once they have their heads
warmed with a particular object, rarely lose sight of it; and
Love is a Spright, which, however it may flutter and frolic
it in young tenements, when it takes possession of your old
ruined castles, is devilish tenacious of its haunts, and is not
easy to be laid by the exorcism of any but the person who
has raised it.

Condemned then by all the laws of honour and prudence
not to play false to my own challenge, after very cooly finishing a game of billiards, which had borrowed somewhat
upon the precious instants of my appointed hour, I drove to
Lady Oldborough's with an excuse in my mouth, and something not so favourable to her as perfect indifference, in my
heart.

I did not deserve the being so happy as to have any accident favour me with a disappointment, or to find the lady
herself indisposed to be satisfied with my apology for making her wait, for, rather than upbraid me with my want of
punctuality, she chose to give her watch the lie, and observed how good I was to come at least half an hour before
my time.

I found her just risen from before her toilette, where she
had doubtless taken a great deal of pains to very little effect.
Her dress for the occasion presented an appearance odd
enough, as it aimed at a medium between the negligent dis-

habille, and the cumbersome full dress. A gown, stiff with embroidery and loosely enough wrapped round her, gave no further expression than was necessary for her interest that it should, of a shape which most surely was not that of a nymph; whilst a bosom bolstered up, obtruded its false evidence, without avail. Our senses are not such dupes. Modest enough, not to be wholly insensible of the ravages of time and industrious to repair them, she had exhausted all the powers of paint, powder, laces, and jewels, to forge herself a face and figure more supportable than ordinary: but nature is hardly ever seen to yield to the efforts of art, which we are even cruel enough to impute as crimes to the women, though they commit them purely in favour of our pleasure. But if they thus egregiously deceive themselves, they deceive none of our sex, who are worth deceiving. Who sees not the difference between the dead colours produced by the toilette, and the inimitable roseate ones of nature? between the bloom of youthful smoothness, so florid to the eye, and delicious to the touch, and the spurious glaze of varnish, presenting nearly the disagreeable shine of a coarse enamel? The face in short can neither be hid, nor sufficiently sophisticated; the deception, therefore, of dress is as silly and inconsistent as that of a merchant who would attempt to pass a bale of dowlas under the false package of cambric wrappers, whilst a principal part of the contents was left staringly open, in contradiction to the fraud. Ornaments indeed, sparingly used and employed with taste, may heighten indifferent beauty, but they as surely serve to render age or homeliness more conspicuous and, of course, more disagreeable.

Such was the natural effect then of poor Lady Oldborough's treacherous auxiliaries. I viewed her with a smile, which in the blindness of her passion she doubtless took for a smile of approbation. I betrayed some marks of awkward confusion, that I owed to certain inward self-reproaches, which she kindly interpreted as a transport, or ecstasy, that did not allow me the liberty of expressing my sense of my happiness. Such a prepossession one would not, however, have suspected in one of her experience, and yielding to me on the terms understood between us: but what is there less consequential than passions at any age, but especially on the verge of dotage?

Not without some violence, however, could I assume something of a countenance befitting the occasion, after some shew of faint reluctance on her side, some hints of discretion —a word which came very unseasonably into mention from her—and a world of pretty little grimaces, meant for expressions of delicacy, which did not extremely become the widow of five husbands, she gave me her hand, and I led her to my chariot, she glowing with desires, and myself feeling only the coolness of one who had no desires of my own, and could have wished to have had none of hers to satisfy.

With these ideas, the way to my pleasure-house gave me no occasion to complain of its length. We arrived then, and the conveyance which carried Cæsar and his rare good fortune landed us safe. I introduced her then to my little temple of joy, and, in the decency of doing the superficial honours of it, stupified for a while the less pleasing sense of my engagement to do the more essential ones.

Women are not naturally born for liberties which dishonour them. Lady Oldborough was, at least as she pretended, and which I was too indifferent to examine scrupulously into the truth of, at the first of her campaigns of this sort. She was then obliged to act as if such a situation was not familiar to her, and accordingly the novelty of this adventure, the taste of my house and furniture, the delicious convenience of such places for transactions of polite gallantry, were all topics which served to amuse our first awkward minutes. She admired especially the downy air, the commodious cushioning of a superb sofa, with a warmth of expression in which its obvious destination had doubtless some share.

Presently an ambigu was served in, in which nothing was omitted, that could flatter the taste, or stir up the sensual powers. My attendants, duly disciplined to the orders of the house, disappeared, as usual, and a dumb-waiter supplied us with the most generous wines. These were not unnecessary preliminaries, at least to me, whose nerves, as high-strung as they were with health and youth, felt too much the absence of desire, not to want the being invigorated and aided by the warmth of good cheer.

We supped together with the confidence and ease of parties in full agreement. I began myself to enter into the spirit and humour of it, to consider my situation in a less disagreeable light, and to think it droll enough for me to divert myself with the nature of my conquest. I grew gradually more pleasant, more free, and more disposed to put an end gloriously to this adventure. Even my imagination deigned to

come in to the assistance of my constitution, and, by soft-
ening the defects of the present object, as well as piquing my
curiosity, began to press Desire into the service of Sensuality.

But Lady Oldborough's own indiscretion had like to have
nipped in its bud this laudable disposition. For not content
with manifesting a fondness more cloying than provoking,
either with an eye to excite me by a view of my reward, or
trusting triumphantly to the power she flattered herself with
having acquired over me, she ventured to toast Agnes to
me. Nothing could be more injudiciously timed. It served
to awaken an idea of comparison highly prejudicial to her
present interest. I could not recall to mind the youth, the
freshness, the prodigious beauty of Agnes, without forming
such a constrast of her charms, to the spectacle I had before
me, as bred a momentary disqualification, equal to that of the
monsters of the opera. In vain, for some moments, did the
twice too tender Lady Oldborough redouble her ardours.
They redoubled only my disrelish; and I saw myself on the
point of freezing by a fire-side.

Partly through the necessity of gaining time to recover
myself, partly through mere ill-nature, and to see how she
would take it, I slackened my advances and declined into
that sort of respect, which is to women in certain situations,
an injury the more exquisite, in that they cannot so very decently complain of it. I enjoyed then, for a little time, her
perplexity and distress, with all the barbarity of a tyrant who
delights in the tortures of his subjects. But if by this means
I forced Lady Oldborough to make a foolish figure enough
to herself, that which I myself made was, candidly speaking,
not a much more respectable one. At length, however, my
vanity served her more effectually than either her wishes or
my own. The dishonour, which I suggested to myself would
redound to me from a blank entertainment, stood me instead of a goad. These thoughts, conspiring to fill up the void
of desire with the heat of youth, now resuming its force,
helped me to go on in the undertaking, for which I had, not
without straining, taxed my abilities.

I addressed myself then with the best grace I was master
of to acquit myself honourably of a function, which was
not the more agreeable to me, for the now considering it as a
sort of duty. I had commanded, and, what is rare enough in
such cases, I had forced my imagination, on which the springs
of pleasure so sensibly depend. Nature was now at my or-

ders. My attacks then began to partake of the warmth of
my emotions, and became decisive enough to quiet the lady's
alarms for fear of carrying back her virtue, as untouched as
she had trusted it with me in hopes of better treatment. I
was now plainly her man; but who can paint what she
seemed in those instants?

Her countenance enflamed and reddened so as to deepen
the artificial layer of tints that overspread its surface; eyes
twinkling and glimmering with those occasional fires: and
languishingly fixed upon me with a certain timidity and diffidence, as if they were asking charity: her neck, bare in
some places, through the disorder of a tippit, which had
faithfully answered her intentions, in giving way to the
slightest pull, discovered the peels and cracks of a varnish,
which had not been proof against the variety of its inflexions.
Her hands, the fingers of which appearing the longer for
wanting the plumpness of juicy youth, had the air of pliers
or nippers, with which she either tenderly gripped mine,
or sleeking them over my face, numbed as they touched me,
and made all heat retreat before them; the whole in short
of her person, spread before me like a desert of dried fruit,
exhibited such a picture of amorous fondness, as was even
more ridiculous than distasteful, and had nigh quelled my
best of man. But as I was now in the pride of my spring, well-
bottomed, and my blood fermented strongly in my veins
as to threaten the bursting its turgid and distended chan-
nels, so that love was rather a natural want in me, than
merely a debauch of imagination. The sympathy of organs
established between the two sexes, sensibly exerted itself, and
drove all delicacy or distinction of persons out of my head.
I became then quite as naughty, to use her own term, as she
could have wished, and piquing myself upon doing things
conscientiously, I repeated a ceremony, which in some respects resembled that of the doge of Venice, when he weds
the gulf by way of asserting his dominion. I had now triumphantly founded mine, and inspired her not only with a respect, but with a gratitude, which was not perhaps the less
serious and engaging, for the motives being such pleasant
ones.

But that nothing might be wanting to my satiety, I was not,
I found, to be let off without a most cloying after-course
of sweets and dears, which almost overbalanced my self-satisfaction at the proofs of my prowess, from whence I pres-

aged to myself the most advantageous successes, whenever
my constitution should act with the whole force of imagination on its side.

I was soon, however, relieved by the welcome arrival of
the instants of our separation, instants of which many a loving couple openly deplore the cruel necessity with as much
inward joy, as captives feel in the crisis of their ransom and
deliverance.

I gave my hand to the lady, and led her to my chariot, in
which I was to set her down at her own door. In the way
thither, she shewed so much love and tenderness for me, that
merely out of good breeding or politeness, I could not
squeeze in any intimations of the service I expected she
should be of to me in my designs upon Agnes, towards whom
my stream of passion now ran with redoubled violence, as
was but natural from the comparison my officious imagination had suggested to me, and yet more so, from the coolness
of my senses towards the present object, which proportionally reinforced my flame for the other.

Determined withal, in favour of the main point I had in
view, I had too great a share of insensibility and presumption, to forego my advantages. I fancy, too, that I made Lady
Oldborough feel my consciousness of them, in a way that
could not much flatter or please her. My style to her was
more assuming than became a lover, or even a husband, more
in the imperative than in the optative strain, and by that time
we arrived at her house, and there parted, I left her pretty
sensible that I did not consider as her *last favours* those she
had just bestowed upon me. Such an express declaration
would have appeared too crude, and close on the heels of
them, and accordingly I thought it the very extremity of politeness to spare it her, till a decenter season.

After then sacrificing a few days to a forced complaisance, my impatience drove me to such explanations with
Lady Oldborough in respect to Agnes, as she could neither
avoid comprehending nor expressing her resentment at, as
far as her fear of offending me, in a point she saw I was not
to be trifled with, would permit her. A conqueror may submit to request, but does not therefore submit to a denial. She
did not fail accordingly to expostulate tenderly with me, on
the barbarity there would be in exacting such a disgraceful
service, especially from her; as well as on the indignity of
such a conspiracy against the innocence of a young creature

under her protection. Her remonstrances, in short, had not fault in them, but her having bethought herself of urging them too late. Possibly had they come from any but herself, I might have listened to them with more calmness and deference, but in her they appeared as so many prevarications, which rather insulted my authority, than convinced my reason. I was unhappily too, at that time, of too impetuous a character, too much hurried away by the violence of my passions and the heat of my blood, to have much relish for that heroic merit, which is annexed to the sway of reason. I could not then easily part with the hopes of a possession I had taken such uncommon pains for, nor relinquish the reward I flattered myself that I had earned. I had known, I had seen, that the accomplishment of my desires entirely depended on Lady Oldborough; I had taken all my measures upon the foot of this presumption, and I was not of a humour, nor indeed generous enough, to bear a baulk of this sort with much patience or resignation. I was, besides, confirmed in my resolution by the behaviour of Agnes herself, whose constitutional coldness and apathy began sensibly to break way, and she grew more disposed to let in an enemy the less effectually guarded against, in that it is nature which unbars the gates to it. More beautiful than Venus, and more simple than her doves, if she was thus charming, it was more than she knew or cared for, though she had been a thousand times told so. But none had succeeded in making any impression on her silly insensibility, till a natural sentiment of jealousy, which she probably could herself give no account for, had advanced my affairs with her, to say nothing of the language and whisperings of an instinct common to all living beings, and which doubtless began to operate on a girl of her age and full formation. This instinct, by the bye, however the men ungratefully affect to despise and decry it, is probably often their best friend, even with those prodigies of virtue, who surrender to their lovers with the flag of sentiment flying abroad, whilst it is this very instinct which, from under the hatches, gives the word of command for striking.

Agnes, ignorant of the art generally used, and which seems so innate to women since they are mistresses of it even in their first weaknesses, added to the merit of her sentiments, that of the pure simplicity of the golden-age, in the escape rather than the expression of them. I soon found her melting so fast into my arms, that I could easily have dispensed with any obligations of Lady Oldborough's, but barely that of her not opposing me.

But this alteration in Agnes had as little escaped her observation as mine; and she treated the discovery more like a woman jealous and exasperated, than as a lucky incident which would save, or at least lighten her of, the incumbence of a criminal complaisance to those desires of mine, of which she had contracted an implicit engagement to procure me the satisfaction.

To say the truth too, I had not entirely deserved the best of usage from her. For (not to mention the coolness and neglect, with which I had repaid her fondness, and made her, by keeping too little measures with her, sensible of the ingratitude with which it is not uncommon for youth to reward the favour of those who at a certain age are unhappy enough to be plagued with a state for it) I had received too cavalierly those remonstrances of hers, to which, as they were the results of her regard for me, I ought at least, in favour of the motive, to have shown more tenderness. But I was naturally too hot and impetuous to bear the least thwarting, where I thought myself so much the master; and I had not yet, in my converse with women, learned enough of their dissimulation, to play it upon them, in favour of my ends with them.

I found indeed no direct obstacles to the consummation of my success with Agnes, but now they were not the less invincible for being oblique. I might see her as often as I pleased. I could single her out, draw her to a window, talk to her, which by the way only served the more to tantalize me, as I discovered that I should, upon occasion, have little or no opposition from herself; but I could never come at her alone. It was only in company, or at such hours and places, where all essential privacy was impracticable, that I could gain admission to her. The evident nearness to my point, which such insufficient opportunities pointed out to me, at the same time that I could neither bring things home, nor well complain openly of the impediments of my progress, tortured and wearied me to a degree that tried my patience beyond its bearing.

Lady Oldborough's finger was too plain in these incessant disappointments of my desire, for me either not to see it or her motives. They redoubled my ardours for Agnes, and my resentment against her. Yielding then at length to the vehemence of my passion, I became cruel and ungenerous enough, upon one of those occasions of privacy with herself, of which at least she was not sparing, to talk to her in a tone, in which I neither respected her nor myself. I upbraided her with duplicity, with breach of faith, and what was yet more inhuman, with her fondness for me. I knew she dreaded an open rupture with me, and though I was not so lost to decency and honour, as to mean such an extremity, I was not, in the blindness of my passion, ashamed to drop her distant hints of leaving her house, and never seeing her again. The acrimony which a fretful eagerness threw into my expressions, and the menacing tone which I lost myself so far as to assume, without working the effect I wished, had another which, as stale, as worn, as easily seen through, as the trick is, in the service of that sex, I had not experience enough to be prepared against.

Lady Oldborough, after giving me a tolerably quiet hearing, seemed overwhelmed, and unable to support herself under so heavy a storm; and after certain convulsions of face, which certainly did not extremely beautify it, fell into a fainting fit. This was a novelty which accordingly made a forcible impression on my good-nature. I was at once alarmed, and sorry for my petulances. Could the traitress have viewed me, (as not improbably she did, through half-closed eyelids) my confusion and grief must not have a little diverted her. I held her up for a few instants in my arms; and at length carried her and laid her tenderly down upon a settee, where I composed her as decently as I could. I was preparing to leave her there, in order to call for help; but I felt she held me so fast by one of my hands, which had, I know not how, got locked in hers, that I could not without violence disengage it from her grip. Then she squeezed it with such convulsive grasps, and fetched such deep-heaved sighs, as made me tremble for fear of her being in the agonies of death. In this idea, I burst from her, got to the bell, and rang for assistance. But before the servants came up, madam thought proper to come a little to herself, and sitting up on the couch, with a wildness in her eyes and a faint voice, just articulated in breaks a few mournful ejaculations. I was cruel ——I was barbarous——I should be the death of her——no matter; she had deserved it all——and worse——but not from me.——By this time the vehemence of my ringing had brought in two or three of her attendants, to whom she only complained of a violent fit of the head-ache, and bid her woman get her some volatile-drops. They were accordingly brought: and I was for some time idiot enough, to believe that those were the drops she wanted to relieve her. We were once more left alone. And I began to make some apologies for my vivacity, which I could not give utterance to, without a tenderness of tone, that shewed her I was melted into compassion for what I had made her suffer. With too much experience not to know the advantages of this soft season, with too little delicacy not to seize and make the most of them, Lady Oldborough, who still kept her post upon the settee, and had insensibly drawn me to sit down by her, listened with her head languishingly reclined upon me, and now and then convulsively clasped me. She said little, sighed much, and looked a great deal more. The situation was new to me, and I was at first no doubt awkward and mistaken enough in my means of consolation. But I must have been less than man, could I have long held out against the designations of the sole specific in cases of this sort, which her eyes tenderly turned upon me, and her fond caresses left no room to misunderstand. Penetrated then with concern for the extremities I had come to with her, and perceiving that I could not well atone for them, but by proceeding to others, and unwilling to lose the merit I was coxcomb enough to attribute to myself with her for past indulgences, by now leaving her with so much reason to complain of my brutality, I employed myself so efficaciously to console and repair the injury I imagined I had done her, that we parted for this time better friends than ever. For now convinced that she had owed entirely my complaisance to my expectation of hers, and to a momentary fit of compassion. she had given up the point of attaching me to herself. She assured me then very cordially, and with great seeming sincerity, that since she was not to reckon any longer on solely engaging me, she would rather bear the tortures of dividing my affection, than part with the pleasure of receiving sometimes marks of it, though she were to owe them to no more than my gratitude.

Content with this intimation, I believed and left her. On cooler reflections too, I began not to be so dissatisfied with myself for having carried matters with so high a hand. The issue of the fainting fit had greatly relieved me from considering it in the tragical light, I had at first viewed it. I began even to suspect the reality of it, and indeed it was a remains of weakness in me, that I no more than suspected. Could the laws of honour have allowed me to have made a confidence of my adventure to Lord Merville, he would doubtless have set me right, and not have suffered me to have been so egregiously the dupe of my candour and inexperience; but I was fated to acquire my knowledge at my own expense.

In two or three meetings I had afterwards with Lady Oldborough, she amused me with a false confidence of the progress of her dispositions in favour of my designs upon Agnes, which I was the easier to believe her sincere in, from the increased artless demonstrations of love, or at least liking, I met with from Agnes herself. I seemed even so sure to myself, that, like a master-engineer, I thought I could have named the very day the place would surrender to me: but in the fairest of this prospect I found myself stopped, as it were, by a haha wall, the very instant I expected to enter it at discretion.

I had told Lady Oldborough a day before that I could not dispense with attending my aunt, next evening, to an opera, but that as soon as I had reconducted her home, I would come and sup with her and Agnes, and hoped to have the pleasure of finding them both disengaged. Accordingly about eleven I came to my appointment. I found Lady Oldborough waited supper for me; Agnes was not with her. On the terms we were then, I thought myself authorized to complain a little peevishly at this baulk. I imagined her absence was a little paltry finesse of Lady Oldborough's, to procure herself an opportunity of privacy with me, which I could scarce forgive her the being so silly as to hope any good from, towards answering the ends I supposed she had in it. I took no pains, of course, to dissemble my ill-humour, whilst she vainly took a great deal, to quiet and recover me to any tolerable temper. She assured me that Agnes had positively begged her to dispense with her company for that night, and had retired to her apartment early, on the plea of indisposition. "The truth "of this," added she artfully, "you may satisfy yourself of to-"morrow, as you will have all liberty of access to her; and, as "I am really myself sorry for the girl's being out of order, it "will be cruel for you to punish me for what I can so little "help, and even doubly feel for the pain it gives you." This she pronounced with so much seeming candour and veracity, that I actually suspended my suspicions. Supper was served in, and we sat down duly enough on both sides. After supper, just as I was meditating my escape, and preparing as tolerable an excuse as I could think of, my lady's woman came in, and taking her mistress aside, spoke to her with a great air of mystery, and with great emotion and vehemence. They stood at a reasonable distance from me, and I could just overhear, as her servant's voice occasionally raised itself, the interjections of——"what will this world come to?——had long "suspected something extraordinary,——who would ever have "thought it?—such a creature too!—I was almost afraid to "tell your ladyship of it.——I should not deserve to eat your "ladyship's bread, if"——here, as in other breaks, the fall of her voice left my curiosity grievously in the lurch. Lady Oldborough, whispering something in her ear, too low for me to hear, dismissed her, and returned to me with all the marks of confusion, anger, grief and vexation, as legible in her countenance as she could have wished. She kept withal a profound silence, as if at a loss for expressions to give vent to what she felt; less than I now saw and had heard would have provoked my desire of knowing what was the meaning of it. I pressed Lady Oldborough urgently to relieve my suspense. She hesitated a little, and acted the utmost unwillingness to break the matter to me. I easily conjectured that Agnes was what all this mystery related to, but had not the least guess of the nature of this novelty. At length she broke out in a most bitter exclamation, that Agnes was ruined, undone, vilely, vilely sunk and lost. The colour which rose into my face at this, the quiver of my lips, the passion which I felt at my heart, and which lightened in my eyes, readily betrayed to her, that I was more disposed to look on this information as a trick than truth. But this she was no doubt prepared for: she then told me that she herself would never believe, nor desire me to believe, less than ocular demonstration, which, she added, she was afraid would not be wanting, for that her woman assured her, she was at that instant in the arms of her paramour, a young man, the choice of whom did her taste as little honour as her reputation; that she expected, in short, her woman instantly back again, who was to lead her to be a witness herself of the infamous scene: that if I pleased, and would give her my word and honour that I would command my passion, I should myself partake the discovery with her, but that for many obvious respects she would not have the creature exposed, less for her own sake, than that of her poor friends,

and the honour of her own house. I stood, at the hearing of
this, overcome with surprize. I aimed at speaking. Rage and
vexation choked up my words: I could not refuse so fair an
offer as that of seeing the proof with my own eyes, yet I
dreaded it as the death of those desires which were so dear to
me, and in which I had treasured up, by anticipation, such an
exquisite feast for my senses, and in truth for them alone.
Whilst I was thus undecided, and stood like a statue, her
woman returned, and entering the room, where we were,
stood pausing, as if waiting for Lady Oldborough to speak
privately to her; but this she declined, and to shew she had
no reserve for me, with an air of confidence and ingenuity,
bid her woman speak out before me.

Upon which this Mrs. Burward, whose looks by the bye, I
had never much liked, as I fancied I saw something in them
fit for treasons, stratagems and spoils, and who had doubtless
returned me the aversion I had never dissembled for her,
broke out with all the malignity, which her face was of an
admirable cut and hue to express, and which was not now
much embellished to me, by the nature of the discovery.

"She had long suspected, that she had, Miss Agnes's for-
"wardness; but she never could have thought her capable of
"taking evil courses,——that she seemed so innocent! well!
"to be sure there was no trusting to looks:——that, on miss's
"excusing herself particularly though mightily pressed by
"her good lady to sup with her that night, on pretence of
"being out of order, she shrewdly imagined there was some-
"thing more than ordinary at bottom,——that she watched
"her waters narrowly,——and as *good-luck* would have it,
"she had found out the whole *plot*.——That the intrigue
"could not be of yesterday's standing, since it was with
"young Tom Stokes, a neighbour's child in the country, who
"had been observed even there to be more noticed by her,
"than he should have been.——That this sweet-heart of hers
"was come to town, not above four days ago, as she sup-
"posed, after Agnes, though when he came to the house, he
"pretended he was only up on an errand to see some rela-
"tions, who had promised to do for him; that miss had seen
"him, and that she could not well tell how, but that, with all
"her simplicity, she had been cunning enough, to conceal
"and harbour him all the day till night, in her bedchamber,
"where he then actually was locked up with her: that it was
"the greatest *mercy* in the world, she had discovered such

" doings——that she would not for the world's worth have
" concealed them from her good lady, and that if she pleased,
" she might with her own eyes satisfy herself of the truth.
" ——That she was sure, by the silence and darkness in the
" room as she could perceive through the key-hole, that they
" were gone to bed together, for she had taken care that he
" should not escape."

Whilst this recital lasted, it was hard to say what I felt. Indignation, contempt, regret of so much time and trouble thrown away on a worthless object, all mixed, and made
me feel at once their blended impressions. But soon no passion was stronger with me than that of curiosity, to which I
annexed at least the benefit of undeception, one way or
another.

I urged Lady Oldborough then to accept immediately of
her servant's offer, which she agreed to, on re-exacting from
me a solemn promise, that nothing should tempt me to any
violence or *eclat*. A promise I readily gave her, in the security
that my rising scorn would enable me to keep it.

It was now one in the morning. Mrs. Burward took the
lead with a candle and a pass-par-tout key in her hand, and
directing us to tread softly, marched at the head of the silent
procession, Lady Oldborough dolefully leaning upon me, as
if the extremity of her grief had rendered such a support indispensably needful to her. After going up the private stairs,
and passing through a range of apartments, we came at length
to that of Agnes. Our conductress stole her key softly into
the door, opened it, and let us in.

Lady Oldborough made me observe, for I was almost blind
with the fury of my passion, the hat and clothes of a man,
lying in disorder upon the chairs near the bed. They served
to confirm Mrs. Burward's information about the person, as
they seemed those of a plain country farmer. At this
I snatched pretty abruptly the light out of the woman's
hands, and leaving Lady Oldborough to sustain herself as well
as she could, hurried towards the bed, and drew the curtain.
Agnes, the beautiful Agnes, whom I had thought so innocent,
lay under the bed-clothes, which covered every thing but her
face and hands, buried in the profoundest sleep, which even
added to her charms new graces of tenderness and delicacy:
no! never appeared she to my eyes more lovely and more
despicable. For behold! on the side of her a young fellow,
with his hand passed under her neck, and clasping her as it

were to him, lay snoring, with his eyes fast enough shut, to defy the effect of the light glaring in them; which I naturally attributed to the fatigues of his chamber-confinement of the preceding day.

I was so enraged, however, at the rascal's tranquillity and happy posture, that I was wishing for a cane or horsewhip, just to have given him a hearty remembrance of his good fortune of that night: I was lifting up my hand, to present him at least with some token of good will when Lady Oldborough stopped me, and with a beseeching look, which silently put me in mind of my promise, drew me away gently from the guilty scene, and accordingly we left the chamber with as much precaution as we had entered it.

As soon as we had recovered the room in which we had supped, Lady Oldborough did not fail to value herself upon, as well as praise me, for *our* command of temper. She observed that there was no medium, between acting as *we* had done, or proceeding to such extremities, as they indeed deserved, but which for superior respects were better avoided; but that she would take care to pack her off instantly, and not keep her disgrace at least within her doors.

I heard this with the utmost unconcern. The sight I had just been regaled with, had on reflection, instead of adding to my indignation, perfectly cooled it. The revolution in my sentiments towards Agnes was seemingly complete: my contempt had so thoroughly taken place, that but for shame of having so much misemployed myself in the pursuit of her, I could have laughed heartily at this adventure. To Lady Oldborough, then, who affected to ask my advice, by way of sounding my pulse, how she should proceed, I answered with the most frozen indifference, that I did not pretend to experience enough, in cases of this sort, to direct her ladyship what to do; that it was enough I knew very well what I was to do myself: but that she might depend on my secrecy in all events and consequences.

Upon this I precipitately retreated, and left Lady Oldborough in some consternation at the tone I took it in; she who had probably counted on being a gainer, by all that was detracted from Agnes. But she had overshot her mark; for now, full of the most determinate detestation and contempt of them both, I quitted the house, with a fixed resolution never to set my foot in it again.

I was not indeed very justifiable for thus involving both,

on these appearances, in my renunciation, but the whole of
the part I had suffered my passion to prevail on me to act,
now appeared to me in so ridiculous and even criminal a
light, that I could not well bear the thoughts of either, so that
now the destruction of my desires became a sort of reason to
me, or supplied the place of it.

The next morning I received a letter from Lady Oldborough, acquainting me with having that instant sent Agnes
away, to do penitence in the mountains of Wales after such a
connivance at her gallant's getting off, as she supposed *we*
had agreed on, as the best salvo. The letter concluded with
an intimation how welcome a visit would be, to comfort her
for her affliction on this occasion.

But she could not have applied to a person on earth less
disposed, after what had happened, to afford her consolation.
Unmoveable then in my resolves, I sent her an answer, such
as was fit to cut off all further commerce; and on receiving,
and sending back unopened several consequential letters
from her, I arrived at disembarrassing myself from an affair,
which was grown highly disgustful to me, and in which I
was not soon to know how much and how basely I had been
abused.

It was not till some months after, that Lady Oldborough,
upon the marriage of Agnes in the country to a gentleman of
worth and honour, in favour of which this patroness of hers
had parted with a very considerable sum, completed the
reparation she owed her, by sending me, (for I constantly
refused to see her) an authentic and well attested narrative
of the deception which had been practised upon me, and
which I was ultimately not sorry for, as time and other objects had favoured my disengagement, and as it justified me
so amply to myself for my usage of Lady Oldborough, which
as it happened had no other fault but that of not being bad
enough.

The truth, in short, was that the whole of my discovery of
Agnes and her pretended gallant was a device, and that a
coarse one enough employed on any but a novice, and framed
and executed by Lady Oldborough and her worthy confidante. The person in bed with Agnes was a lusty country
girl, picked out and disguised for the purpose, and equally
innocent with her of their hellish designs upon us; as they
were both thrown into that deep sleep, which had deceived
me, by the common operation of drugs given them for that

effect, it is easy to imagine how the rest came to be artfully disposed, as the hat and clothes and hour of the night.

In the meant time, Lady Oldborough, whether by her own suggestions, or by conjectures naturally enough combined, reaped even honour from my desertion, and the sending away of Agnes. It was presently whispered about, that finding my assiduities began to grow too serious, and to alarm her for her charge, she had not only broke off her acquaintance with me, but sent Agnes very discreetly out of harm's way. For my part, I was far from being sorry that the story took this turn: I had even good-nature enough to encourage it, as most certainly, when the interest of my passions did not mislead me, it was not in my nature to be ungenerous to the sex, or to make an ill use of any secrets I came at, in the course of my commerce with it.

END of the SECOND PART.

MEMOIRS

OF A

COXCOMB.

PART III.

THERE is nothing like a disappointment, for throwing one into the arms of philosophy for consolation. The baulk I had met with in my designs upon Agnes, had heartily mortified me, though perhaps not more than the consciousness of my rare success with Lady Oldborough, whom I now heartily detested with a less reason than I was then sensible of her deserving. Yet my coolness on the discovery had been only a temporary illusion, in which my pride had helped to smother my vexation, even to myself. But when I was alone my rage returned upon me with tenfold violence, and as soon as I got home, I relieved it by a copious expectoration of spleen, which I vented in a ranting soliloquy against the sex. And then alone it was, that I forgot Lydia, purely that I might not too positively involve her in the fulmination of my general censures.

"The women were all, ay that they were, nothing but living magazines of levity, art and folly. The only wise were those, who by treating with them, merely on the foot of their subserviency to their own pleasure, without ever suffering it to be in their power to give them a moment's pain, preserved their great character of superiority. The complaints of being made fools of by them ought to begin at home."

These ravings, with some scraps of poetry, theatrically tattered away, and which were certainly not panegyrics upon a sex, whose power never stands more sensibly confessed, than in these impotent sallies of rage and railling, eased and composd me into the most philosophical serenity. As my passion, too, had never been of a nature to break in upon my rest, a few hours' sleep restored me so perfectly, that I waked in no other disposition, than looking out for a new mistress, with whom to repair my loss of time and trouble.

I was then so thoroughly humbled, that I was once more determined to take the readiest; a disposition in which, however, my natural impatience and the love of an easy satisfaction of my senses had some share: my senses, I say, which I was sure were always true to me, whatever the favourite objects of them might be. I made it then with myself a point of justice not to punish them for what was not their fault.

I was full of this commodious casuistry, when Merville came to pay me a morning-visit. I saw him with the more pleasure, as I had undergone less raillery from him, for my attachment to Agnes, than I was sensible I well deserved. He proposed to me then a party of pleasure, for the evening, at one of the most celebrated houses in town for the accommodation of such travellers as are bound on voyages to the land of love, and who are not over curious of what bottoms they venture upon, provided they are trim vessels and pleasing to the eye. As there is then no insurance-office, yet erected for the security of those adventurers, especially against the case of poisoned returns, which often obliges them to make disagreeable quarantines, every one runs personally his own risk. Merville was himself an admirable pilot, not only as he knew the chart perfectly well, but as he was defended by his experience from embarking farther than was consistent with his safety. No man besides had ever declared a higher contempt for all the false and insipid delights of this course than himself. Not was it inconsistent with his regard for me, to engage me once in such a party, if but to give me a right, from my own personal observation, to share with him the honour of holding them as cheap as he did.

I the readier came into his scheme, as I was now clearly disengaged from Agnes, the mystery of which I suppressed to Merville, as much out of pride, as from any point of honour.

We parted on the terms of my accepting his engagements, and met again that evening at the Play, after which we proceeded, to finish the remains of the night, to one of those shambles in the neighbourhood, in which, with a barbarism of taste scarce inferior to that of the cannibal markets, human flesh is exposed and set out for sale; and the terms of the craft generally used to put off the goods to their customers, or cheapners, are so nearly those of a carcase-butcher, that one may reasonably enough deduce from them the affinity of these genteel trades. "See here, my masters! here is a charming piece of flesh! oh this is a delicate morsel for the spit! here is a substance to cut up, so juicy, so meaty, so young, fresh out of the country, none of your overdriven cattle, neither handled, tainted, nor fly-blown; plump, white, and lovingly worth your money:" with the rest of the puff in this style, or rather not quite so delicate.

Our company consisted of Lord Merville, and besides myself, three more, the Duke of—— Lord Melton, and Harry Burr.

The party was made upon the Duke of——'s losing a supper upon a wager: the scene of payment was settled by his adversary, and the plan of it left to Merville, who was to bring whom he pleased with him. The Duke of——, besides the illustrations common to him with the rest of the nobility, was distinguished by that of having with the fortune of a prince the soul of an usurer, and of exhibiting the rare personage of a young hunks. Thus his only virtue, frugality, was an arrant imposition on superficial judgments, and was at bottom the meanest of vices, since it was far from wearing the genuine air of that worthy economy, which is not to be safely or commendably neglected, even with the greatest estates. His parsimony was visibly the dirtiest avarice, added to all the other impertinencies and follies that dishonour the commonalty of those of his rank. If he paid his tradesmen ready money, it was not from principle, or tenderness due to all trading industry, but merely as that rarity gave him a sort of title to screw them up to harder terms. The management of his household, all breathed more the narrowness of his soul, than that spirit of order and regulation, which it is even a point of taste to establish in a family. Even the pleasures of the sex, which were never to him more than the gratifications of a purely animal instinct, in which his chairmen or porter observed as much delicacy as his Grace, could not in the softest moments unlock the gripe of his contracted heart, and nothing was commoner than stories of his sordidness and brutality to his mistresses, who were constantly ill used and ill paid by him. Conformable, however, to his manners, was the coarseness of his appetite, which coincided deliciously with his darling penury, by directing his choice in his amours to the cheapest objects; those in short less likely to prove ex-

pensive to him, than in a rank of life nearer his own level.
The public opinion of a character, so little respectable as he
was, could not escape even his own knowledge of it; but besides that the saving half a crown would have proved at any
time a specific consolation to him, under the united censure
of mankind, he had naturally a most serene insensibility upon
that head. Not indeed that noble carelessness of it, which
proceeds from a consciousness of right, but from that contempt of reputation, which constantly goes with the contempt of virtue.

Then friends he had neither the taste to relish, the merit to
create, nor indeed the impudence to expect. He modestly
contented himself with giving that name to those muck-flies
which swarm round any dung-hill eminence.

Contrasted to this character in, perhaps, as indefensible
an extreme was that of Lord Melton, to whom the wager
had been lost. He had not been above three years emanci-
pated by the death of a rigorous father, who had kept him
under a restraint much fitter to inflame, than moderate, the
natural impetuosity of youth, and drive it headlong down the
flowery precipice of pleasure, on the first snap of the curb.
And accordingly as he came at once to the full possession of
his liberty and estate, he laid about him like a fury unchained,
and let loose upon the town. Void of all experience of the
world, and an enemy to all advice, the physical taste of
which from the manner in which he had been drenched with
it, he could never after endure; his fine person became the
prey of every drab that would poison his blood, and drain
him in every sense; and his purse the resource of every
sharper of every rank, who, considering it as his property,
made no scruple of taking his own wherever he found it. In
so short a time then he had irretrievably foundered his estate
and constitution. His estate, in tasteless, silly profusions,
which had produced him no return but ridicule from those
who were enriched by them: his constitution, in one continued succession of excesses. Thus by too greedy a grasp at
pleasures, he had really tasted none, so constantly did any
enjoyment in view, cut the throat of the one in actual possession. In the arms of one mistress, he was less sensible to the
present joy, than to his wishes for another in perspective,
so that he could never gratify his desires for the obtrusion of
new ones, which kept deriding him, like the horizon, that
flies for ever before the approaches to it. He had aimed at

the character of a voluptuary, and fell so short of it, as to be nothing more than one of those debauchees, those woeful sons of pleasure, of which one sees so many scarcely living objects about town, who with pale jaundiced faces, hectic constitutions, and reduced legs, preach from example the virtue of temperance, stronger than whole libraries of sermons or morality.

As for Harry Burr, this facetious gentleman was one, who, having very foolishly spent a small income of his own, by associating with young fellows of superior fortune, and by that means bought his experience of the brittleness of those friendships founded upon a bawdy-house acquaintance, was now grown wise enough to make the most of the present minutes, and lived by reprisals on the rising rakes, and by which means he had made some of them refund his losses by their fathers. He possessed then so thoroughly all that branch of town-knowledge, which centres nearly in the rounds of Covent-garden, that no party of debauchery was esteemed a complete one, without his comptrollership and presence at it. The bawds accounted with him, the gamesters fee'd, the whores courted, and the waiters *respected* him. In short he was the beau N—— of all that important province. He had taken Lord Melton under his protection from his first launch into the ruinous extravagancies of the town, and had taken especial care, that no one should impose upon him, without his coming in for a competent share of the pillage. With regard to this person, my coxcombry was of great advantage, as the insolence and haughtiness, which made a part of its composition, served me to awe and keep him at a distance.

It was in this company, however, that I was destined to make my first campaign of this sort in form. For though I had had several parties of gallantry at my little pleasure-lodge, with not the most straight-laced of women, they had been always conducted with a spirit of decency and order, unknown to these hackney seraglios.

As soon as we were let into our assembly-room, the patroness of the house waddled in, and welcomed us with a most nauseous familiarity, chucking one under the chin, and slapping another on the shoulder, with all that coarse, vulgar style of freedom, so fit to open a man's eyes on the level he lets himself down to in suffering it from those creatures. Then, Dick, Harry, Tom, were all her forms of compellation, accompanied with a silly, hollow laugh, which she meant for

an expression of joy. "So, my killbucks, you are come I see,
"——it is an age since you have darkened my doors—ah!
"rogues, I have got such goods——such roses and lilies——
"none of your rotten regiment——but where the devil did
"you get this young smooth face? I never saw him before
"[meaning me]; is he come to lose his maidenhead here? ads
"me, if that is the case, I have his match to a hair,——a girl
"with an eye like a sloe, and a hip as hard as a green apple.
"She will do for him, my life on't."

This greeting, joined to the figure it came from, drew a
laugh from me, in which she was too gross of sense to distinguish contempt from approbation. I begged her, however,
to keep her hands off me, the fat and oiliness of which gave
me no relish to the touch of them. And, to say the truth, this
majestic dame was no exception to the general rule of those
of her vocation, who break as naturally into fogginess and
corpulence, as the rest of the publican tribe, which may be
one reason, too, why, their sensations of pleasure being
buried in their fat, they can the more quietly manage the
duties of their function, and see with less pain their old personal customers go by their doors.

Yet, one would naturally enough imagine, that these superannuated suffocks should consult their interest so far as to
keep as much out of sight as possible, if but to stave off an
idea that cannot but be unfavourable to their trade; the idea,
that the pupils whom they produce as objects of pleasure,
should be of the same species as themselves, and must, if not
cut short by diseases or accidents, as naturally come into that
form of being, as young pickpockets grow up into house-
breakers and highwaymen.

As for mother Sulphur, which was a name *de guerde*, given
her by one of her customers, and the propriety of which
had fastened it upon her: there could be nothing even more
shocking or disgustful than her appearance. Only imagine a
tartarphiz, begrimed with powder and sweat, that could not,
however, conceal the coarseness of a dun skin; a mob, that
with all its pink ribbons, was forced to give way, all round, to
the impatience of confinement of stiff, bristling, grizzly locks,
every hair of which was as thick as a pea-straw; then this
gorgonhead was sunk between her two shoulders, and carried in mock state, something in the style of the crown and
cushion; descending from which blessed landscape, to where
the creases and plaits of her breast triumphed over all the

dirt and ceruse that encrusted it, the sight, if not the scent, was feasted with two pailfuls, at least, of uberous flesh, which had outgrown the size, and neither in hue and consistence deserved the names of breasts. I go no lower than a *busto* description for the sake of nice stomachs. But as her whole figure was of a piece with this sketch, it will be easy for an imagination, unwilling to lose any part, to supplement the whole of this lovely original. It was, however, more natural to take such a scare-pleasure for a priestess of Diana, than a minister of the Cyprian queen. The sight of her was at least enough to lay in a month's provision of chastity.

Lord Merville, who had had the arrangement of this party left to him, to the visible discomfort of Harry Burr, who looked upon him for that time as an usurper upon his juridiction, asked her how trade went on: she thanked *heaven*, never better, and that, for her part, she was satisfied; she had a neighbour's share. She did not doubt, if the Lord was pleased to *bless* her, but that she should have, before long, one of the genteelest bawdy-houses in town. I was growing sick of her cant, when Merville, who saw how I suffered, fell to asking her what forwardness the dispositions were in that he had given her directions about. "Ay," says she, "gentle-"men, if you would always give a body orders in such good "time, you might be better served, and to be sure, I have for "this bout done my best to *oblige* you." Upon this, Merville desired her to send in, together with the girls, the largest bowl of arrack punch in her house, to which she signified her ready obedience by a gracious nod, a frightful grin of joy, and disencumbered the room.

Presently entered, with the liquor ordered, a fellow, or kind of tyburn-smart figure, in the double quality of a waiter and master of ceremonies to the *ladies*. The old woman had had her instructions, and there were five bespoke for our entertainment. Accordingly they whisked into the room with that unceremonious familiarity which breaks out in a silly giggle, and half-curtsies. Harry Burr, whom Lord Merville's request had restored to his usual superintendence, resumed his function with great importance of dignity and aspect. He presented then the girls to the company with a gracious smile of protection, and assured us upon his *word* and *honour*, which was, upon these occasions, as authentic as a bill of health, that these were all fresh and sound pieces, and at the first of their appearance in that *character*, and that he would pass for them all partly upon his own knowledge, and partly on the venerable mother Sulphur's assurance, who, he was certain, durst not impose upon *him*, or *his* company!

The truth is that they were all very young and very pretty figures. The oldest was not twenty. Their dress, too, was that of drabs of distinction, and such as became the high rank of a house of the first note in town; yet, all their finery had a certain paltry patchwork, frippery air, and a dash of the tawdry-fine, which could not escape any one, the least acquainted with the dress of real high life, with which these creatures have so often to boast momentary connexions, and in which they are, however, so far from catching the air of it, that nothing ever betrays their invincible strangeness to it, than when they attempt it, and mistake flippancy and pertness for ease and freedom.

Some of them had besides, toward repairing the ill effects of their night vigils on their complexion, tricked it up with some red, but so coarsely, that it was discerned with half an eye and gave them such a finished look of their trade, as was far from being the advantage to them for which they meant it.

For my own part, I who was then too vain, too insolent and too presuming on my person, to debase it to the embraces of these devotees to the public debauchery, who raised in me only sentiments of compassion, and none of pleasure, I could peruse their charms with perfect impunity. I considered them as the unhappy victims of indigence; as the objects, in short, of charity, more than of desire. I wondered how such figures could pass, not indeed upon country-bumpkins, apprentices, lawyer's clerks and the like, but upon young fellows of fortune, fashion and spirit. I could not conceive by what infatuation some of the first rank in the kingdom could sink their taste of pleasure into scenes of it, too low for description, and rake for their delights in the sinks of the stews. Surely, if women of true worth and distinction, were to consider who those wretches are, they are so often sacrificed to, the excess of the disproportion would prove their consolation. They would disdain to regret any so low of taste, as to content themselves with such carrion-quarry. Unfortunate creatures! at once the sport and scorn of those who deal with them, and who well know that for the most part these slaves of necessity are obliged to feign and forge joy, in order to give joy.

It was then but natural for me with these sentiments, to aquiesce with the utmost ease in the distribution of these fair ones to their owners for the night. There was then no scrambling for them. The Duke of——, with an air of authority and engernes that I was much more disposed to laugh at than resent, laid claim to his duchess, who was neither the handsomest, nor appeared to be over-much exalted or pleased with the preference. She knew his Grace. Lord Melton waited for Burr's signal of distinction, before he would venture to throw his handkerchief: though, if he was not belied, he was so far broke down, that a nun might have picked it up without essentially endangering her vows. Lord Merville, upon mine and Burr's refusal of precedence, for expedition's sake took the one next him; after which Burr, with the most nauseous humility and designing selfdenial, forced me to make a choice, which I let drop with unaffected carelessness, on evidently the least amiable of the two left, doubtless to the no small inward diversion of so great a connoisseur, who could not keep the pity of my taste to himself as far as his looks could betray it. Merville alone construed me right, and took the first opportunity to tell me so. As for the girl who fell to Burr's share, she made such a face, as one may suppose of a captain of a privateer, when he falls in with one of his own trade, where he expected a Spanish galleon. Our being thus paired threw, however, a sort of order into our assembly, and every one of us behaved at least, as if we liked each our partner. I was not come there to give myself the airs of a young Cato, and went of course with the current. A compliance, which was not only due to my knowledge of life, but necessary to my views of making the right use of scenes, in which I should have thought my taste for ever dishonoured to have found a pleasure. Every thing went smoothly on. The girls began their usual part. They acted gaiety in the way on earth the least fit to inspire it, and pretended a fondness, which, considering the motives of it, could not be returned with contempt enough.

Merville, who was, in his fits of humour, as malicious as a monkey, observing that his *Dear* hummed an air then in vogue at one of the gardens, was barbarous enough to take the hint, and asked her to sing for the diversion of the company; which she was so good as to comply with, after the usual forms and grimaces, as "lord, she wondered any body "could of all things desire her to sing,—she had got a sad

" cold, to be sure,—she would, however, endeavour to *pleas-*
" *ure* the company,"—then primming up, she set out with a
squawl that kept me on the rack the whole unmerciful length
of a sad song, at the end of which Merville had the impudence to cry out *bravo!* and his Grace, entranced to the point
of repenting his not having chosen her, *encored* it, upon
which encouragement the poor girl was on the point of renewing her complaisance at our expense, when Merville, in
whom compassion began to take its turn, eluded the second
torture, by observing that it was cruel to take the advantage
of so much sweetness and condescension, and succeeded in
silencing her by dint of compliments.

But who can paint, or who would wish to see painted, all
the follies and nonsense of this motley assembly, bad warm,
and worse cold? the lust-toying of the men, and the repulsive
false fondling of the women, or, what was yet more nauseat-
ing, that sort of mock modesty which these sometimes affect,
because they are often told that modesty pleased our sex, and
which becomes them yet worse than the most abandoned
impudence: as all art, when it is not exact enough to be mistaken for nature, is sure to turn doubly to the disadvantage
of those who employ it. Who does not hate imposture, or
not expect to find it in them?

After a little time thus spent in these preliminaries, the
chat, by Merville's management, landed at length on a question commonly enough proposed. "How came you first upon
"the town, my dear?" and a question which they are generally prepared for, and take special care to have a moving
story, ready cut and dry, in which they stick all the lies that
may be useful to them, without suppressing such truths as
may not clash with their designs, or which may spread over
the whole a colour of probability.

One was the daughter of a reverend clergyman, who had
brought up a numerous family in too genteel a way, and being left destitute by his death, she was betrayed into this
course by a woman who pretended herself a friend to the
family. She had never thought to have seen the day, and endeavoured to squeeze a few drops, that honestly refused
coming to her assistance.

Upon this, I could not escape observing that the girl, who
was devolved to my share, was endeavouring to stifle a titter,
and, by the way, though the least pretty of the five, she appeared the archest, and most sensible of them. I asked her

what straw it was that tickled her upon this occasion. She whispered me as conveniently as she could manage it, that that unfortunate daughter of a reverend clergyman had, to her certain knowledge, no other relation to the church but being taken off the steps of St. George's porch, Hanover-square (where she was loitering for want of a lodging, and eat up with the itch) by one of her quondam landladies, who seeing this girl with a pretty face and tolerable shape, had taken her home, washed, purified and clothed her, by which means she became, after a subaltern course of prostitution in her house to half the town, qualified for the preferment, she was now raised to, in this stately bawdy house.

As the question went round, they had all some very tragical circumstance to relate of their family, and of the rogue that had betrayed and left them; upon all which my peculiar had some arch comment or remark 'till it came to her own turn, when she said, very naturally; "Gentlemen, if you have "any curiosity concerning me, I hope you will be so good "to suspend it, 'till my story is _made_ too; at present, I have "not one ready, unless you will be contented with the plain "truth which is, that I am the daughter of an honest chair-"man, and as soon as I came of age to feel desires, having no "education to awe and instruct me of the danger of humour-"ing them, I honestly gave way to their force, and was soon "let into the great secret by a young prentice in our neigh-"bourhood, since which after various adventures, I came at "length to harbour here." Upon this ingenuous confession, her companions frowned, the men laughed and probably did not think a whit the worse of her for it.

I was, however, amidst all this entertainment and repeated observations, "how merry we were," growing into the most wearisome impatience, when the waiter coming in, relieved me with the news of supper being upon table, which was no farther welcome than as it promised me, at the least, the diversifying our dullness.

We adjourned then to the supper-room, where we found the table covered with the most exquisite viands, in the preparation of which all the refinements of modern cookery had been exhausted, all the foreign delicacies had been made to contribute, and all the seasons had been forced. The wines were proportionably rich, and chosen. Burgundy, Champagne, Sileri, Aix, and Tokay were profusely ready at call, as Merville, who had traced the plain of this entertainment,

took care to signify to us. Upon which, I was not a little
diverted at seeing the Duke of——change his colour to a
silly pale. He had, as before observed, lost a supper at discretion to Lord Melton, who had agreed to refer the arbitration
and management of it to Merville. The duke had come into
this readier, as that being ashamed to name a sum as small as
he could have wished the payment stinted to it, he was in
hopes that Merville would have behaved in the affair, like
any of his own stewards, who knew his aversion to expense,
and would have accordingly made court to his reigning passion. But Merville, who had no more respect for him than
his personal character deserved, had proposed to himself
great joy, in giving him the fret by this piece of innocent and
meritorious perfidy. He had then studiously spared no article
of the most expensive luxury, which his own perfect knowledge of every branch could suggest to him, towards inflam-
ing the reckoning, the great no-jest of which to the Duke
of——was that he by this means gave a miser's feast without
having the merit of giving it.

We took our places then with no other respect to rank or
order than every one placing his fair partner next him; when
it was not the least part of the treat to me, to observe the
girls, some of them giving fairly way to the impulse of their
appetites, and falling on as ravenously as a starved carter,
whilst the others acted the delicates and eat so divinely, pick-
ing of small bones so prettily to preserve their shapes, a
nicety which they however immediately renounced as soon
as they found that we took no notice of them. And it was not
long before their repletion with eating and drinking height-
ened their good humours to a point that threatened an excess
of it. The wine especially had begun its usual operation of
substituting sincerity to falsity, nature to art. The female
tongues had now acquired such a volubility, that in the necessity of giving a loose to them, and being put by all the guards
of their little cunning, they began to shew themselves in
their original true characters, and drop their masks and
bridles. It was then, that occasionally they came out with
some oaths, that savoured of the liberties of a guardroom,
or produced some flowers of the fish-market or Covent-
garden: freedoms which are so far from turning of some
stomachs, that they are welcomed as provocatives by some
debauchees of the first rank.

We were then in the height of this miserable mirth, when

the sudden apparition of mother Sulphur engrossed our attention.

She had bounced into the room, almost unobserved, 'till with a gesture that demanded silence she obtained an audience from our curiosity to know the meaning of this irruption.

"Gentlemen," says she, with an impudence peculiar to all of her vocation, and which they take for a grace the more "I beg pardon for disturbing you, but I have such an excuse. "Well! to be sure you are in luck! I have such a bargain this "instant put into my hands—a pure untouched virgin. I will "put my hand into the fire upon it; and as I can light of no "good thing, that I am not willing to communicate to my "*friends*, I would not delay giving this honourable company "the preference of the offer. She is but this instant come to "my house, and it is with a deal to do, that I have managed "so as to get her. Now, gentlemen, you are to agree amongst "yourselves, which shall be the happy man. We shall not dis-"agree about the price. There is not a sober substantial citi-"zen but would think such a maidenhead dog-cheap at an "hundred pieces; and I ask you no more than fifty. I have a "conscience, that I have. Say the word, my heroes, and she "is yours, upon honour. It is no bargain, if you do not like "her. See for love, and buy for money."

Every one of us, however before provided with each his bird of paradise, appeared, at least, alert and alive at the proposal of a new face, and a maid too. The impressions, however, were different.

The Duke of——, who loved pleasure, but loved his money yet better, had pricked up his ears at the beginning, and hung them down again at the mention of the price.

Lord Melton sucked it in the greediest, and as he had hardly ever received a favour from any woman, that he had not been soon after obliged to run and make a confidence of to the doctor, was so keen on the opening to him of a safe enjoyment, that he seemed to have forgot his present physical incapacity for it.

Lord Merville betrayed no great eagerness to close with a proposal of this nature, from his being used to consider them in a very problematical light.

As for Burr, whose sensations were worn out, and to whom these proffers were no novelties, and generally preconcerted with him, he shewed no more concern than was in character for one to express, who was a pillar of the piazzas.

For me, as I had no relish for any of the present objects, I was delighted with the thoughts of a new one, and my curiosity adding its spur to that of the wine in my head, I seconded the good old lady's motion, with the utmost zeal.

Upon Burr's declining then and giving up all pretentions with a modesty which made us all laugh, the point to be decided was, which of us four should have the first cut of the haunch. Merville insisted, as he told me afterwards, purely to yield up his right to me, if the prize fell to his share; but, in short, after a few discussions of means to adjust the precedence, we agreed to draw cuts. We did so, and the benefit-ticket fell to me: upon which I received the compliments of all the company, except of the poor girl who had been destined to me for the night. But I immediately consulted her consolation in the most specific manner by putting a purse into her hands, which could not fail to have its due weight, since there were above twenty pieces in it; as I thought myself bound in conscience to pay, since it was no fault of hers, the fine for what I did not do, as old men pay it for what they cannot do.

Upon this, the old lady rolled out of the room, to bring in the candidate for initiation; it having been universally pre-resolved upon, that we should all see her: a point which I was now rather pleased with, as it humoured the vanity I took in the preference, and was in course not sorry of having witnesses to my little triumph. It was true, I owed it to chance. But what of that? Does not chance preside more in matter of choice made by women than any thing else? And chance for chance perhaps, the way of drawing cuts would not succeed worse, in general, than what we daily see in most matches or intrigues, that have been brought about by the caprice of it, only in another manner.

My imagination was, however, now set to work, and my head tolerably well warmed with the more poignant pleasure which I prefigured to myself there was in the leading, rather than in following. And though I well knew that nothing was commoner than counterfeits of this sort, and that some, even of my acquaintance, had been so woefully bit, as to have had one of those town-vestals, who never let their sacred fire go out, imposed upon them for untouched virgins; the idea, and which my own desires treacherously took part with, that such a trick of the trade was beneath the

lignity of this most princely bordel, confirmed me in my
scheme of acceptance; and in the humour I was then wound
up to, I am conscious I should have more admired, than
been tempted to imitate, those heroic selfdenials, I have met
with in history on the like occasions.

In the mean time, I could hardly conceal my exultation. I
looked on my companions of the night with come compassion, and I waited with great impatience the return of our so
obliging landlady.

At length she came, handing in this copy of a bride, this
pure and well warranted mistress of her maiden-flower. As
the door opened, the general stare had been directed to it,
and modest miss, in preservation of character, advanced towards us, leaning upon her introductress with her eyes declined, as not daring to lift them up in so large and mixed a
company, especially on so critical a conjuncture.

As the person then most interested, my looks were doubtless the quickest upon their march, and informed me, on the
instant, of this precious maiden being no other than the individual Diana; once my Diana, and now any body's Diana.

My first emotions were, to confess the plain truth, a med-
ey of surprize, shame and indignation. This was a re-meeting for which I was in no sort prepared; and one of my first
ideas was that it must be a trick preconcerted and forelaid
for me.

I recovered, however, presently, and, before even she had
made me out, burst out into so violent a fit of laughter, as
surprized the company in their turn, and bringing the eyes
of this unfortunate girl upon me, she immediately knew me,
gave a scream, and fainted away, perhaps in earnest; for less
than such an accident might have shocked and overpowered
the natural weakness of her sex.

Merville, without precisely knowing particulars, easily
conjecturing that we were old acquaintances, ran to her re-
ief, on seeing me put out of my laugh by her fainting, and
too disconcerted to attend even to such an office of common
humanity. The alarm was general; the girls all gathered
round the distressed princess, and busied themselves about
recovering her to life again. Vexed, too, and fretted as I was
at my part in this scene, I yet could not help being diverted
with the tragi-comic phyz of the old conscientious beldam,
who was watching my looks to compose her own by, and
displayed such a state of suspense in muscles ready to take

their cue from the reception I should give to this discovery
as would have delighted me to have kept her as long as she
deserved on the rack of it, had my own impatience not
interfered. As the old woman was then lifting up her hands
and eyes, crying out now and then, "who would ever have
"thought it?" for want of something better to say, or rather
from not knowing what to think, and Diana was now come
to herself, I asked in a dry severe tone for a private room,
which to be sure there was no want of in that house, and, by
a whisper to Merville of the name of the girl, removed all his
anxiety about the nature of the explanations I was desirous
of having with her.

I was then immediately shewn to an apartment, to which I
civilly and coolly desired Diana to follow me, and left the
company to resume their course of entertainment, to whom
this novelty had given a short interruption.

As soon as we were alone together, I was master enough
of myself, and of the air of the world, to put on a brow of
awe and interrogation; how it came, that after I had made a
handsome provision for her for life, and had given her posi-
tive directions to stay in the country 'till I sent for her, I
now met with her in such a place and upon such an errand?

Diana, who was in too great a surprize, to have the presence of mind necessary to cook up an extempore fiction,
and was too much humbled by the circumstances I found
her in, to dare deny me the satisfaction I deigned to exact
of her, made a shift between sighing and sobbing, to give me
her history, since I had left her, and of which I afterwards
verified the reality.

She then told me that in the impatience of not hearing from me, and of some little mortifications she had met
with in the country upon the account of her connexions with
me, which could not, as she said, be kept a secret, and where
they were not so polite as to treat her slip as venially and
slightly, as the frequency of these accidents makes them pass
in town, she was *advised* to come to London, where she proposed to wait upon me. (At this I gave her a look extremely
fit to assure her of my not being flattered with the compliment.) That she had accordingly taken a place in the stage-
coach, where she had contracted an acquaintance with one
of those Irish fortune-hunters, who are not suffered in, or
are driven out by the contempt or justice of their own nation, to seek a livelihood in ours, the mob of which, with the

grossest injustice and unconsequence, lumps conclusions from these outcasts against a country which produces a nobility in many points superior to that of their neighbours, and a people naturally brave and generally genteel, and who deserve a better fate than a subordination, which does not at least seem so grateful a reward for their constant exertion and co-operation in the cause of liberty. This digressive remark will, I hope, be excused, as the homage due from candour to truth, and paid it in the teeth of the vulgarest of prejudices. It was then one of these adventurers, who had liberally bestowed upon himself a commission under the commodious travelling name of captain, that lighting upon this silly, half-bred creature on the road, soon found out that she was game for him: and, as he easily passed upon her both in point of character and fortune for what he pleased, under favour of a good person, he soon got into her confidence, and made his harvest of it. His success then was neither very difficult, nor extraordinary. After making himself the master of her, by a fleet-marriage, and as unauthentic a one as either of them could wish it, he soon prevailed on her to convert the annuity, which had been too loosely tacked to her, into ready money; and having got possession of every thing she had, left her one fair morning without a shilling to help her, and decamped in quest of new adventures. In this extremity she had been ashamed to have recourse to me, and, by the inducements of her landlady where they had lodged, she had been driven into this wretched course, in which, however, this was not less than the fourth time she had been *made* a virgin, and produced in this very house upon that footing.

I was, on the hearing of this, too much moved with compassion, to make her any reproaches. And as for the hag of the house, she was beneath any thing but even a mirthful contempt. I saw then nothing in her proceeding, but in a ludicrous light. But as to Diana, whatever her fault might be, I felt and disdained to dissemble to myself that I was originally the author of it, and of course in point of justice, as well as that I might reconcile myself to myself, bound to repair the disorder I had occasioned. I could not bear to think that any act of mine should *procure* for the public, and add a victim to it in the once object of my private pleasure. Resolved then to remedy an ill I had not at the first, for want of experience, sufficiently provided against, I took a note of

her lodging and immediately sent her away. How I after
wards took care to settle her in a way more secure agains
such scandalous necessities, without however renewing wit
her, which I was sufficiently guarded against by the condition
in which I had found her, is a point which circumstantiating
would only favor too strongly of egotism; and having natu
rally no place amongst the follies I am in the course of con
fessing, I readily and properly pass it over.

After giving Diana the necessary instructions in seeing her
out of this execrable house, I returned to my company. My
eclipse had not lasted above an hour and a half, and in that
time the wine and warmth of dalliance had given them a
Bacchanalian air, which to me, who was sobered even by the
scene I had gone through and the reflection obviously arising
from it, appeared in its true and genuine light of rejoicings
from the noise and nonsense of which one would hold escaping to a desert a cheap ransom. The men, except Merville,
who possessed the great art of reserving himself without being
remarked to reserve himself, and of course without incurring
the ridicule or offense of singularity; the men, I say, appeared
in too great a disorder of their senses, to enjoy any true feast
of them, and the women in high colour looked like so many
furies, that had violently driven the Graces from the side of
Venus, and taken up their post.

As soon as I came into the room, I was immediately sur-
rounded and attacked with questions without order or measure. Merville, who saw my confusion, good naturedly helped
to extricate me, and furnished me with a hint by observing
that I looked pale and out of order, to plead an indisposition,
which in the more than one sense was no more than true. I
pretended then that I was taken so ill, that I could not satisfy
their curiosity just at that time, and proved so great a
comedian, that Merville himself was ready to take his own
suggestions for reality, and being besides willing to improve
this opportunity into a plausible excuse for his own escape
from a party of which he was heartily weary, he obtained
leave of the company to see me home, as I was particularly
under his protection for the night. I saw his drift, and humoured it by closing eagerly with the proffer of his taking
me home in his chariot, my own not being so much as ordered.

Thus we accomplished our deliverance. As soon as we were
alone together, Merville remarked to me, that low and disgustful as the ribaldry of such revels must appear to any who

were not devoid of all taste for distinction of pleasure, such, or no better than these, were chiefly the orgies in which the common run of our young nobility stooped to mix purest of their blood with the puddle of those kennels of filth and venery, and in the grossness of which they contracted an habitual disrelish to the joys of sensations, seasoned with sentiments and disembruted by love. That ridiculous, as he owned, the whine of a passion to be, when romantically pursued, he questioned whether even the pains of such an extreme were not preferable to the pleasures of the other. That to recover a truth of taste in even voluptuousness, we should, after all, be obligated to return to the simplicity of the old times, when men loved like men, neither like mere brutes, nor in the air like the sheer Platonics. That at present it was matter even of compassion to see so many promising youths sacrifice their healths and fortunes to despicable systems of debauchery, and rush headlong into a ruinous course, in which their persons and purses were, literally speaking, the spunges of the meanest and dissolutest of mercenaries in one sex, and of the most dangerous sharpers and sycophants in the other. That, in short, great as the misfortunes which they might bring on themselves might be, they could not possibly be greater than the reproach they would one day have to make to themselves for their want of all taste and elegance: ingredients which may be truly called the spirit of pleasure, since they confer upon it a kind of immortality, which hinders reflexion from putting it to death.

This sermon of Merville's took the faster hold of me, and found the welcomer reception, for its recalling strongly to me the delicate and dear distinction between all the sensual gratifications, in which I had indulged myself, and my unextinguished passion for my ever adorable Lydia. Lydia! to whom I had first owed all the rapturous feelings of an innocent, virtuous love: Lydia! to whom I owed all the little checks I felt in the career of that worthless coxcombry, which consisted in my seeking to reduce women to my point for the sake of my pleasure as well as my vanity, which last came cruelly in for its share, with my libertine taste for variety in leaving them. But these sentiments had only their reign of a moment. The excuse I framed to myself, out of the uncertainty of ever seeing Lydia again, and present objects prevailed over these protests of love and reason, and soon re-subjected me to the mis-rule of an imagination too

easily inflamed, and too indelicate of appetite, to refuse it
subsistence on the feast at hand, in preference to much
higher out of reach, or placed at too discouraging a distance
of perspective.

It was then I acquainted Merville with the consequence
of my last meeting with Diana, of whose history I had before
made him a confidence, and with the dispositions I was in
towards her, which he was not content with approving, but
afterwards assisted me effectually in the execution of them.

As soon then as he had seen me home to my apartment, he
took his leave of me for that night. I was now alone, and on
reflecting on that revel-riot, in the midst of which I had left
my happy companions of the party, I could not help con-
gratulating myself on the different figure I now made to my
own view, cool, free, and tranquil, from what I painted to
myself, and what I probably should have made, had I gone
all the lengths of these worthies, heated, muddled, and fear-
ful of dismal consequences to my health. Of this, however, I
was sure, that without affecting a false merit I had denied
myself to such pleasures with infinitely more satisfaction
than I should have found in taking a fulsome fill of them.
In short, I was naturally too much the true voluptuary, to
mudsuck my pleasure in such dirty dull debauches, or to
content myself with joys, that had not some degree of
taste for their sanction and seasoning. I had besides too much
of pride and self-value, to barter that florid bloom, that
freshness and vigour of my youth, of which I was not a little
vain, for very little or no pleasure with those rank retailers
to the public of rottenness and diseases.

The refusal of the door to one folly was, however, far
from implying the exclusion of another; since the current of
my constitutional desires, banked off by one dam, turned its
course with the more impetuosity to gallantry and plans of
attack upon women, whose favours should not be quite so
much in the hackney style, or so liable to penitential consequences.

I was now under a necessity of looking out for a new conquest, and London is happily a place, in which with any
thing of a tolerable person and an easy fortune there is, with
very little industry, no great fear of losing much time or
trouble in achievements of that sort. My late disappointment
with Agnes had humbled but cured me of ever designing
again upon idiot-beauty, and I was determined that at least

in my next adventure it should not be a simpleton that should make a fool of me; which was, however, a needless precaution, since a woman of true sense is never the woman by whom a man need apprehend the being made a fool.

I had remained then but a few days without any particular attachment, and not without being in a hurry to form one, when at a visit to one of my relations, an old lady, I saw for the first time the celebrated Lady Bell Travers, who was just returned from France by the way of Bath. This lady was a daughter of one of the highest rank of our nobility, and had married very young without her father's consent, who, charmed with the double advantage of getting rid of a girl, the custody of whom began to be pretty difficult, and of an handle for not giving her a groat, treated this act of undutifulness with the utmost acquiescence, without ever approving it or coming to a reconciliation, that must have naturally been an expensive one. As for her husband, who was a man of considerable fortune, he had fixed his choice upon her, yet less upon the account of her person, which was, to do her no more than justice, a very desirable one, or even of her birth, than from his having seen reason to expect being thwarted, and having his pretentions rejected by the father, on account of certain dissentions between his family and hers. As soon then as he saw himself in the quiet, uncontested possession of her, and that she was left upon his hands without the least stir or opposition, the indifference of her friends begat his, and as if the life of his passion had been tied to the difficulties of gratifying it, the instant they failed, his passion died with them. But Lady Travers had too much penetration and acuteness of sense, (as what woman is there that wants it on these occasions?) not to feel the difference, as well as too much spirit not to resent and revenge herself. From the first then of her discovering the remission of his taste for her, she took care to lead him such a life, that with too little dissimulation of his coolness, if not aversion, and too much indolence to support the spirit of it, he suffered her to subdue him to a point; that taking him by this weak side, his superior love of ease and quiet, she made at length what terms she pleased with him; and he thought none too extravagant, that could purchase him the joy of a separation and deliverance from a domestic torment.

Emboldened with this success, Lady Travers hoisted immediately the flag of independence, and made all her advantages of her irregular condition, being now, properly speaking, neither maid, widow, nor wife. She launched out then into the world with a very competent stock of personal charms and a great fund of spirit and imagination, which, according to custom, she applied to the service of her pleasures, and of her turn to scandal, by which means she was the envy and dread of her own sex, and occasionally courted, but never thoroughly esteemed, by ours. She was not, at the time I got acquainted with her, less than at the latter end of the season of pleasing, and yet she had amply preserved the power of it. Besides it was a kind of fashion to have had her, and who knows not the tyranny of fashion even in points of taste, which one would imagine from their nature the least liable to come under it?

For my own part, who had seen much younger and greater beauties than she was with impunity, I was struck, at first sight, with the taste and magnificence of her dress, the nobility of her manner, a travelled air, and a certain freedom and superiority, with which she commanded the conversation, and rather decided than gave her opinion upon all the subjects of it. She displayed, in fine, a sort of imperiousness much after my own heart, which began by awing, and ended by captivating me. I conceived now that I had met with my match, and promised myself, without looking further, that I would try what was to be won or lost with one whose reduction was, however, with me rather a point of ambition than of love.

At first, indeed, she hardly vouchsafed me the honour of the least attention or regard. My youth, which though at bottom was no discommendation of me to her, but had not yet attracted her examination, made her treat the lead I aimed at taking in the conversation, as a kind of usurpation on her prerogative; and, though few could fill the coxcomb-character with a more audacious self-sufficiency than I did, I had the mortification to find a woman, who durst outbrave me, and expressed pretty plainly, not only by her looks and contemptuous smiles, but by some shrewd hints occasionally dropped, that she took me for nothing better than a forward, petulant boy, spoiled by the complaisances of a world, which she was above, to my rank and figure. This insolence of hers, for such I construed it, piqued my vanity, but then it provoked a desire of dealing with one, whose superiority I could not conceal to myself. I figured to myself such a high joy, such a triumph, in demolishing her haughtiness and lev-elling her to my purposes, that I believe I should have been at the expense of some submission, rather than not accom-plish them. By chance, however, I took a more effectual course. For, in trying masteries of pride, the most long-breathed ever wins the field. Adhering then stiffly to the air of control I had begun with, I not only dissembled the im-pressions she had made upon me, but the chagrin and humili-ation I felt from her procedure towards me. Upon this, I re-doubled my presumption, and without giving up one point to her, right or wrong, in the face of a company whose admiration and dread she was, I arrived at appearing so ridi-culous and contemptible to her, that she began to pity me, and think it a matter of real compassion, that such a pretty fellow as I was, an appellation which she allowed me with great seeming scorn of it, should be such a consummate cox-comb. The term indeed she politely spared me, but put the full equivalent of it into a periphrasis, as clear as one would not have wished it.

The great point with women is to be taken notice of by them; no matter, whether for one's good or bad qualities, if one has but the merit of a pleasing person. With that advan-tage, one may safely rely upon them, for turning even one's faults into recommendations. I played away then my fire so briskly, that Lady Travers, from contemning and pitying me, as well she might, fell to envying me for my spirits and in-trepidity. She had not been prepared for so determinate and well supported an assurance in one of my age and inexperi-ence of life, and I began, as was no more than natural, to suc-ceed in virtue of a quality, which, if resolutely, is rarely em-ployed without success.

It was not then without my great inward exultation, that before we parted for that time, Lady Travers included me in an invitation, which she gave to others, to see her at her own house; and which she particularized to me by a smile of protection, and telling me with a tone extremely softened, that she hoped I would not grudge her the pleasure of con-tributing any thing in her power to the settling a better un-derstanding between us, and that she should set me down on the list of the company she admitted to visit her; and which she did not doubt I would find not inferior to the best in England. This she said to me, as I was leading her to her chair, and as this was a prevenience of the request I was meditating, I received and answered it with a warmth of acknowledgment, very fit to convince her how much I was pleased with it.

The next morning I waited on her, and was admitted without hesitation to her dressing-room, where I found her at high toilet, and nobody with her but her woman, who was dressing her, and one next to nobody, the Lord Tersillion, who was paying his most formal and insignificant devoirs to her, in a visit of ceremony.

As soon as I came in, she treated me with all the easy familiarity of a long established acquaintance. A chair was set me on one side of the dressing table, in which I spread myself as unceremoniously as I was received. Her woman stood over her, combing her hair, which fell over her shoulders and neck in an agreeable confusion, and gave the sight fair play enough to discover a perfectly white skin; and I could easily observe that she was not shy of shewing me her independence upon art, and that she was still able to hold it out against the dismal necessity of making a mystery of the operations of the toilet.

As for her visitant, he was one of those figures of state, whose gravity and solemnity compose so high a burlesque; equip them with cap and bells, and they would not subscribe half so rich a jest. Then a trivial, unmeaning face, drowned in a voluminous white wig, when his chin was in motion with talking, gave one the idea of a white rabbit at feed.

My coming in had bred a short interruption of the conversation, which this Mock-Machiavel resumed, and in which he gave both of us the yawns, with the unmerciful repetition of a speech he had lately made in the house, and which, however, for any thing I knew to the contrary, might be as intrinsically important, as any that had been made there for twenty years before. And after some pindaric transitions from subject to subject, of all which the central point was to convince his audience of the vast consequence he was of to public as well as private life, he at long length relieved us, and went out, if one might judge by his air of self-satisfaction, intimately persuaded of his leaving us penetrated with as high a veneration and respect for him, as he had for himself. What was this, however, but coxcombry, only of another species than mine?

As soon as he was gone, Lady Travers lamented to me the

necessity there was of letting such *people* in, by way of keeping measures with them, not for the good, but for the hurt, which the most worthless of them were not incapable of doing. That for example, that solemn personage having engrossed for his own use all the little interest he had with the present team of state, could do no service to others, but that, withal, his admission every where, upon the foot of his rank and title, gave him opportunities of doing mischief. That, for the rest, he was one of those *things* made up of fashions and forms, who being reckoned by number, and not by weight, compose that *high* and respectable order of beings, so vulgarly called amongst themselves the great world. That he had, like the rest of that populace, his town-house, his seats, his equipage, and all that follows in their stale, dull rote of life, the grand distinctions of which consist in being sold, or devoured, by their dependents, poisoned by their cooks, and enslaved by all the nonsense of shew and ceremony. That with a much larger estate than was necessary to support even the splendour of life, he had been mean enough to carry his whole stock of importance to the old market, in which he hugged himself, not without reason, for his having oversold it, tho' at no better a price than his obtaining much such a grace of distinction and preferment, as the hackney-coaches have to boast of, which are driven about town, with the arms half worn out of some ancient family, under the royal mark and number.

Lady Travers, who did not easily give out, when once her hand was in, was running on, when I barred her the box by begging her to consider that such an animal was game not worth stooping to; that there was neither joy nor wit in sousing such as were beneath mention, and, properly speaking, could not be abused. This was a remonstrance too just in itself, and too much in her taste, for her not to acquiesce in it, and accordingly she dropped a subject too trivial even for an expletive, and asked me pardon for having omitted at first to thank me for the proof of my readiness to accept the offer of her friendship, in the quickness of my visit upon it. This was furnishing me the cue I wanted, and accordingly, to my assuring her that inclination had robbed my duty of any pretentions to merit in the payment of it, I added every thing I could best think of to introduce me advantageously, by beginning with engaging her vanity in my interests.

As impatient, however, as I was of coming to a point with her, I was very sensible that my designs had measures to keep with so superior a skill, in the exercise of gallantry, if I was in earnest to secure the success of them. I was far from being modest enough to despair of Lady Travers granting me what I was well assured she had not refused to many others. I was no stranger to her turn for tenderness and sensibility, and, if I might trust to very authentic chronicles of her reign, I could have called over a pretty numerous list of her favourites. I had especially been told that striking deep into the *vertua*, she had made herself renowned at Rome for her private studies in a *Villa* near it, of the antiquities of nature in the finest modern editions of them; so that it could not be her character for rigour which could overawe, or discourage me. I had besides my own full-sufficient fund of presumption, which, together with my having desires enough to put me into action, without having too much of love to check the ease and freedom of that action, might have told me that I was entitled to make such a jest of any resistance of hers, as should be very fit to abridge it. But then I knew, too, that Lady Travers was a woman of too much experience, too well acquainted with consequences, not to be mistress of her own moments of yielding. She was not to be attacked with the common-place protestations of pains, ardour, dying, and all that soft nonsense, which is the vulgar idiom of love, and the lullaby of a raw girl's virtue. Neither was she to be attempted in so summary a way, as to wound the dignity she affected, if not as a virtue, at least as a grace, essential to raising the price of her favours, and exalting a pleasure, which is commonly very slight, or of short continuance, without having had its due preliminary digestion of desire. And I fancy men would not be much mistaken, if they were generally to look upon the resistance of the sex, as kindly meant in favour of their greater satisfaction, and take their measures upon the foot of that presumption.

With no opinion then of Lady Travers's virtue, and a very high one of her experience and management, I imagined that I might safely rely upon herself, for preparing and determining the accomplishment of my designs upon her, whenever I should have raised her taste enough, to appear important to her own pleasure. My point then was simply to give my person all the value to her I possibly could, and to excite her desires in favour of my own, as I had no reason greatly to fear that she would love herself so little, as in mine perversely to deny her own satisfaction. She was none of those dupes.

My plan of operations was accordingly, in an instant, concerted and resolved in my head; in pursuance of which I took care in this my first visit, to make no direct court to her. Our conversation turned upon generals; but when some of the reigning beauties were occasionally mentioned, I did not fail to observe of Miss Beryll, that she had bad teeth; of Miss Powers, that she had a coarse and clumsy hand; of Lady Laval, that her hair was harsh and sandy; all which was in other words praising Lady Travers in those points, in which she manifestly excelled; as it was hardly possible to have whiter, evener teeth, a delicater hand, or a finer head of hair than she had. Then I had to do with one, upon whom no compliment was ever lost, or without merit, that included a detraction from any other.

She had besides, with all the appearances of wit, the rage of being thought one; a weakness which had been fomented by the complaisance of poets, who had flattered and consulted her, and of authors who had read their works to her, from all which she had furnished herself with a fund, if not properly speaking of wit, at least, of a specious, fluent jargon, which dazzled and imposed upon the vulgar of her admirers. She had, too, seen most of the courts in Europe, and had picked up crumbs of politics enough to have set up ten modern ministers. With so much knowledge of the world, she only wanted knowledge enough of herself, and of her own interest, to avoid making too great a display of her acquisitions; as too knowing an air in women only gives them a masculine look, which becomes them no better than whiskers and jack-boots would do.

Too conscious of having great advantages over me, to suppose she should ever give me any but what she pleased herself over her, she set out with treating me as a young fellow of no consequence; and even took care not to dissemble her superiority over me. And I on my side set myself to humour this foible of hers, by making an assiduous court to her vanity, and pretending to take lessons from her, 'till she took it into her head, that it was a kind of charity to take charge of the finishings of my education, and to form me. The pleasant charity that, when I think of it, of forming a young pupil, and bestowing upon him the improvement of his mind, wrapped up in all the blandishments of his senses!

I had not then long attended her lectures, before I had established some pretensions. I could not, all coxcombry apart, escape observing that I had played my figure in her eyes with some success. I had caught her viewing me with attention, and with those looks which carry breviate-commissions of pay in them, and which it would have been rather stupidity than modesty to have mistaken. She had besides, at times, insinuated some of those leading questions about the state of my heart, which are never motioned by indifferent curiosity. My answers had seemed to satisfy her, and I daily saw reasons for not despairing.

A woman who knew so perfectly as she did the value of time, who had not herself much to lose, and who by her condition, as well as by her way of thinking, was above the ordinary restraints of form, or the grimaces of affectation, was not a woman I was to fear would let me languish for her favours longer than was necessary, or that would trifle with her own inclinations; consequently, it was not a very unconscionable length of time before that, after having acquitted herself of what she thought she owed her pride, she began to consider of putting into a course of payment her debt to pleasure, which desire exacted, and of which I now stood a fair candidate for an employ in the collection.

That my pride, too, might not want the favourite feast of rivals sacrificed to it, I had the pleasure to see several pretenders to her favours, ill enough received, or dismissed, whilst all the marks of favour and distinction were even ostentatiously reserved for me. I was admitted to her at most hours, and those of the greatest privacy, when her door was refused to every body else, of which, however, I had made such ill use, that I do not doubt of my having often given her the comedy with the appearances of my bashfulness and timidity. I knew very well she had not been always used, nor was indeed of a temper to be pleased, with over-respect, but to say the truth, she had got a greater ascendant over me than I cared to confess even to myself, and I was a good while awed, and withheld by no other obstacles than what my own imagination had created me.

I had dined with her one day, at a countryhouse of hers upon the Thames-side near Chiswick, when after dinner and a party at picquet, we adjourned *tête-à-tête*, to a tea-room at the end of the gardens, and situated in the corner of a terrace that overlooked the river. Nothing could be more joyous than the prospect, nothing more commodious than the furniture; every chair was an ottoman, or demy sofa. Here it was the tea was ordered, the lamp set, and we were left to ourselves. But this was no novelty; and I had certainly brought with me no particular notion of this being my occasion.

Yet nothing could be more poignant than the dishabille in which she had received my expected visit from town. An Armenian of white satin, so loosely wrapped round her, as rather to invite a ruffling than extremely awful; a tippet artfully adjusted to humour the half discoveries of a fine neck; her hair playing free in a style of noble, negligent uncorrection, all together composed her a slattern elegance of undress, that she swam in with an ease and a grace, the natural air of which is never familiarized, but to women of the highest form of breeding, and is ever so ridiculous in the unavoidable stiffness of their copyists.

As I had never seen her so handsome, or so dangerous, I was scarce master enough of my desires to give my expression of them a due share of decency, and yet I scarce durst think myself advanced enough to state them to her. I began, however, at all hazards, to treat the tea-drinking as matter of form and pretext, and drawing my chair, ventured to take hold of her hand, sighing and barely not trembling. She abandoned it to me in a style of carelessness, as a matter of no consequence, and I moulded it in mine at discretion. Encouraged, however, by this passiveness, I proceeded to press her with increased vivacity, and grew rather more enterprizing than was exactly consistent with the declarations of my profound respect. It is a term, however, never better employed than in the midst of the widest breaches of it. She desired me at length, when I was reducing her to take a little more notice of what I was about, to have done with liberties, which she had not expected I would permit myself: but in these expressions of her displeasure, the tone of her voice had nothing very severe or imperious: on the contrary, she seemed favourably fluttered, and I could plainly read the emotions of her senses and the looks of her desire; when, all of a sudden, she recalled an air of austerity into her face, and withdrew her hand hastily from the lock of mine, as if upon sudden recollection. I ventured to ask the reason of this shift of humour.

"It is not," said she, "that I am either disconcerted or of-"fended with your designs upon me. I should act a part "much beneath me, if I dissembled to you, that you are in all "senses far from disagreeable to me. I prefer even the degra-"dation attached to the declaration of my sentiments, to the "constraint of concealing them. Yet, if I know myself (con-"tinued she with a sigh) I wish less for the pleasure of com-"plying with my inclinations, than for the power of preserv-"ing your esteem by overcoming them. You are young, and "with the means of pleasing peculiar to that age, have not "you the dangerous faults of it too? Can you, ought you to "wish, that I should run the risks of your levity and indis-"cretion, or consign to your keeping a happiness, which must "depend on so frail a tenure as your constancy? I do not by "constancy mean that of a passion, which you will not the "less scruple to promise me, for knowing it is not in your "power, nor perhaps even in your idea; but of your friend-"ship and esteem, to which these weaknesses are ever fatal. "If the love I should, and not impossibly, have already con-"ceived for you, could bear an infidelity, of which I am not "enough the fool of my own desires, not to foresee the ne-"cessity; yet my pride could never brook the reproaches I "should imagine you would make me for having overlooked "the disparity of our ages. You would, probably, have too "much good-nature, too much politeness, not to spare me the "wound of hearing them from you; but to what purpose, if "I could not forbear whispering them to myself? Even the "ridicule, which the eyes of the world, as well as your own, "opened upon this transient caprice of yours, will not fail to "suggest to you, you will have the cruel injustice to impute "to me, and disclaim your share in it, by laying the whole "burthen of it upon me, and hate me only the more for my "having the less deserved it of you."

This was a theatrical sally for which I was not prepared, and had too little experience to answer without premeditation. I could not dissemble to myself that there was an air of probability ran through these objections: they even staggered my resolutions, and dazzled me to a point that I did not presently see how much they were out of time and out of place, in the heart of such an opportunity. I was not quite so clear then, as I have been since, that the plain English of

ll parleys of this nature is, *capitulation*. I very simply then
applied myself to demolish scruples which she had not, by
dint of a rhetoric, confused, unseasonable, and only fit to
prove my noviceship in adventures of this sort. Yet, I could
plainly enough observe that she heard all my protestations,
with an impatience and absence, that might have shewn me
her head was not upon any thing I could *say* to her. I confess
it, however, with shame, that I was some time before I could
recover from the damp with which she had struck and
stopped me in mid-career. She had, in short, against her own
intention, re-inspired me with such a respect, as made me
consume the time of action, in that silly apologizing, which
is rather calling the guards, than benefiting by their being off
duty. I behaved then so ill, that I believe the critical minute
would have struck in vain for me, if Lady Travers had not
kindly won upon herself to relinquish her heroics, and re-
descended to a more explicit encouragement.

On seeking then to read my fate once more in the oracles
of it, her eyes, I caught them turned towards me in that arch
and sly askance, with which women mean to hide, and never
more effectually betray the tenderness of their looks. Emboldened now, and once more resolved to repair the ridicule
of my timidity, I repossessed myself of her hand; and ventured even to press her bosom with one of mine, and discomposed her tippet. On her part, little or no opposition: 'till I
soon convinced myself that every pulse in every vein was
beating a point of surrender. Yet she was still enough her
own mistress to act a sort of defence which obliged me to
graduate my approaches, 'till by a gentle and sly scalade, I
made myself at length master of the post of honour.

Plenary possession was, however, far from abating my
ardour. The pride I had placed in subduing one of her port
and figure had added a piquancy to the extreme sweets of a
pleasure, in which my senses had found their account beyond their most sanguine expectation, that made me look on
myself with a rapture of complacency and exultation, which
may be called the self-apotheosis of a coxcomb. I had entirely forgotten the list of my predecessors in her good
graces; and when the memory of them re-obtruded, I treated
them but as so many rivals sacrificed, or supplanted by my
superior merit; as if women, in their transitions from one
lover to another, were ever influenced by that consideration.
But such are the illusions of vanity, such the joys, of self-

deception. As for Lady Travers, she seemed entranced anoverwhelmed with the sense of her defeat, and though thes
situations could not be extremely new to her, she had the ar
of throwing so much engaging confusion, such a modes
delicate diffidence of the power of her charms into her ex
pressions, as obliged me to give her all the tenderes
re-assurances both of my gratitude and esteem. Then sh
was too expert, and deep in acquired knowledge, to overdoz
the immediately following moments with that mis-time
fondness or those cloying endearments that sink satisfactio
into satiety. She kept then so just a measure in every lool
and gesture, as secured to her the recalls of my desire, with
out her departing from the admirable policy of sufferin
them to appear more my own mere motion than a complai
sance to her wishes: as an artful minister never fails of pass
ing his suggestions for his master's own thought. And let m
observe, by the way, that the nicest of a woman's play is th
after-game of discretion.

I thought now of nothing so intensely, as of deserving th
continuance of Lady Travers's indulgence to me; whilst on
her side she gave herself up without the least reserve, and
with a loose indeed, to the gratifications of her taste for me
We became from that instant inseparable. Having then long
before exhausted the whole quiver of scandal, and left the
malicious world nothing new to say of her, she was resolved
to let it see how little she was governed by her respect for
it; in virtue of which noble indifference, she made up to herself in ease and pleasure, what she lost on the side of reputation.

She produced me at her assembly, which was open every
night to what passed generally for very good, if not the best,
company in town; a term, however, which does not carry
with it a very high idea, when one comes to decompose and
simplify the qualifications of the individuals comprehended
in it.

As Lady Travers was far from deigning to make a mystery of her connexions with me, neither could I perceive that
she was the less respected for them. She had taken the lead
in life, with so high a hand, and had secured the suffrage and
countenance of so many who were at the head of taste, and
understood raillery upon affairs of this nature, that she could
very easily despise or dispense with the approbation of the
rest of the world. And indeed the world seems to have come

o an amicable enough composition with those superior
women, who have formed to themselves a fund of merit independent of their sex, and benevolently pass them those
very weaknesses, for which it tears to pieces without
mercy those of it, whose whole of pretentions being chastity,
have had the misfortune to forfeit their character of it. Yet
what is the merit of this chastity in many of them, but that
of a constitution which has spared them the temptation
from within, or of a form which has spared it them from
without?

It was then at these assemblies I appeared always with the
ease and freedom of the master of the house, and the more
so, in that I never permitted myself any particularities to
Lady Travers, who on her side treated me with as much
indifference and cool politeness, as if I really had been her
husband.

It was at these conventions, too, that I could not help
viewing with eyes of great compassion some grave personages, who, by their rank and situation in life, one would
hardly have suspected of having much time to lose, reduced to
so miserable a confession of the insignificance of their existence, either to public or private life, and to themselves, as to sit
down with great earnestness and importance to a card-table,
and trifle away whole centuries, (to measure time by its
value) in an amusement, fit only for tasteless frivolous idle-
ness, or for the gratification of one of the most worthless of
the human passions.

Here I could observe some women, unamiable enough in
all conscience already, render themselves yet more so, by
their unmasked meanness, their gaunt eagerness after gain,
and the fury which rose in their countenances in the unfavourable turns of their game, passions of which even the best
bred of them are often not the mistresses of concealing the
deformity, and which must destroy in the men every idea
of tenderness and respect to them. Be it, too, remarked, that
women, in general, are the bubbles of their fondness for
cards. If they play with the men, they are overmatched by
their superior skill; for there are so few women that ever arrive at playing well even those games which require the least
attention or combination, that the exception hardly deserves
the name of one. If they play amongst themselves, they hate
and despise one another too much, not to lose their temper
at least.

Others again retrenched themselves into sheer conversation, and affected to look down as from an eminence on th triflers at cards, whose ridicule, however, they unhappily justified, by the subscription of as great an one in the man agement of their alternative. As surely even cards may vi with smattered politics, party-spleen, characters and com parisons of players, adventures at the public gardens, jubilee drolls, dissertations upon dress, little scandalous stories, an all the rest of the common-place trash, which constitute the quick-stock of wit and humour, I repeat it here, in th commerce of not the lowest life.

I was then in one sense obliged to the casting-weight of passion, which by engrossing, defended me from being mor carried away with the shallow stream, than was just neces sary for me to avoid the reproach of singularity. It was not however, with total impunity that I gave way to the torren of a disorderly passion. Merville and my other friends wh saw my weakness, were not content with pitying, and en deavoured in vain to break or divert the course of it by serious hints or salutary raillery. No wonder, however, tha I could not listen to the remonstrances of friendship, when I was ensnared and entangled to the point of being deaf t those of love. Even my sentiments for Lydia, if impossibl to be erazed from my heart, were at least long absorbed ir this ruling passion of my senses; in which, too, I drove wit such fury, that my constitution, overdrawn upon by the fierceness of my desires, and even by the vanity I took in the pleasure I gave, began to give signs of suffering by my un moderate profusion.

Lady Travers, who joined to the charms of her person consummation in all the mysteries and science of voluptuous ness, employed such successive varied refinements of it, tha she appeared new mistress to me upon every re-approach Whether her travels had not procured her these advantage I will not say, but she united in herself the profound fire o the Spanish, the sentimental tenderness of the French, and the elegant neatness of the English women. She was alone a seraglio of beauties.

Such even was the magic of her attractions, that some transient sallies of occasional infidelity had, in consequence of a comparison, in which my senses gave judgment highly in her favour, only served to bring me back to her, more re inflamed, and more desire-drunk than ever.

How could I then resist the tyranny of a passion that was founded and established on pleasure, or suspend services which carried so richly with them their own reward? Lady Travers indeed, from reasons of self-interest and of an experience not unfamiliar to her, often recommended moderation to me, but while she preached that necessary virtue, her presence made the practice of it impossible.

It has been remarked that excesses carry with them the principles of their own destruction, and generally involve with them the cause of them, by bringing on upon the spur decline of passion. Mine, however, stood proof even against the force of an intemperance, which battered me to ruins. All my sprightliness, vigour, and florid freshness, the native attendants of healthy youth, began to give shew of drooping, and flagged under the violence of the heat, with which the constancy of fire in my imagination melted me down into current love. My tender aunt was, without so much as dreaming of the true cause, afraid of my constitution taking a consumptive turn. Merville, with juster judgment, after experiencing the fruitlessness of his friendly advice, had fairly given me over, on the foot of the maxim, that violent ills cure themselves. But it was reserved for Lady Travers alone to disgust me of Lady Travers.

I had been now near two months under the absolute dominion of an unremitting lust for her, when one day, about two in the afternoon, I came to Lady Travers's, and finding the street-door open, slipped by the porter unperceived, without any design of being unperceived, and as I was perfectly acquainted with the disposition of the apartments, made my way directly to her bed-chamber-door. I opened it, and found nobody there. I instantly recollected that she was gone to an auction, to which the evening before she had desired me to accompany her; and I had excused myself on the account of a business that was to command me a great part of the morning. This business I had dispatched, and the force of custom had mechanically carried me to Lady Travers's. This was a liberty, too, I had often before taken without any consequence. Finding myself then alone, I amused myself with the first stray-book about the room, during the time of my waiting for her return: my expectation of which was answered in a few minutes. I heard her footman's rap at the street-door, and a whim suddenly took me, that I would hide myself, without, however, any other

view, but that of playing her an innocent trick by bolting o
and surprizing her. Accordingly I took my post in a kind
dark closet let into the wainscot, in which were kept a fe
books, some bottles of cordials, and some toilet lumber c
shelves which hardly afforded me room to niche myself witl
out some uneasiness. I shut the door of it upon me, whic
being in carve work, symmetrically with other parts of th
room, gave both sight and hearing fair-play, through th
interstices of the foliage; and all this, both thought and ex
cution, was the work of a moment.

Lady Travers came in alone, in her morning-dress, gave
transient glance, very likely without meaning, round th
room, and rang the bell; upon which I proposed keeping t
my entrenchment till she should have dismissed her atten
ant. Presently, her woman, her trusty confidante, Mrs. Ve
gers, appeared to the bell. Lady Travers asked her if Sir Wil
liam (meaning me) had been there. "No, my lady." "Well,
says she, with a carelessness that piqued me heartily, "it is n
great matter: go and give orders at the door, that I am no
at home either to him, or any one else, and return instantly.

The general order of exclusion, out of which, too, I ha
heard myself specifically not excepted, and which I could s
little expect, mortified and indisposed me to pursue m
project of surprize, and while I was deliberating what coun
tenance to put on my appearance to her, Mrs. Vergers re
turned; and Lady Travers asked her if she had taken car
to provide the woman she had ordered her. "Yes, my lady
she is in waiting."——"Well then, you may bid Buralt com
to me, if he is able; if not, I think I must go to him."——"May
it please your ladyship, he is a great deal better; he has bee
down in the steward's room already."——"Let me see hin
then, and the nurse may come at the same time."

Upon this, Mrs. Vergers went out upon her errand, and
remained in a profound muse, upon what should be th
meaning of this odd condescension. I knew there was one
Buralt in the house. I had seen him without ever having
taken the least notice of him, nor had I ever remarked tha
Lady Travers had distinguished him from the rest of he
domestics. He was by birth a Swiss, and of a very ordinary
coarse figure. She had picked him up abroad in her travels
and had brought him home with her. I had heard, too, tran
siently, some time after my acquaintance with his mistress
that he had been at the point of death; but she had never, to

me, laid any stress upon his illness. I was then admiring within myself the sudden excess of this charitable concern, without justly penetrating either the motives or the extent of it; when the door opened, and this Buralt came in, leaning upon Mrs. Vergers, with his knees knocking together, a wildish stare, and all the symptoms of debility and pallid faintness. They were followed, at a little distance, by a plain, modest-looking country-woman. As soon as this Buralt was come the length of the bed, he let himself fall upon it, without the least ceremony, whilst Lady Travers busied herself with examining the nature of the woman's milk, and the terms of her agreement. After which she brought the nurse to the bed-side; but as soon as the poor woman viewed more narrowly the object to whom she was to give her breast, she recoiled with visible horror and affright. Nor without reason; for it is hardly possible to figure to oneself a more ghastly spectre than what this wretch exhibited, wrapped in a kind of blue coat, that sat on him yet less loosely than his skin, which was of a dun sallow hue. His eyes goggled from sockets appearing sunk inwards by the retreat of the flesh round them, which likewise added to the protuberance of his cheek-bones. A napkin in the shape of a night-cap covered all his hair, (except a platted queue of it, and some lank side-locks) the dull dingy black of which, by its shade, raised and added to the hideousness of his grim meager visage.

It was this figure, however, that this superb, this delicate lady, employed herself to support, bolster up with pillows, besides her own arms, so as to place him in a posture to receive the benefit of the restorative which she had prepared for him, in the milk of this nurse; and the fondness and humility with which she performed this tender office obviously enough reminded me of the libidinous lady in one of Scarron's novels.

She could not, however, prevail over the nurse to conquer her fears and aversion, so far as to suckle this babe of delight, but by dint of increasing her hire; and then, with her face averted, she gave him her breast, which he fastened upon, and looked more like a sucking demon, or a *vampire* escaped from his grave, than a human creature. He presented, in short, a horrible caricature of the story of Roman piety, where a daughter saves the life of her condemned father by the nourishment of her breast.

I stood in the mean time motionless with surprize, without

other sense of life, than in the sharpness of my affliction which exceeded, at first, even my indignation. There was no possibility of mistaking the motives of all this wonderful charity. The apprehensions of them, from my own experience, too sensibly began at home with me. I was more than once, upon the point of breaking out, and adding one more figure to the group before me. My pride, however, stepped in to my rescue, and, by representing to me the unworthiness of the object, prevailed over the rage which impetuously prompted me to exhale it, by covering her with confusion. Reproaches would indeed have relieved the vexation with which I was bursting, but then they would have done her too much honour. It was then myself, that I respected, more than I spared her. And after all, I was only wounded in the loss of a pleasure, which the habit of it had endeared to me, and upon the grossness of which this scene had opened my eyes; a scene, too, which had not the greatest right to surprize me, considering all that I had before known of her character. I felt, however, pangs in the first instants, as for the severance of a limb, but the immediately consequent reflection of its being a rotten one helped me to support myself under the agonies of my pain. I had then barely the patience necessary to see the whole disgustful transaction without breaking covert.

The nurse was dismissed with orders to come again, and Lady Travers, after several expressions of tenderness, which closed up the evidence of the nature of her concern for this chamber-satyr, proposed seeing him herself back to his apartment. This was a circumstance which luckily paved the way for my escaping, without the necessity of coming to personal explanation, any pleasure in which my rising scorn had not, however, without difficulty enabled me to renounce.

As soon then as I saw the coast clear, I sallied out of my hiding-place, and with a perfect indifference about my being seen or not by any of the domestics that might be in the way, I got to the street-door, and finding nobody in waiting in the hall, opened it, and let myself out with a most thorough determination never to re-enter it.

In the heat of my emotion, and in the urgency of my passions with me, to give them a vent by communicating this most woeful disaster of mine, I hurried to Lord Merville's, and happily found, not only that he was not at home, but that I could not expect to see him that day, for which I was afterwards not sorry, since, all as my fury subsided, I confessed to myself that this chance of his being out of the way had saved me the ill grace of a complaint, and the folly of exposing to him, unnecessarily, a scandalous secret; my own concern in which did not suffer me to make the best of figures in it, and which was so much better to be passed over in a contemptuous concealment.

I was, however, so faint and overcome with all the agitations and conflicts which I had just undergone, that I threw myself on a chair at Merville's apartment, 'till I could recover a little breath. It was then I desired his servant to furnish me the necessaries for writing, and my recent rage dictated me a letter to Lady Travers, embittered with all the gall and vinegar that overflowed from my heart. It was, doubtless, a curious piece, and, to the best of my remembrance, stuffed full of the most virulent invectives, and concluded with a complete self-dismission from her ladyship's service, with a recommendation of her for consolation to her gipsy-adonis, as soon as she should have recruited and set him upon his legs again.

When I had finished this most unheroic epistle, I went home, and sent it by one of my servants, with an order simply to deliver it, without waiting for an answer. And indeed Lady Travers was wise enough not to attempt to answer it. For what could she have said so well as saying of nothing upon a discovery so flagrant and so unsusceptible of palliations? Neither did I ever enquire how she took it. Probably, it did not operate so very violently upon her, as I would, at the time of writing it, have wished or presumed it. Those who are capable of such a conduct are not generally very sore: the habit of deserving reproaches sears them to the sense of them. Lady Travers then, who had often boldly drove two or three intrigues abreast, could not either be very delicate of feeling, much confounded, or at a loss to find a colour for my sudden desertion of her. Nor could I help being told some time after, that she literally followed my advice in one point, for she placed her minion, as soon as he was recovered, at the head of her household, and that, no doubt, with her hearty consent for the world's thinking just as it should please of it.

There is in some cases a consolatory enormity, and that which I saw in this of mine, combining with my natural levity, soon inspired me with sentiments of the coolest resignation. Even the satisfaction of seeing myself free from an engagement, of which I now saw all the indignity, made me heartily ashamed of the pain which my undeception had cost me. I grew ever hard to return into favour with myself, for having wrote in such outrageous terms to Lady Travers; not only as it betrayed a sensibility which she did not deserve, but as it was inconsistent with the considerations of compassion which began to occur to me. For I soon came to see Lady Travers in no other light, than as one of those unfortunate characters, constitutionally subjected by the violence of their passions to those weaknesses which too often debase those of the highest intellects beneath their own notions and principles; and who, by this means, become lessons of humility to man in general, by shewing him, in the examples of others, to what excesses intemperance and misrule of appetite are, at times, capable of carrying even the wisest: at the same time that they should inspire him with a salutary diffidence of that strength, which human pride is too apt to attribute to reason.

Thus, however, Lady Travers lost at once all the merit of her favours, and all the power of her beauty to give me either pleasure or pain. The discovery of such an abandoned cheapness had now sunk her in my esteem, beneath the rank of those unfortunate commoners, who having none of those respects to break through, which she owed to herself, have besides the plea of necessity to intercede for them. Those unhappy creatures follow vice as a trade, and treat it as a drudgery. But Lady Travers went such sousing lengths in it, with the less excuse, as she had so many more obligations from birth, fortune and nature, to have at least spared herself the indignity of such a choice. Taste and distinction, if they do not justify, they at least ennoble weaknesses. As there are virtues then which are their own reward, so there are vices which are amply their own punishment. And I did not doubt, but that even her own self-contempt would sooner or later do her justice on herself, even if she could be proof against the sense of thus losing me, for whom she had openly pretended a violent passion, and in which she had at least found the solid amusements of one.

As a quickness of consolation is not one of the least enviable perquisites of the coxcomb-character, the sum of my reflections presently amounted to a radical cure, and I began to be less provoked than ashamed at the smart of it. As nothing, too, is more natural than the skip of levity from extreme to extreme, I now felt the joy of my disengagement, with such a sincere gust, that I conceived I might safely embark afresh in new adventures; if not for the pleasure I might expect in the course of them, at least for that I figure to myself in getting rid of them. Such are generally the plans of a coxcomb's reformation, such his use of his experience.

In these laudable dispositions, I declared war within myself against the whole sex. Not that I was yet fool enough to put all women indifferently under one cover and superscription, or to lump conclusions against them from those objects of my amusement or contempt. But the truth is, that I had contracted a very low opinion of the mass of them. I had not observed, in their favour, that most of them treated none with more ridicule and contempt than such of our sex as were in awe of, or really respected, them: and that nothing was more sure of commanding success with them, than precisely the not deserving it; a humour, of which, however, they have had the honour of setting the fashion to Church and State.

Possessed, as I eminently then was, of the sort of merit necessary to make all the fortune I wanted with them, I was determined to profess gallantry at large, to cultivate no serious attachment, nor entertain any passion for that sex, other than that of the bee with the flower-tribe, pillaging upon the wing the sweets of one, and fluttering on to the next.

In this course, however, whatever airs of superiority I had inwardly presumed myself capable of, my fondness for ease, and certain remains of that undebauched natural candour, which is the character of youth, made me find one great inconvenience in that it was so much easier to get a mistress, than to get rid of her. But then this discount was balanced again by the service the noise of an infidelity to a stale mistress did me in the getting a fresh one. Women, naturally enemies to women, and from that principle incapable of union enough to make a common cause against a common enemy, seem rather to treat the most notorious perfidies, as recommendations. Thus the ill usage of one woman, besides that it flatters the hatred of another, it provokes her vanity to the dangerous trial, whether the presumed superiority of her charms may not give her the honour of making a fool of one, who has made fools of thousands. A project, however, by which numbers have been cruelly drawn in, with this comfort to them, indeed, that their examples will give as little warming to, as they themselves had taken it from, others.

I set out then full speed in the same career, which I had seen pursued by a number of coxcombs, whom I heartily despised, and in which, most certainly, I never found those rapturous joys, the hopes of which had seduced me into it. More passions, too, than one fell short in their account, since I could not dissemble to myself that those women whom I undertook, and over whom I prevailed, were either too weak to give my desires the pleasure of a proper resistance, or too worthless to give my vanity leave to live upon the reputation of having subdued them. To particularize them farther, would, after all, be abusing the privilege of my character to trifle. I could scarce be more insignificantly employed in writing the History of my own Times, than in that of those immemorables, with whom I lumbered the list of my conquests, and who were consequently far from being matter of triumph or record.

Men are only great grown children, as fond of new play things, and especially as apt to be cured of their eagerest fancies, as that age is of its liquorishness for sweet-meats, by a surfeit. Thus arrived at the topping my character, after having, in the course of it, obtained the honour of passing for the most splendid, happy, dangerous coxcomb in town, I grew cloyed and sick of my successes. The frequency of indulging benumbed my sensations, and I was suddenly taken torpid in the midst of my good fortunes. I began as well to disrelish the facility of the sex, to whom I was so ungrateful, as not to give it the least credit for all that it spared me, in the very little expense it put me to, of time, modesty, and sincerity, as to despise myself for my own cheapness. For I had even descended, in the wantonness of a promiscuous chase, to women, and those not in the lowest walks of life, whom I thought myself obliged to swear previously to secrecy, and that they would never divulge the honour I did them.

I saw myself then with pain in the wretched enough condition of those pleasure-sated Sultans, who, in the midst of their overstocked seraglios, overtaken with the languors of satiety, and drugged even to loathing, with all the passive obedience and non-resistance round them, find at length

how essential the heart is to the preparation of a feast worth
the appetite of the senses; and are obliged, for the interest of
pleasure itself, to renounce their prerogative, in order to receive it at the hands of love, its only sovereign dispenser.

Then it was that Lydia once more rose to my rescue, triumphantly, and dispelling the clouds and fumes of a debauched imagination, resumed a flame which was to burn the
purer and fiercer for its victory over the fuel of a grosser
fire. Her memory now revindicated fully the possession of
me. I felt severely, but salutarily, that nothing but the true
love-passion could afford me a happiness, to which my taste
could set its face. And as nothing preaches so powerfully
or leads more surely into a return to reason, than the experienced insufficiency of a course of folly and vice, even to the
end of pleasure, aimed at in it, I was not yet so grossly abandoned, or so much an enemy to myself, as to withstand my
own self conviction, however ungratefully I had stood unmoved to the tender remonstrances of my relations and
friends.

Variety exhausted, indolence and, above all, my sensible
experience of the futility and nonsense of the course in
which I had been bewildered, had all favourably disposed
me to a suspension, at least, of my follies. But then it was reserved for love alone to secure to me the benefit of this disgust, and to detach me effectually from them. My heart, at
last rouzed and resuming its importance, made me sensible
that it was made for love; that nothing less would worthily
satisfy its delicacy, and that in playing false to that passion I
had, to my own wrong, renounced the truest, greatest pleasure, to which humanity can boast its inheritance. I remembered now, between raptures of delight and pangs of regret,
the first instants of my susception of it. All the sweet emotions I had felt at the sight of Lydia, and had never felt for
any other, rose in review before me, and movingly re-
proached me with the wilful murder of my own happiness. I
wondered how, or by what infatuation, I could sacrifice a
divinity to objects beneath even the honour of being her victims. I could not conceive then a more mortifying degradation, than what the error of indistinction, and the violence of
those tasteless passions had plunged me into, only to make
me feel the more sharply their comparison with the noble
one, to which I had seemed to give up my pretensions. I
judged, I condemned myself then, and the severe conscious-

ness of my follies began to do Lydia justice on myself, for a
toleration of her absence, which had worn too much the air
of indifference.

I had, it is true, not punctually obeyed her orders to me, to
suspend any enquiries after her, but I had not disobeyed
them enough to acquit me, even to myself, of an accusation
of neglect. But in this violent reflux of the tide of love, I determined nothing so strongly as repairing my failure, and
going personally in quest of her, with a diligence that should
leave no hero of a romance, in pursuit of his princess, the
odds of comparison to his advantage.

I had long settled within myself that, for many obvious
reasons, it was not in the British dominions I was to seek for
her. I imagined with justice that so finished a beauty,
attended with the circumstances before related, could not
have remained so long in obscurity, or concealed from such
perquisitions as I had imagined, I durst venture, without giving her cause to complain of my having too glaringly vio-
lated her injunctions. And, to say the truth, I had delayed
from instant to instant my fixed designs of commencing an
effectual search, in the momentary hopes of her own mani-
festation to me. But my impatience was now risen to such a
pitch, that I decided within me that a longer acquiescence
would be an injustice to myself and an indignity to Lydia.

As soon then as I had given my resolutions a degree of
consistence requisite to carry them into execution, I prevailed with my aunt to indulge me with her consent to proceed upon my travels, and as Lady Bellinger was at length
grown to think that I could scarce employ my time worse
abroad than at home, I obtained it even from her fondness
and regard for me; upon the condition, however, of my attending her down to Warwickshire, where certain indispen-
sible affairs required her presence for a few weeks, and of
my bringing her to town, after which I was to dispose of the
time of my out-set at my own discretion.

I came into this condition (though certainly I would not
have refused her any she should have been pleased to exact
of me) the readier, for that I looked upon that country as
the central point, from which I was regularly to begin my
enquiries on the spot where Lydia first disappeared, and
thence date my departure in the search of her.

Upon communicating, too, my design to Merville, he,
without entirely approving the romantic part of it, with his

usual warmth of friendship, offered to accompany me abroad, though it was not long since he was returned from the tour of Europe; and finding me unwilling to abuse his complaisance by straining it so far, he forced me in my retrenchment by engaging, and making a point of my acceptance, with Lady Bellinger, who was greatly pleased and relieved by it of any apprehensions for me, under a conductor, of whom, with no more than mere justice, she had the highest opinion.

Our equipages were then ordered to be got ready with all expedition, that we might set out immediately upon my return from the country.

Whilst these dispositions were making, I could not help feeling with the purest joy the restoration of Lydia to all her empire over my heart. I compared myself now with the figure I made to myself, in the days of my most triumphant coxcombry, and found it a virtue to be vain of my gains by the change. A delicious calm had now succeeded to those gusts of folly and intemperance which had made me take a gulf for a port, and carried me with such violence down the dangerous stream. I seemed now to breathe a fresher, purer air. Sentiments of all another merit, sentiments more delicate, and infinitely more voluptuous, filled my heart, and added to the sweetness they brought with them the joy and self-gratulation of an escape. I tasted now, with the highest relish, the difference between pleasures, which reflection is sure to redouble, and those it is sure to destroy and erect pain upon their ruins: between, in fine, those delicate desires, which are the rectified spirit of the highest passion, and those instinctive ones which are the sediments of the lowest.

I had, however, something to suffer from my impatience, my doubts, and my fears: but even that suffering was compensated by the worthiness of their motives.

At length every thing was in readiness for our preliminary journey into the country, when, on the eve of our setting out, I went with Merville, by way of dissipation, to a maskball given by the Duke of N——, at his own house in——.

Nothing could be more splendid than the assembly of the company there, or more elegant than the entertainment, in which taste wondered to see itself for once in alliance with magnificence. Merville happening to separate from me, I sauntered about the apartments, with an indifference natural to the sentiments I had lately taken up, and which made me decline any particular notice of the ladies, in the conviction that the best precaution against a relapse is the not depending too thoroughly upon a cure.

I was in this careless disposition, when early, and before any number of the company thought proper to take off their masks, mine, too loosely fastened, dropped off, and I took no pains to retie it, being rather pleased with the ease and freshness of which this accident had, without my meaning it, given me the benefit. I could not, however, escape hearing a gentle exclamation of surprize from a corner of the room, to which I was, at the time, nearest. A motion of curiosity directed my eyes thither, and I observed three ladies clustering together, and whispering in a way for me easily to discern that I was the subject of it.

This alone at first drew my attention towards them, and with a liberty familiar to these assemblies, I examined them to see if through their masks I could penetrate who they were.

One of them especially engrossed the whole strain of my conjectures, being superiourly distinguished by a delicacy of shape, and dignity of air, which not only attracted my eyes, but gave my heart a palpitation, of which I could not conceive the meaning. I could not be weary of admiring the graces which composed her every gesture, and all that nameless charm, that powerful unaccountable, which, mocking definition, is, without being precisely beauty, the very soul and spirit of it. I tried to command away my eyes from so dangerous an object, but in vain, whilst my heart mutinously determined them upon it, in direct rebellion to my will. Alarmed at these violent emotions, which I began to consider as regerminating seeds of those follies which I had hoped were entirely killed, I was then meditating my retreat, when one of the other ladies advanced towards me, and slipping her mask, for an instant, aside, let me see she was Mrs. Barmore, one who visited frequently at my aunt's, and was besides a near relation to Lord Merville, whom she took for her text, and asked me if he was at the ball. I assured her he was, and at the same time, urged by an impulse stronger than myself, I could not resist the opportunity of joining company, in the hopes of discovering who this fair unknown might be, who had given the peace of my breast a disturbance, to which it had been long disused. Mrs. Barmore herself seemed to favour this inclination, by continuing the conversation with me. My *incognita*, in the mean time, kept a profound silence, which did not hinder me from imagining that I observed a certain air of concern and agitation diffused over her, and which communicated to me a disquiet the more distracting, for my ignorance of any particular cause for it. As for the other lady, she talked to Mrs. Barmore of indifferent matters, and occasionally made me a compliment upon my habit, which, however, was neither very remarkable, nor very curiously chosen, being simply that of a huntsman with his accoutrements for the chase.

By this time, Merville had joined us, and presently, as if upon sudden recollection, Mrs. Barmore asked us if we had seen Lady Gertrude Sunly, who had the day before been introduced at court. Merville declared he had not, upon which I answered very coolly and carelessly that I was in the drawing room at the very juncture, and in the crowd of the circle when she was presented. The next question in course put to me was how I liked her. To which very giddily, and without considering the interest which Mrs. Barmore herself or her company might take in the opinion I should give of her, I answered that I had seen her long before without knowing who she was, but that I had perused her even with attention, and had seen nothing very extraordinary in her person. That she had a good shape and skin, a face too that was not very exceptionable, but that the features of it had no play, nor air of life; that she had one of those tame, unmeaning countenances, that wit never went with, and that altogether she was a figure common enough, and such as one might view without too much risk: and this, I added, I might say from my own experience. Mrs. Barmore shrugged up her shoulders at this impertinence, and told me with some acrimony that I was not only very difficult, but singular in my opinion; that the whole town was, and would be against me in this decision of mine. This tone of contradiction, instead of enlightening or proving a hint of reserve or reparation to me, pushed me deeper into my plunge, especially as I could not associate the idea of this Lady Gertrude with what I saw of, and felt for, the young lady who was with Mrs. Barmore, and whose mask could not conceal certain marks of concern and impatience, which broke out at what I had said. As for the third lady, she was entirely, by her size and stature, out of the question. The truth, too, was that I had been the whole day so dunned and pestered by num-

bers, with the terms of "a prodigy of beauty,——a miracle
"of Nature,——the finest creature under the heavens," with
other exaggerations of this sort, applied to this Lady Gertrude, in whom I had seen nothing but what was barely tolerable, that on this occasion I could not command myself
from giving my spleen a little vent, and accordingly, instead
of receding from what I had advanced, or giving it at least
a palliative turn, I filled up the measure of my absurdity, by
the indecent eagerness with which I thought myself obliged
to support my opinion, insomuch that the third lady pulled
Mrs. Barmore by the sleeve, and beckoning her to follow
her, took the young lady away, leaning upon her arm, and
left Merville and me pretty abruptly. Mrs. Barmore just
stayed behind long enough to let me know the excess of my
impoliteness, for that it was Lady Gertrude in person, before whom I had spoke with such apparent slight of herself.
That besides my being extremely in the wrong, in point of
judgment, I must have been either absent, or thoughtless indeed, not to take the hints that she had given me. That, for
her part, she was entirely clear of any malicious design of
drawing me into the scrape by her interrogation, how I liked
the lady; for that she had grounded it on a reasonable sup-
position, that there could not be two opinions of a beauty so
universally allowed to be one, as Lady Gertrude was. That
therefore her question was purely an innocent trap for a
compliment, which she thought it had been impossible to
have refused her by any one who had ever seen her. Upon
this she left me under my confusion, with my mouth open
and a silly excuse sticking in my throat, which she saved me
the confusion of bringing out.

Yet, to say the truth, I was less displeased with myself for
the blunder I had committed, than at the baulk I could not
dissemble to myself this discovery had been to those sentiments and emotions I had felt at the sight of this Lady Gertrude under her mask, and whom I had seen with such perfect indifference without one; and in this idea, I could not
help telling Merville laughingly that it was greatly her interest to wear it for life.

In the mean time I was so disgusted with myself, for the
impressions of which I had found myself susceptible on this
occasion, and so damped with my disappointment in the object of them, that I presently after took leave of Merville,
hurried out of the ball-room, flung into the first chair in

waiting, and came home with a redoubled impatience to begin my journey, upon which I accordingly set out with Lady Bellinger, the very next morning.

As soon as we were arrived at our seat, and I could dispose of an instant's leisure from the crowd of friends and neighbours who came in to pay us their compliments, my first visit, (and I proceeded upon it with the devotion of a pilgrim to the shrine of his select saint) was to the cottage, which had been consecrated to me by the residence Lydia had made in it. Here I found Mrs. Gibson, who still tenanted it, alive and transported with joy to see me, and especially her grandchild Tom, whom I had brought down with me, and of whom I had taken a care suitable to the importance of his recommendation to me, from having had the honour to serve Lydia. Nor did I think it beneath me to be pleased with seeing the force of blood take place, and break out in the pure language of nature, which entertained me with a scene, not without its worth, if but for its movingly presenting to me the power of simple undebauched sensibility in this low, rustic state, to bestow a happiness too often adulterated or smothered amidst the clash of interests or the dissipations of high life.

As soon then as the good old woman had satisfied the pleasing duties of natural affection, I indulged myself with the commemoration of Lydia to her. And it can only be conceived by those who have truly loved, how high a rank and interest the circumstance of her having lodged this sovereign of my heart, gave her with me. It is the character, it is the privilege of that imperial passion to ennoble every thing that has any relation to the object of it. I knew she could not have heard any thing of her, with which I should not immediately have been made acquainted, and yet I could not help asking her the vain question, her answer to which in the negative had the power to afflict, without the right to surprize me.

The idea, however, of my now being upon the spot in which I had, for the first time, seen Lydia, carried with it, in the midst of the most wishful regret of her, a peculiar sentiment of sweetness and delight. A thousand tenderly interesting images crowded to my memory, and flattered the resumption of all my passion for her. Every thing I saw round me, to which my remembrance could annex any relation to her, wore in proportion a stamp of value and an aspect of joy, that seemed to hail the momentary presence of her to my enchanted imagination. The air, methought, had a local virtue, and felt more balmy, more serene, from a consideration of the place in which I now breathed, and returned the respiration of it modulated into sighs, which relieved the tender anxieties of my breast. A soft and not unvoluptuous melancholy stole upon me, which I indulged and cherished, under the whispers of my hopes, that I should yet find again the only person on earth, capable of restoring me to myself and to the world, which without Lydia was no more to me than the wilds of Tartary, or the desolate wastes of Russia.

I did myself then some violence to quit a spot so necessary to me, but during my stay in the country I neglected not one instant of leisure, in which I could return to it, and enjoy, in the bosom of solitude, those soothing pleasures of love-pensiveness, so preferable to the tumult of irregular passions, or to the comparatively cheap, indeed, joys of promiscuous company or dissipated life.

Retreats into the country had never appeared to me in any other light, than of a duty to cultivate, at certain seasons, the old *English* hospitality if but to give the mine workers of agriculture their just encouragement, in their share in the circulation of the revenues produced by them. This, too, I allowed to be no more than a grateful return for the enablements draughted out of the country, to live in town, the capital seat of society. But then I could annex no ideas of a very lively pleasure, to the acquittal of this kind of land tax. The examples of those mutton-headed self-exiles, who dare not in any point think or live out of the fashion, of those who are obliged to retire on the retrieving plan, or of those who affect a rural recess, (forsooth!) with an air of philosophical self-importance, or withdraw in fits of heroic spleen from a world unhappily fallen under their disgrace, and to which they are perfectly insignificant; all these were far from disinclining me to a choice, which I saw they did not make, of keeping to town. I had often then beheld, without the least temptation to envy or imitation, those cavalcades, called grand retinues, which appeared to me rather like funeral processions, in which some lifeless corpse was carrying out of town to be deposited for a time in its burying-place, in one of those temples of dullness called country-seats, where yawns are the form of worship; neither had I, at times, diverted myself amiss with scenes of fondness, I had seen acted between many a woeful pair of turtle-*doves*, who had taken shelter under shady bowers from the disturbance of an envious world and passed most lovingly the live-long hours, phyz to phyz, in cooing over the old slobbered tale of "my "dear, and my dear." Yet with all this railing, with all this my distaste to the general insipidity of a country-life, which I perhaps pushed to a coxcomb-excess, I could not help confessing to myself that such a companion as Lydia was very capable of making me dispense with all the wearisomeness and even ridicule of it: of infusing into it all the spirit I could wish, and of indemnifying one, by her presence, for all the pleasures of the universe besides.

With these sentiments, it was not natural for me to neglect any measures conducive to a point that was so much a point with me, as the recovery of Lydia. I went then to Warwick myself, where I made all the enquiries imaginable, and all resulting in vain. I proceeded then on my search, 'till, at length, I arrived at Bristol, where, by the minuteness of the description with which Tom had furnished me, and by proper diligence and exactness in my dates, I found, at length, how much more effectually one is self-served than by commission. For, on examining, by advice, the port-entries, so far backward as was necessary for my purpose, it appeared that a Flanders trader had cleared out thence for Ostend, on or about the day that Tom lost sight of the coach in which Lydia went off, the master's name Ebenezer Tomkins; whose habitation too, by farther enquiry, I discovered was not above a short mile out of town.

Justly then ashamed and enraged at myself, for having so long delayed procuring myself a satisfaction that I might have come at with such obvious ease, I proceeded in person to this Tomkins's house, who I was informed was then actually at home, on his return from one of his trips. On my meeting with and exposing to him the purport of my application, he very frankly told me all that I believe he knew, which was in sum that his vessel had been freighted at a very liberal price for some time before, to proceed, with permission of wind and weather, at a minute's warning by one who called himself Mr. Bernard, for himself and his family, consisting of three gentlewomen; that he believed they must be persons of note, by their sparing no cost for accommodation and provisions for the voyage. That he had no discourse with them, as they kept close in the cabin, 'till he had landed them safe at Ostend; and farther he could give me no account.

Incomplete as this information was, I took it as a good omen for the success of my future researches. I had now traced Lydia to her landing-place on the continent, and was determined not to give over my chase, 'till I should have perfected a discovery, to which I now annexed all the satisfaction and happiness of my life.

I returned then to our seat with an impatience for my return to town, redoubled by the light I had obtained, and I was only withheld from hiring a vessel and setting out directly from Bristol, by the circumstances of my travelling-equipage being in London, and of the engagement I was under to Lord Merville for his company in the expedition.

I easily, however, prevailed on Lady Bellinger to expedite her affairs, and succeeded so far as to bring her up to town, at least a fortnight before the time she had set herself for the transaction of them, but which my ardour obliged, and my activity enabled her to abridge without too much inconvenience.

Upon our return to town, Merville came to me, and I could not help observing, amidst his compliments of welcome, a certain air of awkwardness and embarrassment, natural to precede a declaration, which he did me, however, the justice to think would disappoint without offending me. It came out at length, to the following purport.

"I flatter myself, I shall not want much persuasion with "you of the sincerity of my proffers to accompany you "abroad; I will still punctiliously make them good, unless "yourself shall dispense with it. The truth is, that since your "leaving town, I saw, by pure accident, at my cousin Bar- "more's, the celebrated Lady Gertrude Sunly, and could not "escape the fate which inevitably attends all who see her. "Once more, I say, *all*, because even the friendship I have "for you does not give my memory leave to do you so ill an "office, as to take charge of any thing that makes so much "against your taste and judgment, as what I heard you so "rashly pronounced upon that lady at the ball; which, how- "ever, upon reflexion, does not more surprise than please "me, as I own I should be sorry to see you on the ranks of "competition with me. From only admiring her then, at first "sight, since my introduction to her acquaintance through "Mrs. Barmore's interest, that admiration is become a pas-

" sion, but a passion in form, and the most serious business of
" my life. I confess to you then, that I should not without a
" regret, easily excusable to a friend not insensible of
" the power of love, see you too rigorously exact from me the
" accomplishment of a promise, the inconvenience of which
" to you, from your acquitting me of it, bears no proportion
" to the necessity of my presence here, to the pursuit, in
" short, of a point, my success in which will greatly decide
" the future happiness of my life. Not," added he, "that I have
" hitherto made any progress, to which I dare yet give the
" name of encouragement. Lady Gertrude can as yet only
" conjecture my sentiments, by my assiduity, my respect,
" and"——"Courage!" said I, "Merville," and burst out into
a laugh, which at once disconcerted and assured him of my
not taking his disappointment of me in too grave a light;
" why this is little less than stark staring love; what a tragic
" whine was there? Assiduity, and respect too! what solemn
" terms are these! Have you been pillaging for them the old
" obsolete dictionary of the love-cant of our ancestors, or is
" this the identical Lord Merville, who, with all his com-
" plaisance, used to treat my passion for Lydia as a romantic
" flight?—You feel then, my good lord, at length, the force
" of your own suggestions, that to retrieve a true taste of
" pleasure, you must look for it in the natural, genuine love
" passion, in spite of all the fashionable decry it is in. In fa-
" vour then of this reformation I instantly desist, and release
" you from your engagement to go abroad with me, and you
" have not only my consent to stay, but my best wishes for
" your succeeding to your heart's content."

And I spoke as I thought. Nothing, after all, was more im-
personal to me, than this passion of his for Lady Gertrude;
I had seen her at some assembly, before her presentment at
court, when she had not so much as stirred my curiosity to
enquire her name, nor did I know it, 'till I accidentally heard
it mentioned. All that a little chagrined me in this incident
was that, by this means, she deprived me of the valuable
company of a friend, upon which I had in some sort depended, and now gave up, on so superior an objection, even
according to my own sense of things.

This did not, however, contribute to dispose me more favourably to the lady herself, whom I made accountable for
my disappointment. Neither was I over-surprized at this influence of hers. I knew tastes were arbitrary, and though she

had been far from striking mine, I easily allowed that she might please another, without my leave for it.

Merville, thus relieved from his engagement, resumed all his ease and cheerfulness, and offered to get me introduced to Lady Gertrude, before I should proceed on my voyage, in the firm assurance, as he said, that I should be ashamed of having passed my opinion so lightly upon the merit of her person; that he was certain I could not have seen her with my usual eyes; that I, even in point of politeness, owed her a reparation for the rudeness of what she had herself heard me say of her at the ball, and upon which, though she had not, to his knowledge, said any thing, when it was occasionally mentioned, her looks had glaringly betrayed a certain air of pique and confusion, in contradiction to her aim at indifference and unconcern; but that indeed she must have been more than woman not to have resented an injury, especially of this sort.

This was a satisfaction that I would have gladly given both Merville and the lady, even upon my own account, had not I considered my time as too short to spare any instants of it to form and ceremony.

Upon this I told Merville that I constituted him my proxy, and hoped he would acquit me of the reparation to which he taxed me. That, besides, it was requiring of me to do myself an ill office to see a person whom he represented so dangerous, and that would only load my departure with an additional regret. That I might, however, probably see her at some public place, which would save me the formality of a visit, in which case I should——here, Merville interrupted me, with observing that I need not refer any thing to that chance, for that independent of her seeming to understand the value, which reserve and rarity add to beauty, too well to contract the cheapness of those faces constantly upon shew at the gardens, wells, and other parading-places, she had lately especially appeared in prey to a profound melancholy, which had indisposed her to all public diversions, and even to the amusements of private society, to a point that her mother complained of, without assigning any cause for it.

I stuck, however, to my evasion of any visit in form, though Merville did not easily give over his insistence. We parted then, nevertheless, upon the terms of unbated friendship, and he went, as I afterwards learned, to Lady Gertrude's, whom he acquainted of his solicitations of me to see

er, and of my having declined them, purely from the hurry
was in, nor did he omit valuing to them the obliging turn I
ad given to this excuse; but withal he took care not to in-
rench upon the secret I had in general, and before, recom-
ended to him, in respect to the capital and sole motive of
y resolution to leave England. This mark then of my in-
ifference, where I was already so much in the wrong, was
aturally enough received and construed as a fresh insult.

Every thing being now soon ready for my proceeding to
eal, where I proposed embarking for Flanders, I had only
ft myself to pay a few visits of duty or business. And on
e foot of the latter it was, that I could not help calling at
ady Snellgrove's, from whom I was to take letters of rec-
mmendation to a brother of hers, then residing at Brussels.
Ierville was in the chariot, and engaged for the rest of the
vening with me. We found she was at home by a coach be-
g at the door, and were immediately let up to the draw-
g-room, in which she was in company with two ladies,
ho were then upon a visit to her. We advanced towards
em. They had got up at our entrance into the room, and
I was sliding my bow, my heart yet more than my eyes
scerned that one of them was—who? even the Lydia so
ng lost to me, and in pursuit of whom I was preparing to
nge the universe, and to seek for her every where but
here she was not to be. Yes! I shudder yet to think how
ar I was to wandering from the centre of all my wishes, all
y happiness. At this dear and unexpected sight then, I
stood in a trance of surprize and joy, unable to command
y motion, or exert one power of free agency, under the
ppression of such sudden sensations acting unitedly upon
e and keeping every other faculty of my soul suspended. I
zed, I devoured her with eyes insufficient to all the rap-
res and avidity of my heart. But the vivacity of my ideas
pt down the burst of expressions with which it heaved,
d choked my utterance. I was even too much engrossed
y all I felt, to attend to, or distinguish, what impressions the
ght of me made upon her: but the instant of my recover-
g my natural liberty of motion, I precipitated myself at her
et, I seized her hand before she could draw it away from
y grasp, and could not but disconcert her with an impetu-
ity, of which I was not in these moments of transport the
aster. I tried in vain to speak, but my emotions still over-
wered me. And when at length my sentiments forced a

passage, it was only in an exclamation of the name of Lyd
in inarticulate breaks and heart-fetched sighs. Lydia herse
appeared to me, as soon as I was capable of remarking h
situation, if less surprized, not less confounded or agitat
than myself: yet the quickness of discernment so peculiar
the love-passion, that it may be called its instinct, made r
feel a somewhat, if not dry or reserved in her reception
me, at least wanting much of that warmth of welcom
which I should have wished in such a re-meeting. But ev
that remark could not materially dash my draught of d
light. The violence of my sentiments expunged all memo:
or reflexion on every thing but the present object. I sa
Lydia, and that was enough.

The lady, however, who was with Lydia, did not leave r
time to recover myself, before taking her by the hand wi
an air of authority and an unexpected suddenness, which c
off all explanation, led her out of the room, whilst I repr
sented the figure of one petrified alive, without the sense
courage to follow or oppose them. I heard, too, the olde
lady murmur, as she passed me, that I "should not make
"bad actor."

I looked wildly round me, expecting from Merville som
succour or consolation. But he, too, was vanished: so that d
serted at once by my mistress and friend, I remained
a state of stupor and desolation, 'till unable to support m
self under all this distraction of distress, the severer for
quick a shift, I sank down under my weight upon a cha
Lydia still swimming before my eyes, Lydia so ha
pily found and so unaccountably lost in one and the san
instant.

Lady Snellgrove, who was herself astonished at this scen
approached, and asked me what I had done to affro
or drive away Lady Gertrude Sunly and her mother in th
manner.

"Lady Gertrude Sunly?" I cried out. "Is the whole ear
"combined to perplex and torture me? What Lady Ge
"trude? what relation has she to Lydia, to this Lydia, wl
"has just left me in this cruel manner?"

"I do not know what you mean by Lydia," replied La
Snellgrove, coolly enough, "but surely you jest; you cann
"but know that these ladies were the Countess of M——a
"her daughter, Lady Gertrude."

I was, however, so far from knowing, that I was even the

ncapable of believing it, though I was assured that Lady
Snellgrove was not of a turn to trifle with me. But how was
I to believe her against the deposition of my own eyes? We
proceeded then to explanations, in the course of which I
soon discovered that my error was owing to a cause too simple for the consequence of which it had been, and too prob-
able not to give me the chance of an easy clearance of my innocence.

Lady Gertrude had not, as it happened, been the only one
presented that day at court. Miss E——had preceded her,
and it was to her introduction only that I had been witness,
without the least curiosity to ask her name, any more than I
had done, when I had seen her once before. As she was not
then made, if propriety may excuse a vulgarism, to be named
in the same day with Lady Gertrude, this last had engrossed
the public attention; insomuch that when her name was mentioned, upon the occasion of her presentment, I very cur-
rently affixed it to the person whom I had myself seen introduced, and had never once started a doubt of my mistake,
till I was now undeceived and set right; but with what pain
to reflect on all the appearances of wrong, which this un-
lucky error had given me, to Lydia no longer, and now Lady
Gertrude! I had slighted her to her face at the ball, left
the town the next morning, though I was by her supposed to
know she was in it; I had contemptuously refused to see her,
and to crown all, was setting out upon a voyage, that to her
wore more the air of shunning, than of seeking, her. Yet in
the midst of all these subjects of confusion and regret, the
consciousness of my innocence was, not without reason, my
consolation. As my thoughts, too, had flown the compass
round, they could not escape the consideration of Merville
being my rival, and of his sudden eclipse from my side; but I
had not time to dwell upon it, for, company coming in to
Lady Snellgrove's, I was driven away by their interruption
and my own impatience, to pursue my inquiries after Lady
Gertrude, and to procure myself the essential relief of clearing up my mistake to her.

Easy it was to find out where she lived, and as I had no
thought of presenting myself either before Lady Gertrude
or her mother, before I should have smoothed the way by
an explanation, I imagined this could not be better executed
than by a letter which I proposed should be conveyed to
Lady Gertrude by Mrs. Bernard, or her father-in-law, the

little old gentleman who had so fairly put the flam upon m

In pursuance of this resolution, I drove directly home, an
preparatorily dispatched a head domestic of mine with Ton
who knew Mr. Bernard personally, with a note to beg th
favour of seeing him, and, in the mean time, I drew up a let
ter to Lady Gertrude, in which I had nothing to do, but t
flow upon paper the pure emanations of my heart, whic
patheticized the truth too forcibly not to compel convictio

By the time I had finished my letter, my messenger re
turned, and acquainted me that the gentleman was not in th
way that evening, but that the note left would certainl
come to his hands in the morning. All delay was death to m
but against this I had no remedy. It was now that I felt th
want of Merville to unbosom myself to, and, as if my ill for
tune was bent upon not sparing me one circumstance of tor
ture, even that of jealousy rose upon me, in the remembranc
of his confidence to me of his sentiments for Lady Gertrud
In the restlessness then natural to such a situation, I drov
to Merville's, but could neither find, nor get any intelligenc
where to meet with him; upon this I coursed him all ove
the town, through all his haunts or places of resort, and a
to no purpose.

I returned home then, late, oppressed, and harassed wit
the variety of violent emotions and fatigues I had undergon
and then found myself not a whit the nearer to my repos
for its being so necessary to me.

The next morning, pretty early, I received the followin
billet from Merville.

"I have no excuse, Sir, to make you for the abruptness o
"my leaving you yesterday evening. The pain which you
"discovery of Lydia put me to, abundantly acquits that in
"cumbence. In the first heat then of my vexation, the riva
"naturally prevailed over the friend; and I was not ex
"tremely disposed to make you, in a fit of high heroics,
"sacrifice of my competition. Neither then to friendship, o
"even to honour, shall I falsely give the merit of my desis
"ence in your favour, but purely to a reasonable despair o
"succeeding in a pursuit, where you have so much the sta
"of me. I am sensible, too, there has been some devilish mis
"take on your side, and have myself so much more candou
"than to aim at taking an advantage of it, that, even befor
"I shall see you, I propose to wait on Lady M——and a

"quaint her of my persuasion of your innocence towards
"Lady Gertrude, from all that I know myself of it, and
"which will come with the more efficacy from me, as she is
"not ignorant of my sentiments for her daughter. You will,
"on your part, no doubt, neglect nothing that may forward
"your clearance to them. Thus you see, you traitor, that all
"my revenge on you for the death of my pretensions will be
"my sincerest endeavours to re-invalidate yours, and to find,
"at least, in the satisfaction of your wishes, some recompense
"for all that is denied to me in mine. I shall see you some
"time this morning, and now I am my own again, I am truly
"yours.

MERVILLE."

Nothing could have more rejoiced or tranquillized me
than this recovery of Merville to me, unless a reconciliation
with Lady Gertrude, of which I accepted this for a good
omen. I had scarce finished the reading of it, when Mr. Bernard, or rather Mr. Withers, which was his true name, was
at the door, and had immediate admission to me: when not
all the sense I had of his having imposed upon me, and yet
more unmercifully continued me so long in the ignorance of
a point so important to me, could hinder me from embracing and giving him the cordialest reception; and tho' he was
naturally of a dry, stoic temper, he did not seem entirely
unmoved at the profusion of caresses with which I loaded
him. After then the first compliments, I made him sit down,
and not without some gentle expostulations, and to say the
truth, I durst not permit myself any other than the gentlest,
and a succinct explanation of the adventure at the ball,
which I thought no more than necessary to bespeak and engage his confidence, he gave me the satisfaction, for which
I ardently longed, in the following history of Lydia; in the
recital of which he had now renounced all disguise of fact,
or falsity of face and language.

"It may, Sir," said he, "very well have seemed strange and
"unaccountable to you, that a young lady of such birth,
"rank, and fortune, as Lady Gertrude, should in so tender a
"season of life have been forced, in the character of a fugi-
"tive, to take shelter in that retreat, where you first saw her,
"especially in an Age, and in a Country, so very unfavour-
"able to romantic adventures.

"It will then be necessary to go back to the source, and to
"acquaint you with some particularities of the family which
"you may have possibly heard before, in order to introduce
"those which may have escaped your knowledge, and which
"form one of those secrets, that are restrained to the narrow
"circle of relations or intimate friends, especially where scan-
"dal has no very material interest in the divulging them.

"The Earl of M—— has by his lady only one son, Lord
"Sunly, a young nobleman of great promise, and this Lady
"Gertrude, who is what you see her. Lord Sunly was upon
"his travels, when my lord F——, upon an accidental visit at
"the Earl of M——'s seat, saw Lady Gertrude for the first
"time, and, though she was then scarce out of the verge of
"childhood, he was so struck, as to forget the whole distance
"of the horizons between her dawn and his setting, for he
"was upwards of sixty, a widower, and childless. He had
"then no sooner formed to himself the project of a match
"with this young lady, but he signified it to her father with
"that air of authority which he thought became him, as one
"of those leading ministers who dispose of the fate of the
"nation, and taking the Earl of M—— by his weak side, his
"ambition, he shewed him such an access to power, and ac-
"companied his proposal with such tempting advantages of
"fortune and interest, as dazzled my lord M—— to a point,
"that shutting his eyes on every opposing consideration, he
"hardly hesitated his consent; in which he involved without
"further ceremony, and as matter of course, that of the
"young lady and her mother.

"He had the more readily, too, presumed the concurrence,
"or at least acquiescence of Lady M—— in this disposition
"of his, as he had never experienced any material opposi-
"tion to his will from her, as she is naturally of a mild, pas-
"sive temper, and had ever appeared to be thoroughly sub-
"dued by the air of absolute control and authority, with
"which he believed he swayed every thing in his family;
"though, by that submission of hers, and the less of art there
"was in it, the effect of it was the more lasting and secure,
"she had often by giving way in points repugnant to her
"sense of things, seen the fury of the current spend, break,
"and insensibly turn itself in her favour.

"When he intimated then to her, in his usual strain, his
"views for Lady Gertrude, as a measure upon which he was
"resolved, Lady M——, who for many obvious reasons was

" utterly averse to this disposal, without directly coming into
" it expressed no farther dislike to it, than what might be
" construed a natural undecision, in so critical and interesting
" a concern, in hopes that her turn would come to state her
" objections, and to elude, by gaining time for his cooler con-
" sideration to take place, the execution of the treaty, before
" it should be too far engaged.

" As for Lady Gertrude, when she received the advice of
" it from her father, in the style of an irrevocable edict, she
" was too much surprized and over-awed to utter any senti-
" ments at all, so that her silence from consternation and duty
" did her the ill office of passing for a submission, in the midst
" of all her inward horrors and revolt against the proposal.
" Sentiments which nothing could more be made to justify
" than the person and character of Lord F——. For besides
" the disparity of his years, which rendered him more vener-
" able than amiable, and the disagreeable circumstance of
" an inveterate gout, he rather arrogated than made love.
" Incapable of unbending a brow habituated to the austere
" contractions of it in his political functions, he carried all
" the emphasis of tone and gesture, with which he solemnized
" the delivery of his false and frivolous oracles in state-
" debates, into his addresses to the ladies, upon whom, how-
" ever, nothing could be so little apt to succeed as those mag-
" isterial airs, especially without the merit of youth and a
" good figure to set against all the ridicule of them.

" In the Lady M——, her repugnance to this alliance was
" the result of her reason and knowledge of life; but was in
" Lady Gertrude the wisdom of pure Nature, which has sen-
" sibly implanted in that tender age the guard of an instinc-
" tive aversion to those murderous sacrifices of it to the spuri-
" ous powers of Interest or Ambition, which Happiness flies
" from, and disdains; nor can indeed be found, (all romantic
" sentiment apart) but in mutual love alone, which, when un-
" der the protection of honour and duty, ceases to be a pas-
" sion, and commences Reason.

" Lord F——, however, had not the time, if the thing had
" been possible, or his pride had suffered him, to conquer that
" coolness, with which, if he was not made to feel it, his ad-
" dresses were not the less received by Lady M——and her
" daughter. An express from London, requiring his immediate
" attendance in the business of his department in the public
" affairs, obliged him to leave the country precipitately, be-

" fore he had much to boast of his progress with them, and
" perhaps without thinking their consent overnecessary,
" from his abundant dependance on Lord M——, with whom
" he had equal to settled and concluded.

" The family soon after came to town; in the mean time
" Lady M——found that she had misreckoned upon the in-
" fluence of time, and of her own gentle suggestions, oc-
" casionally thrown in against this destination of her
" daughter. Lord M——continued to speak of it, as a point
" unalterably fixed, and with an air of determination that
" made her tremble for the consequences to Lady Gertrude,
" who had rather languished than lived, since her hearing,
" literally speaking, worse than sentence of death pronounced
" upon her; sentence of life with one she could not but detest
" as her persecutor, and dread as her executioner.

" When Lady M——was convinced that the matter was
" going so seriously on, that my lord M——was proceeding
" upon preparations for the match, she tried every insinua-
" tion, every argument, and every measure to divert or dis-
" suade him from this cruel resolution, in vain. He had not
" been shaken by an oblique opposition, and was only the
" more obstinately confirmed by a direct one. He answered
" then in a tone to cut off all further contradiction or remon-
" strance, so as to let her see that there were no extremities to
" which he would not go, rather than be disappointed of the
" schemes of interest and elevation, which he had planned out
" to himself, in the consummation of his alliance.

" Lady M——, pierced at this to the heart, with the threat
" of this imminent blast to the happiness of a daughter, who
" was so deservedly her dear and tender care, gave on this
" occasion a proof, that the mildest, tamest tempers, when
" urged beyond their line of bearance, are capable of the most
" dauntless and desperate resolutions, when generally, too,
" they succeed the better, for no warning of them preceding
" their projection and execution. After seeing reason then
" to give over all hopes of Lord M——'s revoking this dis-
" posal of Lady Gertrude, and determined to put every thing
" to the risk, rather than it should take place; after exhaust-
" ing, too, every practicable expedient she could imagine for
" her rescue, she found she had no chance for it but one, and
" that a desperate one, in withdrawing herself and daughter,
" 'till Time, the intervention of friends, and the enormity of
" the step itself should open his eyes on that of the cause

" given for it. A cause, great enough to force her to lose the
" wife in the mother, and to consult the preservation of her
" child, at so dear an expense, as such a terrible forfeiture of
" duty.

" Nothing, however, now appeared to Lady M——too
" violent, or too hazardous, to save Lady Gertrude from the
" worst of ruin, a compulsion to give her hand, where her
" heart could not accompany, and would more than probably
" never follow it. Upon the foot of this determination, she
" communicated her designs to my daughter Withers, whom
" you know under the occasional name of Bernard, and with
" her she concerted the necessary measures for the accom-
" plishment of the escape which she meditated. For me, who
" had been the steward of my lady's estate in Yorkshire,
" though I had quitted it for some time, on my leaving off
" business, my lady and Mrs. Withers both set upon me so
" urgently, and stated the extreme necessity of this step in
" so fair and forcible a light, that though I was far from dis-
" sembling to myself or them the improprieties both of char-
" acter and conduct, in a measure of such importance as the
" secretion of a wife and daughter from the fury of an in-
" censed husband and father, and the power of a minister
" interested, for his own sake, to recover and re-subject
" them to it, I was at length obliged to acquiesce, and even
" not deny them the assistance for which they had depended
" upon me.

" And here I must do the Lady M——the justice to observe
" that she offered to relinquish with joy this resolution of
" hers, if I should suggest to her any other expedient to pre-
" serve her daughter; adding that she would, then, acknowl-
" edge me her own deliverer from the unfathomable plunge
" she was rushing into, with her eyes open on the dangers of
" it, but which she preferred to the reproaches she should
" have incessantly to make to herself for an inaction that
" should expose her to see her child torn from her arms,
" and made away with, in a manner so barbarous, that
" in both their unexaggerating imaginations death was a gen-
" tle escape from the horrors of such a destiny. That, for the
" rest, she durst undertake that when my lord M——should
" have vented his first fire, and have had time to recover, and
" get disinfatuated from his present dreams of power and
" state, he would receive her again, and treat her as the pre-
" server of a child, equally dear to them both. That, in the

"mean time, she should have recourse to the mediation of
"Lord Sunly, of whose sentiments and concurrence she was
"assured, and who could hardly intercede with his father in
"vain. That gaining time then was gaining every thing.

"I was the less able, too, to stand before the pressure of
"these arguments, for that, bad as the expedient proposed
"necessarily appeared to me, I could not, by what I knew
"myself of my lord's temper, name a better, and to say the
"truth, I knew it was the only one. I saw then, with the most
"tender sense of compassion, my good mistress driven to
"this distressful dilemma of being forced of two evils, both
"very great ones, only to choose the least in her sense of
"them, and that sense perhaps not so unreasonable an one.
"Nor could I consistently with my grateful attachment to
"her, or even my own desire of being instrumental to the
"preservation of Lady Gertrude, refuse running those risks
"of which I saw they were not afraid. I could have wished
"a less obnoxious method, but since there evidently was none,
"I obeyed, where I could not advise.

"There was now no time to lose. Accordingly the plan
"was presently digested and formed under my direction, in
"which it was agreed, that as it might be too dangerous, too
"liable to discovery to keep all together, Lady M——should
"take care of herself, and that Lady Gertrude should be
"under the tuition of my daughter and me. That for fear of
"any accident of detention in any of the seaports, where the
"search would instantly follow the hottest, by contrary
"winds or any other accidents, I should manage them an
"asylum in some obscure and unsuspected corner of any of
"the inland counties, where I was to wait for what further
"orders I should receive from her ladyship.

"Few women would have dared to have formed such a
"resolution, and fewer yet would, with the same steadiness
"and mastery as Lady M——have executed it. She acted, in
"short, upon this occasion, as if she had kept in reserve the
"whole spirit of her life to come out with it upon this critical
"exigency. For with a simulated serenity that masked her
"intentions, she predisposed every thing before the day fixed
"for their escape, when I received from her Lady Gertrude
"and Mrs. Bernard, to be conducted to the Warwick-stage,
"which I had taken as for a family going down out of the
"city, whilst she herself in the character of a plain gentle-
"woman took a post-chaise for Bristol, with a trusty maid-

" servant of my recommendation, who was not likely to be-
" tray the secret she was not let into, of the true name or
" condition of the lady, and there it was easy for her in that
" great and populous city, singly to preserve her *incognita*,
" free from all enquiry or suspicion.

" For the execution of this, my lady had selected a day, in
" which she knew my lord was to be absent upon a party of
" pleasure with Lord F——, his now not future son-in-law.
" At his return home, he found a letter left for him by his
" lady, acquainting him with the motives of this disparition,
" and conceived in the most pathetic terms of remonstrance
" and regret, of firmness and of tenderness, of nature and of
" duty. A fact, however pregnant with such apparent indig-
" nity and revolt, could not be entitled to much alleviation
" from words only. Reason was not made to prevail instantly
" over such a storm of resentment and passion, as such a step
" would naturally enough provoke. Restrained, however,
" by a just pride from giving scenes to the public, he exhaled
" his rage within his domestic, and all as he gave orders for
" an immediate search and enquiry after them, he had the
" command of himself enough to stifle the eclat of this es-
" cape by a deep silence on the ladies having left the town
" without his consent. He relied probably, too, upon the
" efficacy of his measures to find out and recover their per-
" sons, before their secession should take air. But he was dis-
" appointed by the start they had of him, and the preven-
" tional care taken against leaving any traces that might
" immaturely betray them to him. Besides which, he was ill
" obeyed by those whom he trusted with his orders, and
" who were all at bottom in my lady's and in fact in his in-
" terest, as he could not ultimately be more unfaithfully
" served, than to the content of his passion upon this occasion.

" My lady M——though, found herself mistaken in her
" presumption that my lord would soon cool, or hear reason
" upon this point. My lord Sunly, who was wrote to by his
" mother, took the part of his mother and sister, in vain. In
" vain did he write to his father in the most moving strain.
" He continued implacable. It was then soon generally un-
" derstood, that there subsisted great dissensions between my
" lord M——and his lady, but it was known only to a few
" intimate friends and relations that they were gone the
" lengths of so violent a separation, especially as my lord
" M——affected to circulate their being gone to Aix-la-Cha-

" pelle, for the benefit of the waters to my lady, where he
" intended himself soon to follow. The report, too, which
" had been universally enough spread, of the alliance in agi-
" tation, still continued with no other difference than that
" it was to take place upon their return.

      " In the mean time my lady received repeated advices of
" my lord's inflexible disposition, and of the expedience of
" continuing her sequestration, if she meant to reap the fruit
" of having hazarded it at all; so that, tired at length with
" her disagreeable situation, she resolved to repair to Brussels,
" where she knew Lord Sunly was soon to be. It was then
" that Lady Gertrude was obliged to quit the shelter, in which
" she had such obligations to your politeness. A circumstance,
" however which at that time I durst not mention to Lady
" M——, for fear of adding to her anxieties and affliction;
" since if she could scarce justify to herself the rescue of her
" daughter from the unpaternal exertion of my lord M——'s
" power, in marrying her against *her* consent, she would have
" been, but with great reason, the more averse to dispose of
" her without *his*. This would have been too unsufferable an
" aggravation of his causes of complaint, already too great.
" It was upon this consideration then, that you found in Mrs.
" Withers (Mrs. Bernard) so severe a guardian against the
" least advances towards any engagement, that should not
" have had the previous avowal of Lord and Lady M——." [I
confessed here that this objection was a reasonable one,
and gave all honour to that vigilance of Mrs. Bernard,
though I could at that time so gladly have dispensed with
it.]

      Mr. Withers went on, "We got then safe to Brussels, and
" soon after two events contributed to soften and relent my
" lord M——. The one was my lord F——striking up a match
" with a young lady more fashionably prudential than very
" delicate in the disposal of herself; which circumstance, if
" alone, would have only the more exasperated my lord
" M——, but as it happened to be immediately followed by
" my lord F——'s going out of power in one of those fa-
" miliar and insignificant changes of the political drama here;
" when, with as little ceremony as amendment, a set of min-
" isters is as quickly shifted as a set of opera scenes, my lord
" M——grew a little more calm and composed. The peace
" and happiness of persons once so dear to him began to re-
" sume their due weight with him. My lady did not want for

"friends about him to seize and improve the first appearance
"of a lull of his resentment, and being now at ease from any
"disquietudes for Lady Gertrude from my lord F——, she
"made no scruple of proportioning her submissions to the
"measure of her offence, and, for the sake of purchasing her
"peace, gave my lord, on that side, all the satisfaction he
"could wish for, towards justifying to himself the forgive-
"ness of a step so bold, so extraordinary, and so derogatory
"to his just authority. A reconciliation then was soon effectu-
"ated, and the advice of my lord Sunly's having, with leave
"from himself, joined the ladies at Brussels, determined him
"to go in person to them, and realize in company with them
"the journey he had occasionally pretended to Aix-la-Cha-
"pelle.

"Accordingly he arrived happily at Brussels, where noth-
"ing could be more moving than the interview between my
"lord and family. Lady M—— and Lady Gertrude threw
"themselves at his feet, and bathing his hands with tears of
"tenderness and joy, implored the confirmation of his pardon
"in a strain of self-accusation and regret, which disarmed and
"deprived him of the power of pronouncing the least re-
"proach.

"All past bitternesses now merged in the sweets of their
"present re-union. Mrs. Withers and myself were included
"in the amnesty, and my lady had the singular happiness of
"finding that success had done her motives that justice which
"she owned she had no right to expect from means rather
"too irregular, and perhaps as little to be recommended to
"imitation, as the cause that was given for them.

"Soon after they proceeded together to Aix-la-Chapelle,
"where my lord, finding more advantages than he had pro-
"posed to his health, made a long residence, and we had the
"pleasure of seeing a lasting and sincere calm succeed the
"terrible storm that had so unpromisingly parted them.
"From Aix-la-Chapelle, the time of our return was spun out
"in various excursions of curiosity and pleasure, 'till at
"length some affairs at home required my lord's presence in
"the country; upon which, not two days before your seeing
"Lady Gertrude at the Masquerade, he came to town, and
"taking Lord Sunly with him, he went down for some time,
"and left Lady M——and Lady Gertrude here to recover
"from the fatigues of the voyage, so that we now expect my
"lord M——and his son both instantly back to town.

"Upon receipt, however, of your billet, I would not in "justice to Lady Gertrude, postpone the clearing up to you "these particulars, however indifferent they may be, by this "time, to you, and I could not well, without a charge of of-"ficiousness, obtrude them upon you, 'till your advances "should have given me ground for it."

I coloured with conscious shame at this conclusion of his, in which I felt there was couched a sort of reproach, which I had not entirely deserved, and which I would have gladly turned upon himself, but that I thought the time now too precious to waste in expostulations. I begged him then to take charge of my letter of apology to Lady Gertrude, which he readily undertook, on the condition of Lady M——'s leave for it, to the which I neither had, nor made, an objection. Neither did I forget my especial and sincere compliments to Mrs. Bernard.

He took leave then, and left me to my transition from a painful to a not unpleasing inquietude, since I had now a portion of hope mixed with it, sufficient to ferment and inspirit it.

All my preparations for going abroad were now countermanded in an instant, to the great joy of Lady Bellinger, whom I had acquainted with the substance of my discoveries and the revolution in my schemes.

Decision of Mr. Justice Klein
in the New York State Supreme Court
concerning *Fanny Hill*

The Corporation Counsel of the City of New York, together with the District Attorneys of the five counties com-
prising said City, seeks, pursuant to Section 22-a of the Code
of Criminal Procedure, to enjoin the publishing, acquiring,
selling or distributing of a certain book entitled "John
Cleland's Memoirs of a Woman of Pleasure" (commonly
known as Fanny Hill) (plaintiffs' exhibit #1 in evidence)
hereinafter referred to as "Memoirs," or "the book." The
book in question (Library of Congress catalog card #63-
9656) is published by defendant G. P. Putnam's Sons, con-
ceded by plaintiffs to be an old established, reputable publishing firm. Both sides have waived findings of fact and conclusions of law. The action has been discontinued without
costs as against the other defendants (S.M., p. 3).

Section 22-a, Code of Criminal Procedure, provides, in
part, that the District Attorney of any county may maintain
an action to enjoin the sale, distribution, etc. of any book,
magazine, etc. "of an indecent character, which is obscene,
lewd, lascivious, filthy, indecent or disgusting. . . ." Sub-
division 2 of said section provides: "The person, firm or corporation sought to be enjoined shall be entitled to a trial of
the issues within one day after joinder of issue and a decision
shall be rendered by the court within two days of the conclusion of the trial."

Pending the present trial, a temporary injunction was
granted by this court (Marks, J., 7/24/63). The granting of
the injunction pendente lite served, as does every temporary
stay, only to hold the matter in status quo pending a deter-

mination on the merits and the granting of the temporary
injunction can in no wise be considered an adjudication of
the merits. "The issues must be tried to the same extent as
though no temporary injunction had been applied for. . . ."
(Walker Memorial Baptist Church v. Sanders, 285 N.Y. 462)

The publication of "Memoirs" is herein sought to be suppressed on the ground of its alleged obscenity. Since no two
books are exactly alike, each book must be separately judged
and from an examination of the leading cases on the subject
it is apparent that there exists no automatically controlling
precedent.

The United States Supreme Court has set up several standards by which a book is to be judged, and it is well settled
that a book must fail these standards before it may be suppressed.

Two of these tests were announced in Roth v. United
States, 354 U.S. 476, and a third in Manual Enterprises Inc.
et al v. Day, 370 U.S. 478. Still another test was formulated
by our Court of Appeals in People v. Richmond County
News Inc., 9 N.Y. 2d 578.

The tests are as follows:

1) The "social value" test. The core of the opinion in the
leading case is found in the following language:

"All ideas having even the slightest redeeming social importance—unorthodox ideas, controversial ideas, even
ideas hateful to the prevailing climate of opinion—have
the full protection of the guaranties, unless excludable because they encroach upon the limited area of more important interests. But implicit in the history of the First
Amendment is the rejection of obscenity as utterly without redeeming social importance." (Roth v. U.S., 354 U.S.
476)

2) The "prurient interest" test.

"However, sex and obscenity are not synonymous. Obscene material is material which deals with sex in a manner appealing to prurient interest. The portrayal of sex
e.g. in art, literature and scientific works, is not itself sufficient reason to deny material the constitutional protection of freedom of speech and press. Sex, a great and mys-
terious motive force in human life, has indisputably been a

subject of absorbing interest to mankind through the ages; it is one of the vital problems of human interest and public concern."

" '***A thing is obscene if, considered as a whole, its predominant appeal is to prurient interest, i.e., a shameful or morbid interest in nudity, sex, or excretion, and if it goes substantially beyond customary limits of candor in description or representations of such matters.'***" (Roth v. U.S., supra)

3) The "patently offensive" test.

"These magazines cannot be deemed so offensive on their face as to affront current community standards of decency —a quality that we shall hereafter refer to as 'patent offensiveness' or 'indecency'. Lacking that quality, the magazines cannot be deemed legally 'obscene', and we need not consider the question of the proper 'audience' by which their 'prurient interest' appeal should be judged." (Manual Enterprises, Inc. et al v. Day, 370 U.S. 478)

4) The "hard core pornography" test.

"***The inquiry for the court, therefore, is whether the publication is so entirely obscene as to amount to 'hardcore pornography' (not necessarily dealing with deviate sex relations since while there is a pornography of perversion, 'pornography' is not limited to the depiction of unnatural acts)." (People v. Richmond County News Inc., 9 N. Y. 2d 578)

While the standards or tests are clearly defined, their application presents considerable difficulty, witness, for example, the case involving Henry Miller's "Tropic of Cancer". This book has been held obscene in the 9th Circuit Federal Court, (Besig v. U.S., 208 F., 2d 142), in the State of Connecticut, (State v. Huntington, 1962 #24657, Superior Court, Hartford County) and in the State of Pennsylvania (Commonwealth v. Robin, #3177, 1962, Ct. of Common Pleas, Phila. County), while at the same time it has been held to be not obscene by the courts of Massachusetts, Wisconsin and Illinois. (Atty. Gen. v. Book named Tropic of Cancer, 344 Mass. —, McCauley v. Tropic of Cancer — Wis. —, Haiman v. Marris, S 19718, Superior Court, Cook County, Illinois.) On July 2, 1963, the highest court of the State of California declared the book not obscene (Zeitlin et ano v. Arnebergh — Cal. —) yet within 10 days after the seven members of that Court had unanimously rendered their judgment, the highest court of our State in a four to three decision (People v Fritch, — N. Y. 2d —,) declared the book to be obscene.

So zealously is the constitutional right to freedom of expression guarded that the section under which the present action has been brought (22-a, Code of Criminal Procedure supra), contains two unique provisions not to be found in any other statute—(1) that the party sought to be enjoined shall be entitled to a trial of the issues within one day after joinder of issue, and (2) that a decision shall be rendered within two days after the conclusion of the trial.

The book, though undeniably containing numerous descriptions of the sex act and certain aberrations thereof as its central theme, contains not one single obscene word. While it is undoubtedly true that obscenity is not rendered less obscene by virtue of the fact that it has been well written—nor for that matter must a writing necessarily appear exclusively on the walls of men's public lavatories to be considered pornographic—there is present herein an additional factor not normally encountered in cases where books are sought to be suppressed and that is the high literary quality of the book. With respect to the literary quality of the book, defendant produced several expert literary figures as witnesses who testified at some length.

The witnesses, all highly qualified and eminent in their field, included J. Donald Adams, writer, publisher, presently a contributing editor to the New York SUNDAY TIMES BOOK REVIEW, with which he has been associated for forty years, eighteen of which were as editor of said BOOK REVIEW: John Hollander, Poet, Assistant Professor of English Literature at Yale University, book reviewer for many literary quarterlies, The New York TIMES, New York HERALD TRIBUNE, London GUARDIAN and London SUNDAY TIMES; Louis Untermeyer, well known writer poet and literary critic; Gerald Willen, formerly Chairman of the Department of English, Fairleigh Dickinson University, and presently Assistant Professor of English at Hunter College and Eric Bentley, teacher of dramatic literature and chairman of the Program of the Arts at Columbia University.

These witnesses were of the unanimous opinion that the book had great literary merit. Their testimony characterized the book as an historical novel (to a limited extent), containing passages not normally included in a book written solely to arouse passions, and their praises ranged from "extremely interesting" to "skillful". In addition, Mr. Untermeyer testified that the book contained the three great attributes of a good novel: (1) treatment of the subject matter with grace and beauty; (2) skillful and eloquent charm of writing; and (3) characters coming to life. He characterized the book as a "work of art." Plaintiffs did not produce a single literary expert to rebut the foregoing testimony.

Although the instant action is brought pursuant to the Code of Criminal Procedure, it nevertheless is in the nature of a civil proceeding. While plaintiffs need not, therefore, establish their allegations beyond a reasonable doubt, in order to prevail herein, they must, as in every civil action, nevertheless establish their case by a fair preponderance of the evidence. The burden is therefore upon them to establish by such preponderance of evidence that the defendant has caused to be published, distributed, etc., a book not encompassed within the orbit of constitutional protection. In applying these recognized standards, it is the Court's opinion that the plaintiffs have failed to sustain that burden of proof sufficient to entitle them to judgment in this case.

Under the "social value" test referred to in Roth v. United States, 354 U.S. 476, the expert testimony adduced at the trial indicates, and the Court so finds, that the book herein sought to be suppressed is an historical novel of literary value. While each book must necessarily be evaluated on its own individual worth, of interest, nevertheless, is the opinion of defendant's witness, Eliot Fremont-Smith, an editor of the Book Review Section of the New York Sunday Times, who testified that with respect to the depiction of the act of sex, the book involved in this action does not exceed the limits of candor which have been established by the publication and acceptance of books sold through reputable book stores and reviewed in reputable publications during the past several years (SM 152, 155). In addition, the Court takes judicial notice of the fact that many books in circulation today contain much offensive language.

With respect to the "prurient interest" test enunciated in Roth v. United States (supra), taking the book as a whole

and not just those portions thereof which appeal to the sala-
cious page turner, plaintiffs, here, too, have failed to sustain
the burden of proof.

Under Manual Enterprises v. Day, 370 U.S. 478, in addition
to the "prurient interest" test, to warrant a suppression of
the book, plaintiffs must establish that the challenged
material is "patently offensive" to current community
standards of decency.

If the standards of the community are to be gauged by
what it is permitted to read in its daily newspapers,
then Fanny Hill's experiences contain little more than what
the community has already encountered on the front pages
of many of its newspapers in the reporting of the recent
"Profumo" and other sensational cases involving sex.

If the standards are to be measured by what the public has
of late been permitted to view in the so-called "foreign art"
movies, and, indeed, some of our domestic products, then it
is equally clear that "Memoirs" does these standards no
violence whatsoever. "The Community cannot, where liberty
of speech and press are at issue, condemn that which it generally tolerates" (Smith v. Calif., 361 U. S. 147 [171]).

The book can in no manner whoatsoever be characterized
as "patently offensive" when examined in the light of *current*
community standards.

In a case involving a violation of section 1141 of the Penal
Law (sale, etc., of obscene literature, etc.) the Court of
Appeals held such section applicable only to material which
may properly be termed "hard core pornography" (People
v. Richmond County News, Inc., 9 N.Y. 2d 578). In the two
hundred and fourteen years that have elapsed since "Memoirs" was first published in 1749, the book has been in constant, though for the most part surreptitious, circulation and
has been translated into every major European language.
Copies of the novel are to be found in the British Museum
and Library of Congress. Benjamin Franklin is reputed to
have had a copy in his library. The New York Public
Library's copy of the novel indicates in its inscription that
same once belonged to Governor Samuel J. Tilden. Of the
author and the book it has been said: "***While Dr. Johnson
lived in Gough Square, while Edward Gibbon was yet a boy,
long before William Wordsworth was born, an obscure and
harassed Englishman turned out a book which, to judge from

the fascination it still holds for a great variety of readers, is more nearly immortal than anything these and the other great men of the time ever wrote" (Ralph Thompson, "Deathless Lady", The Colophon: A Quarterly for Bookmen, 1935, Vol. I) (pltf's exh. I, p. 27). Were the book "hard core pornography", "dirt for dirt's sake" or "dirt for money's sake", it is extremely doubtful that it would have existed these many years under the aforementioned circumstances. Here, too, then, the plaintiffs have failed to establish their case by a fair preponderance of the evidence.

In view of all of the foregoing and upon a careful reading of the book, it is the Court's view that same is not of such a nature as to warrant the drastic relief sought herein.

While parents would not like the book to be read by their young children, this hardly constitutes a legally sufficient ground upon which to predicate a constitutional judgment that the book is not entitled to the protection of the 1st Amendment. As was pointed out by Mr. Justice Frankfurter on behalf of a unanimous court in Butler v. Michigan, 352 U.S. 380,

> "It is clear on the record that appellant was convicted because Michigan by Section 343 made it an offense for him to make available for the general reading public (and he in fact sold to a police officer) a book that the trial judge found to have a potentially deleterious influence upon youth. The State insists that, by thus guaranteeing the general public against books not too rugged for grown men and women in order to shield juvenile innocence, it is exercising its power to promote the general welfare. Surely, this is to burn the house to roast the pig. ***The incidence of this enactment is to reduce the adult population of Michigan to reading only what is fit for children. It thereby arbitrarily curtails one of those liberties of the individual, now enshrined in the Due Process Clause of the Fourteenth Amendment, that history has attested as the indispensable conditions for the maintenance and progress of a free society." (352 U.S. 380, 383, 384)

While the saga of Fanny Hill will undoubtedly never replace "Little Red Riding Hood" as a popular bedtime story, it is quite possible that were Fanny to be transposed from her mid eighteenth century Georgian surroundings to our present day society, she might conceivably encounter many things which would cause her to blush.

The complaint is dismissed, the temporary injunction is vacated, and judgment is directed for the defendant.

The foregoing constitutes the decision of the Court pursuant to section 440 of the Civil Practice Act. Settle judgment.   Dated: August 23, 1963